CHRONICLES OF THE ORDER BOOKS #1-3

USA TODAY BESTSELLING AND AWARD-WINNING AUTHOR

JB MICHAELS

HARRISON AND JAMES PUBLISHING

THE ANCIENT ORDER

CHRONICLES OF THE ORDER BOOK 1

For my Father, the man who inspired my love for history

For Jack Magnus, ever the champion of my work

For Andrzej, my brother-in-arms

THE ANCIENT ORDER

A Bud Hutchins Supernatural Thriller

By JB Michaels

PROLOGUE

"Stand together, men!" The battle-hardened legionary barked a desperate order.

The devastation surrounding the few soldiers struck fear into their brave hearts. Their brothers-in-arms once full of life and vigor, now lay dead in a most peculiar, inexplicable fashion.

"Shields at the ready! Let it come. We'll push it back together. Togeth—"

A thumping bass sounded once again. Though the sky painted a gloomy gray over the land, the source of this thunder was no storm.

Sweat poured from their helmets. Heavy gasps gave way to controlled breaths. The soldiers packed themselves into a square. Calloused hands gripped hilts of the devastatingly effective short sword—the gladius. Their visibility low, only the small space between their shields showed the danger that charged them. The force that killed their friends. Their fellow men of the mightiest empire the world had ever known—the toughest men born from the blood of their ancestors with the mission to spread the glory of Rome fell in great numbers this day. The remaining thoughts of their homes, their families, their futures, fell to the wayside as the need to survive prevailed.

The rumble of a beast's massive feet moved closer and closer.

"Stand ready, men! Get ready to push it back!"

The loud, guttural roar of the monster muted the centurion's commands and words of encouragement.

"Hold! Iehova be with us!"

CHAPTER ONE

Magnus Vicillius looked out onto the shoreline from the small rowboat powered by men in his charge. The gray sky and the cool temperature did little to welcome the warrior to Britannia. The temperature of the air served as harsh reminder of the wear on his body serving twenty years for SPQR. The Senate and the People of Rome relied on his service to maintain and strengthen the empire.

The neck of the muscular centurion ached. He hurt it pushing a battering ram into the walls of a Germanic fort.

There were many other scars that riddled his back. The barbarians sent out their women in the night to assassinate him and the other officers. He woke upon the first slash of many. Her wild demeanor nearly killed him. Magnus gained the advantage quickly, but his sleepy state caused him much grief. He rarely slept from that night forward. The incident proved his closest brush with death. No battle or bloody skirmishes with men bigger and stronger than he were as dangerous.

Still, Magnus neared the end of his term. In just five short years, he would receive the land promised to him and be able to live peacefully. Away from the frontiers filled with uncertainty and danger.

His reputation preceded him. A greeting party waited for him.

His men jumped from the rowboat into the shallows and pushed the boat up to the beach.

"Greetings, Magnus. Governor Gricola requests your presence immediately." A man dressed in gray robes surrounded by four soldiers looked deadly serious.

"Take me to him." Magnus, in full centurion regalia— full metal breastplate, his large belt which held Marius's mule, his centurion-class helmet with the crimson crest of hair— stepped onto the beach of dismal Britannia. His sandal-boots sank into the wet sand.

GOVERNOR GRICOLA RUBBED his hands on the robe covering his knees. "I sent them past the wall to attempt a peaceful conversion. They have yet to return. I sent for you to investigate and retrieve these men. I assure you I gave them orders to escort the missionary and march on peace and not conquest."

Magnus stood in front of the governor with his helmet under his arm. "The tribes in Caledonia historically don't take kindly to Roman legions marching onto their land no matter the mission."

"Of course, Vicillius. I wouldn't have sent them had I not sent scouts to procure a meeting with a tribal leader who sought knowledge of Iehova or Yeshua or whichever nomenclature they use. Of course, it would be in my best interest to bring Constantine's god to the frontier."

"I shall march with my men upon first light."

"No more time should be wasted. I'd hoped they would

return in the time it took for the message to reach Rome. Alas, they have yet to return."

"I assure you, my men will find out what happened to them, Governor." Magnus stood tall in the lavish, intricate, wood-carved sitting room of the governor's villa.

"That is why I requested you, Magnus. You shall have the full complement of my local auxiliaries manning Hadrian's wall, if you please."

"Though I appreciate the gesture, we'd better not stir up the tribes with another larger force beyond the walls. If we need the might of your forces, I shall send my best messenger for their assistance."

"Remember, Magnus. There is a reason we built the wall. Please come back." The governor stood from his chair and nodded to Magnus.

The centurion didn't know if Gricola's plea was genuine. He'd just admitted that he sent the troop to help convert the pagans of the North to gain favor with the emperor. Over the years, Magnus realized that rarely were the intentions of the patricians in power purely selfless.

"I appreciate your concern for the finest soldiers of the empire. We will be back, Governor."

CHAPTER TWO

The next couple days were spent marching northwest to the walls. Magnus's force of one hundred men were more than up to the task, having quelled barbaric rebellions in Gaul and in the hinterlands of the Germanic forests. The battles of their storied pasts would serve them well in the wilds of Caledonia among the Picts and other tribes that lay stubborn claim to the northern section of Britannia. They made camp at Hadrian's Wall, about a day's march south of the unmanned Antonine wall and the last built physical barrier between Roman Britain and Caledonia.

Magnus removed his helmet and rubbed his scalp. "Tiberius, I want to take three men over this wall and possibly the old Antonine wall. I will accompany them. I need to know what happened, and we mustn't alarm the native tribes with a full century marching into their territory. You must stay with the rest of the legionaries here. I will need horses."

"Very well, Magnus. How will you know where to look for the missing?" Tiberius asked.

"The governor mentioned a tribal leader who sought

knowledge of the Christian god. Upon first light, I will ask the auxiliaries who the tribal leader is and find him." Magnus sat on his blanket in the comfort of his tent.

"You speak of the Christian god as if he isn't yours to worship, Magnus. It would be wise not to use such casual jargon when speaking of Yeshua. Constantinius II is quite the believer in his father's converted belief. Many of the men believe, and I, myself, have grown quite fond of the message considering I have been digging ditches, building walls, bridges, aqueducts, and fighting for the empire the last twenty-four years with nary a sign from the gods that I am worthy of their dominion."

"Tiberius, I am aware of the men's predilection towards the Christian god. I must say I am unaware of your own thoughts of faith. I am Christian outwardly. We must be. It is our charge to be so. Privately, in my heart, I doubt that one man possessed such qualities to subsume and rule over the traditional Roman pantheon. My family gave tribute to the gods my whole life. I find it hard to break such tradition and belief at the request of the emperor."

"Yet you are a centurion, a valued leader of the most powerful army the world has ever known." Tiberius shook his head in frustration.

"I do and say what I must to maintain my position. Unlike you, I have five more years to go before I am granted citizenship. Now, if you would take your leave of my tent. I need rest. Who knows what awaits us beyond the wall?"

"Very well, Magnus. I shall see to it that you have your horses at first light. Any specific men you want on your sojourn?"

"No one specific. You pick. I need rest, Tiberius. Go."

CHAPTER THREE

The sun rose over the green land of Britannia. Magnus decided to wear his chest armor and carry Marius's mule, his tool bag, but would leave the rest of the armor in camp. For this jaunt over the wall, he favored speed and stealth over the usual brute force. He left his tent and waited for Tiberius with his men and horses. They were a few meters away.

"Your full armor will not be necessary. I would suggest taking blankets from my tent and using them as robes. I prefer us to go in quickly and commence with the investigation with as little disruption and attention drawn to us," Magnus barked.

"Meet your men, Magnus." Tiberius pointed to the trio from left to right. "Brayden, Romanus, and Cassius, three of the finest legionaries our century offers, and four black horses per your request."

The gray of Tiberius's hair was accentuated in the dawn's light. He looked older in the mornings. Magnus wondered if he looked as old to these young legionaries.

"Very well, men. I expect Tiberius has brought you up

to speed. We must move with haste and stealth. Upon our exit through the gatehouse, we will ask the local auxiliaries where to find the tribal leader who asked to learn more of Yeshua." Magnus mounted his horse.

The three soldiers grabbed blankets and twine from Magnus's tent and made their shrouds from the dark blue blankets.

"Send Romanus back. He is the lightest on the horse with any news of emergency. The other two should be strong enough to provide substantial defense until the rest of the century can join you." Tiberius patted the neck of Magnus's horse.

"We shall hopefully return before the afternoon, Tiberius." Magnus turned his horse and rode away to the gatehouse walls. The soldiers three followed suit, barely securing their makeshift robes over their chest armor.

THE AUXILIARIES MANNING the wall looked disheveled and dirty. Not the ideal Roman soldier. The frontier and fringe units often didn't utilize the level of discipline and care that the fighting legions did.

"Sir, how may we be of assistance?" a soldier yelled from above them on the earthen and stone wall's gatehouse.

"We are requesting to get through to Caledonia. We have business to attend to. We also need to know the name of the chieftain, he who requested to know more of Yeshua."

"Aye, not a he, sir. A she."

"I beg your pardon." Magnus kept his frustration invisible, hoping he didn't hear him correctly.

"I said the chieftain is female, sir. A she, as it were. Her name is Michaela, and her tribe's village lies just over the first hill you see to the southwest. She commands the respect of the other tribes and is trusted to guard from any Roman intrusion."

"A woman?" Magnus pressed.

His horse neighed, urging him to move forward. Flashes of his near-death experience at the hands of a woman bothered him.

"Yes, a queen like Boudicca."

"Very well. Open the gate. I shall request an audience with this Michaela."

CHAPTER FOUR

This particular section of Caledonia geographically was no different to the land of Britannia, yet Magnus couldn't help but feel a strange and ominous presence in his surroundings as his horse pounded the grassy ground over the hill to the view of the Pict village. The many straw rooftops and stone structures that made up their homes dotted the land below. Strange she chose to build her village here in a low-lying area, yet perhaps she'd learned of Julius Caesar's brilliant and shrewd strategy to build double fortifications around Vercingetorix's hilltop village and starve and weaken the people therein. Magnus looked beyond the village, and there the forest began. Perhaps not a terrible choice for a village since the wilds could provide an easy retreat.

Thoughts of strategy always played in Magnus's mind. He'd hoped he would not have to employ any large-scale tactics on Pict lands, yet it might be necessary.

Magnus checked the twine around his waist. "Men, when we reach the village, I will travel the interior alone and summon Michaela. Two of you stay near the outskirts of the village at the bottom of this hill. Romanus, you stay up here and keep close watch over us. Should anything happen, make haste to Tiberius and bring the rest of the century with you. It, in all probability, won't come to that. Let's hope this makeshift robe helps me blend in with these barbarians."

Magnus made his way down the hill to a village entrance and tied his horse to a nearby tree. He would enter the village on foot. He walked the dirt paths and entered the village. There weren't many Picts milling about quite yet. The hour was still early. Perhaps, the painted people slept well into the day. Magnus never had direct contact with the tribes this far north. A few females opened the doors to their quaint straw, stone, and earthen quarters. A few children ran about on the path. A father chased after them. Their clothes were mostly brown and looked tattered as if the proper regalia of Rome had yet to reach them. They looked dirty. Magnus wondered if he should roll in the dirt more to make himself look rugged. He decided against it.

He approached the man chasing the children about the path.

"Greetings. Where may I find Michaela?" Magnus asked in a very serious tone.

"Mornin' to you too. Say, you wouldn't happen to want any children? I have two that are raring to go and find a new home," the father with a long beard said.

The children giggled while hiding behind a stack of straw.

"I am afraid I have enough responsibility as it is, sir," Magnus answered.

"Oh! I was just havin' a bit of fun with you, mate. Michaela is up the center path." The father pointed to the center of the village.

"What is it that you want, stranger?" A commanding female voice sounded from behind Magnus.

Magnus turned to look upon a short woman with tightly braided hair, a considerably tone musculature, and thick eyebrows that framed piercing blue eyes. "I request an audience with Michaela. It is of great importance."

"You have my attention. In fact, you have had my attention since I watched you descend the hill on horseback. I am also aware of the three other men in your party. Now, what is it you want?" Michaela responded.

Magnus looked at the father. "Is it possible for us to converse with more privacy?"

The father quickly ran and continued to play with the children.

"I shall walk with you as you exit the village." Michaela turned and began walking in the direction from whence Magnus came.

"It is my understanding that you requested a Christian missionary to learn more of the Christian god, Yeshua. The governor sent the missionary and a small dispatch of Roman soldiers to ensure the priest's safe arrival and return. I was sent here to inquire on their behalf and the governor of Britannia."

"I anticipated your arrival, Roman. I can bring you to the sanctuary. I will show you the way with no weapon and no escort as a sign of peace. I have to warn you that I have exhausted my most able-bodied men and finest minds to investigate... I am afraid we have no answers for what you are about to see."

CHAPTER FIVE

Magnus did not enjoy being led by a female Pict through a strange forest in a strange land. His men followed. He had to admit she was adept at riding her horse and guided the four Romans through the forest with conviction. Her knowledge of her land was most valuable, of course, for the task at hand but equally unsettling. The centurion didn't trust her no matter her attempt to put him at ease. She could have easily staged an ambush with a small band of her barbarians hiding in the trees. Perhaps, that is the fate that befell his Roman brethren he was sent here to find.

The cool air whipped through the trees and pushed at Magnus's chest and face. The sound of a steady stream of water grew louder.

Michaela slowed her horse and dismounted. "Best to leave the horses here. The sanctuary is just ahead."

"Very well, men. Dismount. Ready your gladius." Magnus turned his horse to his men and dismounted.

"Shall I stay back with the horses, sir?" Romanus asked.

"Not necessary. We shall secure them to these trees. I want us to stay together unless otherwise noted depending on the situation." Magnus tied his horse's reins around a knobby, thin oak tree.

The four Roman soldiers followed Michaela on foot up a slight elevation that ended in the thinning of foliage and trees that showed the clearing where the sanctuary was located.

Magnus noticed Michaela do something rather peculiar before she entered the clearing. The sign of the crucifix, a Christian act. Had she already converted?

The Pict warrior queen entered the sanctuary. There was a gnarled and mighty oak in the center of the clearing that bordered the steady stream of water that most likely poured from highlands somewhere to the northwest. There were stones with strange swirling symbols that dotted the grass in front of the tree. There were also patches of straw that seemed out of place. Caesar had written of places like this. The Druids practiced their vile religion in similar settings.

Michaela walked to the largest patch of straw. She began throwing the straw to the side in a digging motion.

"Pick a patch of straw and remove it," Michaela ordered.

Magnus moved to help her with the largest patch.

"Men, split up and pick a patch to clear."

The straw was densely packed and heavier than Magnus had anticipated. The straw was deep, at least two licks.

"I fear for what may be buried beneath this straw, Michaela," Magnus said.

"Fear not what you see buried in this hole but what caused the hole."

"Oh no," Brayden said.

"Here is the missionary." Cassius put his forearm to his nose and mouth.

Michaela and Magnus finished clearing the large patch of straw. The contents of the land's indentation were Roman soldiers whose bodies were trampled and forced down into the ground. Some of the bodies were face up, their shoulders partially buried. Their fingers were visible in the dirt. Tips of spears and swords and sword handles were strewn about. Roman shields with emblazoned eagles were cracked and in pieces. Worms and insects feasted on the exposed body parts and didn't seem to care that the straw had been removed.

Magnus pulled a legionary's helmet from the earth. The helmet had been crushed into something one could drink from. The size of a chalice.

The devastation in the clearing bared itself with each straw pile's removal. Some thirty Roman legionaries and a priest crushed and driven three licks into the ground.

CHAPTER SIX

Magnus's eyes closed. His shoulders slumped. His chest heaved. Sadness, rage, and disgust filtered through him in waves. The most lingering emotion he could distill and focus on was the anger. He walked a few paces towards the woods, away from the clearing and the great oak tree.

Michaela followed him. "I assure you, Roman. We know not of what happened here."

"Am I to believe you, a woman whom I've just met? Roman soldiers are dead. Gruesomely driven into the dirt of your pagan sanctuary. Pardon me for not wholly giving of my trust." Magnus wiped sweat from his brow with his forearm then turned to face her.

"What reason would I have to bring you here and show you the dead, if my people were guilty of the massacre? Where is the sense in that?" Michaela's furrowed brow foreshadowed a possible fury should Magnus continue his refusal to listen.

"I will speak no more of this. I will conduct my investigation of this matter as I please. I will be back with more of my men to properly take care of my dead brethren. I am not asking permission. Romanus, ride to Tiberius and send more men. We are returning to your village."

"You shall be allowed to gather your dead. Then you must leave." Michaela stared coldly into the centurion's eyes.

"Very well. Men, let's ride back to the village and wait for Romanus to return." Magnus scanned the Druid sanctuary once more. He memorized the location and secretly prayed to the gods for safe passage of the dead to the afterlife.

A FEW HOURS PASSED. Magnus waited at the crest of the hill that overlooked the Pict village. Michaela had no reason to trust him. He could clearly see the Pict scouts watching him and Brayden. Cassius had been sent to follow Romanus with revised orders. The Pict spies were not hidden from the windows of the stone and straw homes, nor were the stones that dotted the landscape proper cover for the prone Pict acolytes. In the distance, from the direction of Hadrian's wall, Romanus and Cassius rode together.

Magnus patted his horse's neck. "Upon nightfall, Brayden, I want you and Cassius to take out their war chariots and stables. Torch them after you examine their wheels for blood and flesh. Something trampled our men. By then, Tiberius and the rest of our century should be in place."

"Yes sir." Brayden nodded.

"After you torch their chariots, take twenty men and cut off their retreat into the woods. Then await my order to invade. The flaming arrow will serve as your signal." Magnus dismounted his horse and untied the blanket from his waist. His breastplate darkened with the light of dusk. He awaited the rest of his armor.

Romanus and Cassius rode up the hill to meet them.

Romanus dropped a sack to the ground. "Tiberius and the rest of the men march not far behind. They should be here after dark has settled in. Here is your helmet and the rest of your armor, sir."

"Thank you, Romanus. Rid yourselves of the blanket and secure your armor."

"If you don't mind me saying, sir, should we fasten our armor in the open? The Picts watch us," Brayden said.

Magnus picked up and brushed the hair on the crest of his centurion helmet. "It is of no matter. They know we are Romans. The agreement with Michaela was more soldiers to secure our dead. No need to hide. The time for stealth and careful investigation is at an end."

CHAPTER SEVEN

Torches dotted the pathways of the Pict village. Magnus enjoyed the view of the peaceful, serene village. If only it would have remained that way. The moonlight showed the grassy plains on the opposite hillside away from the village. The Roman century marched to their objective.

"Tiberius approaches. Once we lay siege to the village, gather the largest of their Pict men and any weapons they possess. It would not surprise me if you find hammers and other bludgeoning weapons," Magnus said.

"Very well," Romanus responded.

"Cassius and Brayden, time to take out their stables and chariots. Move swiftly. Their spies have assuredly seen our men marching to the village," Magnus ordered.

"On our way."

BRAYDEN AND CASSIUS were men of considerable strength and vigor. They hadn't seen much in the way of all-out war. A few minor rebellions quelled. Still, their experiences helped forge their friendship. Tonight's task proved the most dangerous. They rode swiftly and wide to the right side of the village. The stables were stationed in the northeast corner of the village. The way was clear of Picts. No resistance.

Cassius rode alongside his friend. "Bray, no sentries on duty. Should we be concerned?"

"We should be very concerned, but we have orders. There's a chariot. I will dismount and examine the chariot then grab the nearest torch. Hold my reins." Brayden jumped off his horse and rolled in the grass. He crept to the chariot which was positioned next to an open-air stable with only three horses.

Cassius kept watch from his mount. He held Bray's horse back. There was absolutely no movement. No sounds emanated from the northeast corner of the village. Cassius shook his head and hoped for some stirring as the current situation did little to ease his dread.

Brayden held his dagger in his right hand and approached the war chariot. Moonlight illuminated most of the terrestrial weapon. He ran his hand over the large white bronze wheels. Nothing but dirt blemished them. The wicker and wooden frame appeared as if it had just been washed clean. The throne at the center of the wagon looked pristine and new. This chariot did not bear any evidence of battle use. Brayden figured the chariot was Michaela's and thus, was carefully maintained. Still, the vessel didn't bear the attributes necessary to smash Roman soldiers three licks deep into the ground.

"Bray. The path," Cassius warned and pulled the horses farther back from the village perimeter.

Brayden looked to the path. Three Pict men walked

toward the stable and his location. He crouched low behind the chariot, sheathed his dagger, then pulled his gladius. Their heavy footfalls drew near. He hoped to let them pass. He gripped his short sword tight and took a deep breath.

CHAPTER EIGHT

A drunken male burped. "We should have just stayed the night. Rather than traipse all the way back like a bunch of fools acting as f-fodder for the wolves."

"Nonsense! I am fine, Tom. How 'bout you, Gar?" one of the men said, sounding less drunk than Tom.

If Brayden needed to silence these men, it would be with ease. He could smell the beer on them as they drew much closer.

Brayden held his breath and remained still. He could see the men's legs through the spokes of the wheel.

"That is a fine chariot. Look at her." One of the men stopped.

The other two staggered up to the side of the chariot.

Brayden's eyes widened.

"Look at this craftsmanship. I wonder who could do such fine work. Surely only an Iceni craftsman could do such fine work!" one man bragged.

"Oh no, I am going to be sick..." Another man gurgled.

"Tom, do not puke on my work."

Tom grabbed the wheel and put his head down. He

vomited. Then looked up.

Brayden didn't waste any time. The tip of his gladius struck Tom's throat. Blood poured onto the white bronze. He gurgled more and more. The other two likely thought he still vomited.

"Tom. Just let it out. Don't struggle."

Tom fell to the ground. The other two men bent to examine their friend.

"Tom. Tom. Get up. We have a ways to walk."

Brayden sprang up from behind the chariot. He must have looked like a ghostly phantom in the moonlight. He thrust his sword into the rib cage of one of the other men. Brayden struggled to pull the sword from the second man he felled.

The other man opened his mouth to scream when Cassius's spear struck him in the chest. Brayden used his foot to remove the sword from Gar's rib cage, then finished off the possible screamer with yet another stab to the throat.

"The vomiting one noticed me, Cassius." Brayden shook his head.

"Never mind that now. Grab the torch from the stable entrance and set this chariot alight." Cassius pulled his spear from the Iceni tribesman's chest.

"We have to hurry back and report to Magnus then take men back here to cut off their retreat." Brayden ran down the path and grabbed the nearest torch. His armor clanked and made noise, but the time to worry had passed. He brought the torch to the chariot and dropped it onto the throne.

Cassius pulled the three dead men behind the chariot. The torch's flames spread. The chariot succumbed to the intense elemental force. It wouldn't be long until the Pict warriors emerged to wage their defense.

CHAPTER NINE

Magnus rode to Tiberius at the bottom of the hill.

"They don't expect a full century, although now they assuredly know. They have not readied any battlements or warriors. This shall prove an easy and quick evening's work. We shall gather their largest men and examine their weaponry," Magnus said.

"Yes, something had to have caused our men to be crushed. I understand, Magnus. I will ready the archers." Tiberius stood with full armor readied.

"Send one flaming arrow into one of the straw rooftops. That will signal to Brayden to ready his men. He is to take twenty and cut off a possible retreat into the woods."

"Where are Brayden and Cassius?" Tiberius asked.

Hooves pounded the ground above them at the top of the hill.

"Speak of the devil." Tiberius pointed.

"Speak of the what?" Magnus looked confused atop his horse.

Brayden and Cassius rode to them.

"The chariot was pristine. No evidence it was used in the massacre. Of course, it could have been cleaned. Magnus, I don't think the chariots could have done what we saw in the sanctuary."

"Did you torch it as ordered? Were there any other chariots?" Magnus asked.

"No, we only saw one, and we had to kill three drunken Picts. They were too close and would have seen us," Brayden answered.

"That is of no matter. There will be many more dead Picts before the night ends. Take men and cut off their possible retreat. I want to make sure we can conduct a thorough investigation. Tiberius. It's time."

Brayden gathered his troops and marched on the double-quick.

Tiberius readied the rest of the men, seventy-nine strong, and marched up the hill. They took position at the top and looked down at the Pict village. Magnus watched for Brayden and his twenty men to make considerable distance to their position.

"Tiberius, have an archer ready one flaming arrow and shoot it down into one of their straw huts. On my mark." Magnus raised his hand.

"Magnus, look." Tiberius pointed at the main pathway into the village.

Magnus observed Michaela walking alone with a torch in her hand towards them. "What is she doing?"

"Perhaps she wants to prevent her village from being razed. Perhaps we should listen to what she has to say. She is brave to walk alone," Tiberius said.

"Tiberius, temper your Christian tendencies. She is not to be trusted. Watch our flanks. She could be a distraction. I shall see what she says."

Her torch grew larger the higher she ascended the hill.

"The agreement was a small dispatch of soldiers to gather your dead." The warrior queen came to them with her finest linen and a crossbow strapped to her back.

"We number only one hundred in total. We didn't come to terms on what small means," Magnus answered from his mounted and superior position atop his horse in case she attempted any attack.

"We do not want any violence. I will cooperate with your investigation within reason. What is it that you want?" Michaela pressed.

"We want justice to be served per Roman law. I want to question your fiercest warriors and largest men. I need to examine the weapons at your disposal as well."

"Very well. I assure you, our capabilities, though strong, could not have done that to your men."

"We shall investigate ourselves and will not take counsel from you. Certainly, a biased party who is also suspect."

"Your original troops didn't listen to my counsel, and look what happened to them?"

"That begets that you know more than you have led me to believe."

"I warned them to leave the sanctuary alone. The priest wanted to destroy the stones and clear the sanctuary of any trace of the old religion. They didn't listen. These parts have very different customs and beliefs than yours. I am seeking peace with you as is the Christian way. Is it not?"

"She has a point, Magnus," Tiberius chimed in.

"Tomorrow morning, we commence the investigation. Your largest men. Your weapons laid bare. Bring them out to the perimeter of the village for examination. Romanus, recall Brayden and his men."

"Michaela! Come quick! A fire!" a man yelled from the village.

"You fool! What have you done?" Michaela glared at Magnus and then ran down the hill.

CHAPTER TEN

Magnus observed the northeast corner light up in flames. "The chariot fire has spread. They may have found the bodies too. Alas, they are probably badly burned at this point."

"That may complicate matters. Shall we send men to help, sir? Perhaps as an olive branch." Tiberius looked to his centurion.

"It could have been an accidental conflagration caused by inebriated men. We shall deny it."

Tiberius didn't say a word.

"Have the men rest. We shan't help. If the village burns, it burns." Magnus made sure to see Brayden, Romanus, and the twenty soldiers making their way back to the hilltop.

DAWN'S LIGHT hit the village. Smoke still billowed from the stable. Michaela and a group of her villagers were able to stop the spread of the fire the night before by knocking down the stable, stacking stone, then soaking the ground and flames with whatever water they had in the village. The firefighters and Michaela conversed in the center of the village.

"You mean to cooperate with the Romans who nearly burned our village to the ground!" a burly older male yelled.

"We have no evidence they caused the fire. There were three charred bodies. They could have started the fire themselves. I don't want war. The Romans will commence their investigation then leave."

"Seamus saw at least twenty soldiers near the corner of the village where the fire raged."

"Conor, did he see the Romans start the fire?" Michaela asked.

"No."

"Then let's get this Roman intrusion over with. Do we know who the three bodies were? Is everyone accounted for?"

"So far, no one has reported any missing, which makes me think it was the three visiting Iceni men who brought your new chariot yesterday."

"The Iceni will surely investigate their missing men. Send someone to explain the situation. We don't need any conflict with them," Michaela ordered.

"I shall gather our scattered horses and go myself," Conor said.

"The rest of you, lay your weapons down at the front of the village. Every warrior should present themselves to the Romans."

"Michaela, we have just begun our study of Yeshua. You can't expect all the men to lay down their arms so willingly as this Yeshua would."

Michaela took a heaving, deep breath and stared at Conor. "At their queen's order, they shall."

. . .

MAGNUS OBSERVED the Pict warriors pour out of the village. Some three hundred of them dropped their weapons into a large pile, then stood in a line shoulder to shoulder per Michaela's direction.

"Tiberius, take their largest men with us back to the governor. We may need to destroy the pile of weapons," Magnus ordered.

"Magnus, you only asked for her largest men, and she has brought the village's entire army. She, in good faith, clearly thinks you will submit to reason and seek other answers to the mystery of what happened to our men," Tiberius said, rubbing his chin.

"In good faith...Tiberius, your submission to Yeshua has borne down into your very vernacular. You will do as I command. Round up the fattest and most muscular Picts. Now!" Magnus had tired of Tiberius and of the situation. He had no other explanation other than massive men or war chariots driving the Roman soldiers into the ground. The governor would want to see that justice had been served with the execution of a few large Picts.

Magnus walked with Tiberius down the hill to Michaela, the full complement of the century behind them. They did not lay their arms down. Their shields glowed in the morning light as they moved as one massive iron war machine down the hillside.

The looks on the Pict warriors' faces were tense. Some shook their heads. Others stood strong, loyally following their queen.

"We are here as you asked, my warriors all," Michaela said. "You may conduct your investigation here and now under these terms. The weapons are all here as well. Surely you can see no mace or hammer could effectively smash men into the earth."

"We wish to have the largest men step forward." Magnus didn't trust Tiberius to enact his orders.

"You have eyes. You can simply ask the largest men you see as you walk down the line. I will no longer grant any more of your ridiculous requests." Michaela stood strong in front of her men and before the Romans.

"Tiberius. Do it." Magnus nodded toward the pile of weapons behind Michaela.

"Torchbearers!" Tiberius yelled to a small unit of legionaries, who brought out four freshly lit torches.

"Do you value your weaponry?" Magnus pressed.

"You would leave us defenseless," Michaela observed.

"I want all your largest and strongest men to come with me back to Britannia. From the looks of it, there aren't very many."

"To face execution for an offense they are innocent of."

"Order them forward, or the weapons will be burned." Magnus took a step closer and looked down at Michaela. Her short stature gave him a sense of superiority.

Michaela walked right up to him and met his stare, with intensity and grit. The warrior queen refused to back down.

CHAPTER ELEVEN

The standoff did not last long. A rumbling bass distracted both Magnus and Michaela. They examined the horizon.

"You will regret this treachery, witch." Magnus unsheathed his sword.

"This isn't me. My warriors stand before you!" Michaela yelled as she readied her crossbow.

Underneath his boots, Magnus could feel the steady rhythmic bass. "Horses."

"War chariots. The Iceni. Three of their men were burned. Their village is not far from here. I can speak with them." Michaela looked to the top of the hill.

Magnus did, too, looking over his men who dotted the hillside to the top.

"Men. Turn and ready your shields!" Magnus ordered.

The crest of the hill looked as if it had spewed arrows enough to cast a large shadow over the heart of the Roman century.

"Cover!" Magnus yelled to his men.

All one hundred Romans lifted their shields and formed a vast iron and wooden shell to defend against the volley of arrows. The pattering and smacking sounds of arrowheads on Roman shields filled the air.

"To arms, warriors!" Michaela yelled.

The three hundred Pict warriors ran to secure their weapons in the large pile. Many still wore their shields. Some fell to the ground in the scramble to procure a weapon. Any weapon.

"Roman. They will most likely throw their javelins next, followed by their war chariots, and the Iceni have many. Have your men retreat into the village and regroup!" Michaela yelled.

"I take no orders from you." Magnus looked to the crest of the hill.

Five bronze and white war chariots driven by wild-haired and dirty men took position, each at a spot to force chaos in the ranks of the Romans.

"Your men will be slaughtered on the hillside. Move into the village! I have good relations with their king. They will not attack our village with the women and children inside!" Michaela yelled.

The charioteers raised their javelins as if to signal, and again from the other side of the hill, a volley of javelins and arrows flew through the air. The Roman legionaries remained shielded. The javelins penetrated some of their shields, rendering them useless for the coming close quarters combat. The loud smacks of iron tips meeting wooden shields and cracking wood filled the air. The volley ceased. The charioteers lowered their javelins.

"Magnus! They are about to charge with their chariots, and your angled position will result in slaughter!"

Magnus looked up the hill at his men and the disadvantage Michaela had pointed out. He knew she was right in her tactical assessment.

"Retreat, men! Into the village now! We shall choose our own battlefield!" Magnus ordered.

"Retreat! Retreat!" Tiberius seconded the command.

The century of troops marched down the hillside with shields still raised, covering their retreat, and moved away from the Iceni chariots atop the hill. The war chariot on the left-most side of the crest began to descend the hillside and give chase.

The Pict warriors broke their lines and allowed the Romans to file into the center pathway of the village. Michaela waved her arms and ushered the Romans inside. She then ran with crossbow in hand to head off the charging chariot.

"HALT! HALT!" she screamed at the Iceni charioteer. She aimed the crossbow, likely worried that her decision to shoot the bolt could mean all-out war with her neighboring tribe.

CHAPTER TWELVE

Magnus found himself next to Michaela. He witnessed her steady aim, her resolve, and absolute calm under pressure as the charioteer screamed closer and closer to the village.

"Merely a skirmisher. Don't fire, Michaela. Don't." Magnus readied his spear.

"If he is merely a skirmisher, why ready your spear?" Michaela commented while keeping her aim true.

Screams rang out from behind them. The villagers scrambled. The Pict warriors ran into the village at every opening. Some heard the screams of their wives or husbands. Their children.

Michaela kept watch on the charioteer who was only four meters away. The creaking of the wheels and pounding of horse hooves did little to comfort Magnus.

"I do not wish to attack!" the Iceni aboard the throne of the chariot yelled.

He turned the horses away from Magnus and Michaela and rode past them.

"Something is coming! The trees! The trees!" The Iceni

pointed with his javelin to the treetops at the rear perimeter of the village.

Magnus looked to the trees. The tops of the great trees swayed and raged as if a great wind blew through the forest. Then audible cracks of tremendous tree trunks giving way to immense pressure bounced off the hill and into his ears. Something trampled the ancient forest.

"No! No!" Michaela secured the crossbow to her back and pushed through the Roman legionaries and her own warriors.

"Make way! Make way!" Magnus followed her.

They pushed their way to the center of the village. The cries of a screaming boy made them turn their heads. The small child moved across the dirt path on his back. He moved quickly and unnaturally.

"Something drags the boy!" Michaela ran to catch him.

The boy moved faster and faster away from her.

Magnus looked around. The father he saw earlier ran out of a straw hut. A sudden burst of blood spewed from his neck. He fell to the ground dead.

More cries of children all around. More dragging. Another parent was felled by a force not visible to the naked eye. Bloodied parents and fear-stricken children were everywhere.

A woman ran toward her infant. Magnus tried to stop her. Her abdomen began to bleed as if a sword had stabbed her.

"Michaela! Stop! Don't give chase! You will be killed!" Magnus yelled then ran himself. He shook his head, fully aware that he'd just done what he'd warned not to do.

Michaela was up ahead near the smoky remains of the stable and chariot. All around him, the village's children were dragged into the very forest whose trees buckled and fell to the leafy floor.

Magnus kept his focus on Michaela. She fell to her knees. He hoped she hadn't been killed like the others for fear of the safety of his men and to make sense of the horrendous situation. He wasn't quite ready to acknowledge that his respect for her had grown.

CHAPTER THIRTEEN

"Michaela, it is no use. The children cannot be saved now!" Magnus reached her.

Michaela breathed heavily. She knelt on the ground and looked to the treetops. More trees fell directly in front of her. The children's screams faded into the shaded darkness of the forest.

"The ground shakes. We must move now! Out of the village!" Magnus helped Michaela to her feet.

A monstrous roar emanated from the forest. A loud, high-pitched growl that raked the eardrums of Magnus.

"We must clear away from the village! Move!" He pushed Michaela through the burnt wood of the stable.

He turned around and looked at the vibrating ground. Massive indentations formed in the dirt between the forest and the village's perimeter. Soon, straw filled the air. Rocks from the walls of the Pict huts became dislodged and sprayed and spiraled through the air.

"Our men. Our men!" Michaela ran along the eastern perimeter. "Get out of the village! Get out of the village!"

Some villagers knocked down walls and burst forth from the side of the village to safety. Not as many as there should have been. The massive invisible force of destruction continued its rampage. More straw. More stones. Wood splinters. Huts disappeared into bursting clouds of dust and rubble.

A few Roman soldiers ran out. Magnus worried that most were trapped in the narrow pathways and chaos.

"Form up! Form up!" Tiberius yelled, exercising futility, trying to command order in the chaos.

"No! No! Tiberius! You can't!" Magnus ran behind Michaela.

Blood-curdling screams. The sound of crunching bone and intermittent yelling followed by abrupt muting terrorized Magnus.

The death continued, followed by another monstrous roar. An invisible beast wreaked havoc. Magnus surmised it must have spawned from the depths of the underworld. He shook his head and prayed to the gods. The two leaders stood in abject shock, paralyzed by fear. Finally, the rumbling, invisible force stomped back to the forest, leaving the Pict village's decimation in its wake.

Michaela rested her hand on her chest for a few dedicated seconds before running to the village to look for any and all survivors. Magnus closely followed. The cries of villagers, warriors, and Romans filled the air. A wide swath of structural devastation ran through the middle of the village from the forest perimeter all the way to the front entrance at the bottom of the hill.

Michaela stepped through the rubble of her home, and around her were dead villagers and most likely parents who had run to save their kids. Some were bloodied, others stomped into the ground like the Romans at the sanctuary.

Several tears rolled down her face. The shock of the attack seemed to give way to desperate sadness.

Magnus walked to the front of the village. Many of his soldiers were killed in similar fashion. Stomped and driven by an immensely heavy monster. He was far too upset to rationally count the dead. There were many dead Romans mixed with honorable Pict warriors. Many engagements the Roman centurion had fought in and emerged victorious. This was his first taste of actual defeat. He gripped the hair on the crest of his helmet.

"Mag..." A familiar voice rang out from a group of four downed soldiers a few paces to the left of the main path as if they had nearly made their escape before suffering the same deadly trample as the others. Four cracked shields covered them.

"...nus."

Magnus recognized the voice and cleared the shields from the pile.

Tiberius lay with blood pouring from his mouth. His lower half had been covered with earth.

"My dear friend." Magnus knelt next to him.

"Please take this...and grieve not for me, for Yeshua has saved me. I go now to his kingdom..." Tiberius shook as he handed Magnus a chain with a gold crucifix attached.

Magnus held his hand.

Tiberius coughed and more blood bubbled from his mouth.

"Rest, Tiberius. Rest," Magnus urged.

"*Acta non verba... Yeshua annuit coeptis,*" Tiberius blurted before he was forever silenced. His wounds proved too much to bear.

Magnus held his hand and the crucifix. Grief overwhelmed Magnus, and he took a deep breath to prevent the tears from falling on the face of his long-time friend and brother-in-arms. With his free hand, he shut Tiberius's eyelids and silently wished him well in the afterlife.

CHAPTER FOURTEEN

Acta non verba: Deeds not words. *Yeshua annuit coeptis*: Yeshua favors our undertaking. The words struck Magnus in the most peculiar way. Of all the things to say, Tiberius had chosen to say those two phrases in his dying breath. Magnus grappled with the possible implication and assumption that Tiberius carefully chose those words to be heard by none other than he.

Magnus desired not to leave his side. He felt a great deal of comfort being near Tiberius, even in death. In many ways, Tiberius represented a true partner in their long terms of military service. Tiberius smoothed out the rather rougher edges of Magnus's style of command. Now he was gone. Magnus didn't want to face the future's uncertainty just yet.

"Magnus. Magnus, we must regroup." Michaela walked toward him.

"I am aware." Magnus kept his eyes to Tiberius.

"The forest is vast. We must start the search for the children as soon as possible." Michaela put her hand on his shoulder.

"What of the dead? We can't leave them in such an unpleasant state."

Michaela pointed to one of the Iceni charioteers who came to stand next to her. "My remaining villagers will help with the dead. The Iceni have agreed to forgive the death of their three men and have offered to help rebuild and protect the village. You still have about twenty men remaining. I am sorry. We must try and put a stop to this madness together."

"How do you suggest we find these children and defeat an invisible enemy?" Magnus released Tiberius's hand and stood.

"Malevolent spirits tend to get restless around this time. Samhain begins tonight. Still, I have never seen anything like this," the charioteer said.

"You speak as though spirits haunt this land regularly."

"Part of the reason you Romans built the wall..." the Iceni warrior said.

"I told you, Magnus, there is much you have to learn about our land. I shall take you to our Druid. He is hidden in the forest. We shall seek his counsel." Michaela turned and walked away.

"Send a scout if you need our help in battle. Otherwise, we will do our best to protect our tribes here." The Iceni warrior followed Michaela.

Magnus looked once more at Tiberius and realized he was at the point of no return. The supernatural forces of mayhem had killed his friend and fellow Romans. *Acta non verba*. Deeds of cunning valor and superior strength had been imbued in his very bone marrow since joining the legion. Only action, not words, would avenge his fallen legionaries.

CHAPTER FIFTEEN

Miraculously, Romanus, Brayden, and Cassius survived the onslaught. Magnus marched with them and seventeen other legionaries in a search party along with eighteen Pict warriors led by Michaela. The waning afternoon sun provided the party with decent visibility. The colors of the leaves on the forest floor were orange, brown, and yellow. Some leaves still clung to the branches, but their stubborn hold would prove futile. Winter was coming. The chilled wind caused the hairs to rise on Magnus's arms and legs.

"Magnus! Come to the front. You will join me," Michaela yelled.

"Stay vigilant, Romans." Magnus nodded his head at Brayden and the rest of the soldiers. He walked to the front of the search party to join Michaela.

"He is a peculiar fellow. I am warning you." Michaela pointed to a cave opening that lay ahead.

The orange glow and flicker of a torch showed the mouth of the Druid's quarters. Standing tall next to the entrance of the cave was a large facsimile of a man made from sticks and another larger crucifix made from sticks as well. Perhaps, this Druid believed in Yeshua. Magnus rubbed Tiberius's chain he wore around his neck.

"The peculiar and strange is the norm here. Let's go in." Magnus pointed to the cave.

"And showcasing the slaughter of animals and men alike in an arena is not strange or peculiar." Michaela smiled.

"The Circus Maximus is exceedingly entertaining, I assure you."

The pair of leaders entered the cave. The sound of hammering and water boiling grew louder the farther in they walked.

"Bah! No! No! No!" An older male voice echoed off the rocky and sharp-edged walls.

Michaela and Magnus were careful not to slip on the green moss that covered the ground. A slight turn to the right and the man's quarters were visible. A mess would be giving it too much credit. The clutter of bowls, contraptions, and odd wooden toys overwhelmed Magnus's senses. That and the smell of strong alcohol mixed with honey and oatmeal befuddled him.

The robed man frantically stirred the contents of a large cauldron. "My queen! I knew it. I knew... I assure you, it will be ready and be sufficient and to your liking. Yes. Yes indeed."

"Hutch, we know who commands the real power in the land. We come to seek your counsel." Michaela walked closer to him.

"The brose is nearly ready. It will aid you in the fight." Hutch continued his frantic stirring.

"Hutch, we need to speak with you. What do you know

of this invisible force?" Michaela put a hand on his to stop his incessant preparation.

Hutch finally stopped then sat down on a wobbly, short stool.

"It all started when the first set of Roman priests and soldiers entered the land to teach us the ways of Yeshua. The sanctuary tree became engorged with spiritual activity, much more than usual as the hearts of men have begun to favor Yeshua. A singular, all-powerful force rather than the traditional Danus, Zeuses, Jupiters, etcetera. The priest went to destroy the idols in the sanctuary, and the spirits didn't take kindly to his intentions. I do not know where these particular spirits hail from, but they are certainly not indigenous to our land."

"The trees act as roads for these spirits? You imply that they have come from somewhere else?" Michaela asked.

"You said they began to haunt these parts upon the initial Roman party's arrival," Magnus said.

"Yes, centurion. Your people seem to have attracted these malcontents. I am brewing this drink in the hopes that it will aid you in seeing them." Hutch jumped up from the stool and began to stir once more.

Michaela shook her head and let him stir the pot. "How do we go about defeating them, Hutch? How do we send them back into the sacred tree from whence they came?"

Hutch put up one finger as his other hand stirred. "I know not how to defeat them. I do know that the worship of Yeshua has power. Perhaps Yeshua is the key. His teachings of humility and a better life than the toils of our everyday slog has caught on."

"You are saying that these spirits feel threatened by Yeshua and have attacked, murdered, stolen children, and destroyed villages! What are we to do? Defeat them with blind faith in a criminal of the empire who was crucified centuries ago?" The Roman centurion's chest heaved.

"What is this destruction you speak of? Children?!" Hutch threw the stick he used to stir the brose. "It's worse than I thought! You must go now. Have your men drink this immediately!"

"Warriors! In here now! Grab a cup and drink from the cauldron!" Michaela ordered.

"You must hurry to the sanctuary as soon as you have imbibed the last drop! The spirits will most likely take them there!" Hutch scrambled around his cave dwelling for more cups.

Magnus balked. "I will not have men drink this vile waste."

"Trust him, Magnus. If he says it will help, it will," Michaela gently urged.

Magnus looked into her large blue eyes. Her sincerity and his unadmitted desperation urged him to change his mind. "What have I to lose? Romans, you too!"

The Pict warriors and Roman legionaries made a natural single-file line as the cave's shape dictated to drink the brose.

Magnus dunked his cup into the cauldron and drank from it. The heavy drink tasted of oatmeal and honey. It also burned his throat and warmed him considerably. It tasted better than he thought it would.

"At least it's good, men. Drink up, as the Druid says." Magnus continued to drink.

The line moved rather quickly.

Hutch handed Michaela a leather pouch. "Michaela, you need to take this. I am afraid, Roman. I only have enough of this for one person. She is to have it."

"What is this, Hutch?" Michaela grabbed the pouch.

"It is our traditional blue war paint. Use it only in an emergency." Hutch nodded his head at her as if she would acknowledge his meaning.

"I will save it for when I truly need it. Thank you, Hutch."

CHAPTER SIXTEEN

The search party reached the sanctuary just as dusk hit the open area. There was little light remaining. The dead Romans were still driven deep into the ground. The great tree loomed large, and the stream flowed with a strong current. The area remained eerily dormant of any paranormal activity and the cries of the village's children.

Magnus stood ready for battle, his helmet on, his hand on the hilt of his gladius. He truly looked the part of his centurion role. "We must make torches and set up a perimeter. Also, if your men could help remove our dead? I would be in your debt."

"We shall help, then I shall take my men and split off from you and your men. There are a few places I can search that are big enough to hide that many children. A valley beyond the stream and caves in the mountainsides. Hutch was right to have us come here. The spirits have come from this tree and will most likely have to be forced to return to it."

"I still don't know how we are to fight an invisible and

spiritual enemy. Shouldn't we just come with you on the search for the children?"

"You heard what Hutch said. They will bring the children here. In fact, it is best you leave your dead for now and hide in the brush and observe the area. Set up an ambush."

Magnus lowered his head. He wished he'd thought of the smart, obvious tactic. "You are right. We can hide and wait for them. Should they come with the children, we save the children."

"The moonlight will show this open area. Let's hope Hutch's drink works and we can see our enemy," Michaela said.

AN HOUR PASSED. The pink and purple sky signaled evening's fast approach.

Michaela led her warriors down a ravine formed between two mountains. The valley lay ahead. "I promise we will find your children, Sean. I promise."

"I do hope. I have prayed to Yeshua as you have said to do. I hope so." Sean, a tall and stout warrior, walked next to his queen. He held a massive mace.

"I hope the children will be in this valley ahead." Michaela carried her crossbow and readied a bolt.

"I shall keep prayin— AH!" Sean keeled over, held his stomach, then fell to his knees.

"Sean! What is it?" Michaela put a hand on his back.

The other warriors called out to him.

He raised back up. His eyes glowed bright blue. He pushed Michaela down the ravine. She tumbled a few meters. She spit out a leaf and looked up to her men.

The other warriors readied their weapons.

A thin warrior approached him. "Sean, what is the matter?"

Sean swung his double mace. From the thin warrior's head burst a cloud of blood and teeth. The thin warrior rolled down the ravine to Michaela. His left eye protruded from the socket. His bottom jaw had been forced sideways. Blood poured from his cracked nose. He was dead.

CHAPTER SEVENTEEN

Michaela pushed the dead warrior to the side. She stood up on the incline of the ravine.

Sean continued to swing his mace wildly. The remaining warriors had no choice but to defend themselves against one of their own, driven mad from evil spirits with a drooling mouth and glowing eyes.

Michaela found it hard to believe the sight. Sean's large stature felled three more of her warriors with similar blows to the head. They rolled down to her. Michaela shook her head then aimed her crossbow at him.

The possessed warrior kept his rage fueled like a berserker from the North Seas. He lifted his double mace over his head. Another Pict warrior stabbed his belly while Sean left himself open to the blow. Sean brought down the mace on the back of the warrior's neck. The stab didn't faze him. Blood poured from the wound, yet still he continued to battle.

Michaela shot a bolt from her crossbow. It hit Sean's neck. The wound caused him to hesitate for a brief moment and gave the other warriors enough time to swarm him.

Michaela looked to the sky. Night had fallen over the land. She looked farther down the ravine. The moonlight showed the valley where she'd hoped to find the children.

Michaela realized in that moment that Hutch's brose had worked. Her heart thumped.

"Oh, Iehova, be with me."

Instead of children, she saw at least fifty ghostly soldiers marching toward her and the rest of her warriors. They glowed a similar blue to Sean's unnatural eyes. They wore armor as the Romans did, but their helmets were different and came to a point at the top, some with hair spewing from the point.

Hutch was again correct. They were not of this land and had died in some foreign land, yet somehow lived again in some sinister, otherworldly form.

The sight caused her temporary paralysis. The shock proved too great. She did not acknowledge the sounds of gruesome death just up the ravine from where she stood.

"Michaela! My queen! I have brought you prizes as we have done in the past before your pitiful fascination with Yeshua!" Sean stood higher up on the ravine. His eyes gleamed bright white and blue, and blood poured from his neck and stomach. In his large hands, he held the heads of six more Pict warriors.

"You slaughtered all of them!" Michaela grabbed for another bolt in her quiver.

"Muahahahahahahaha!" Sean laughed and laughed. He raised the heads of the warriors.

Around him were other warriors who lay wounded, but they still clung to life.

Michaela locked the bolt into place and turned. The ghostly soldiers were closing in on her. They neared the bottom of the ravine and started to march toward her. She found herself in the middle of two evil forces.

MAGNUS SET his men to hide behind the trees surrounding the sanctuary. There were two archers left. He positioned them in the branches of two trees on opposite sides of the sanctuary. The Romans waited patiently for some action. They would not wait long.

The cries of children both very small and more mature, male and female, sounded from somewhere beyond the stream and behind the great oak.

Romanus stood next to Magnus, his shield and spear at the ready. Together, they were set back from the sanctuary a good twenty meters.

"Here they come."

MICHAELA AIMED her crossbow then thought better of it. She would have no chance.

Sean's incessant cackling annoyed her. The ghost army closed in.

She fled and ran a straight line that cut parallel through Sean's position and the army's.

"Oh, my queen, where are you going?!" Sean laughed.

Michaela knew the real Sean was long gone.

She ran on the awkward angle of the ravine as fast as she could. The moonlight helped make the ground between the trees visible. Still, she could lose her balance easily. Her confidence in her movement was marred by the cover of night. Every step, every footfall, she hoped she wouldn't fall and be overtaken by the evil spirits.

"She went that way!" Sean yelled.

CHAPTER EIGHTEEN

Magnus squinted. Did his eyes betray him? Or had Hutch's ale worked? The children were dragged in a single-file line by partially transparent blue soldiers. Magnus couldn't quite identify them. They were not Roman, but they looked familiar. The ghosts then put the children in the center of the sanctuary before the tree and atop the dead Roman solders. Magnus counted at least ten children and ten ghostly menaces.

"How are we to fight spirits?" Romanus asked in a whisper.

"I haven't a clue. We shan't let that stop us from protecting the children. Legionaries, attack!" Magnus ordered.

The Romans converged on the open sanctuary from all sides. The blue and transparent warriors simply disappeared.

A few of the children began to cry.

"I can't believe what I just saw," Brayden said.

A few more soldiers reiterated his sentiment.

"That was far too easy. I am afraid we have much to

learn about the nature of our current enemy." Magnus still held a warrior's pose, his shield in front and his sword tucked behind it. "Form up around the children. Archers, come down from your post. We need you down here. Cassius, see if you can't calm them down."

"We are here to protect you. All will be well." Cassius patted a girl's back. She couldn't have been more than four years old.

Twenty Romans formed a square around the center of the sanctuary. Four sides of five solders. The ten children were in the middle. The moonlight provided some visibility but not enough to comfort Magnus.

"Stay vigilant, men. They will most likely be back."

MICHAELA STRUGGLED to continue running at a speed comfortable enough for her to feel safe. She turned to assess the distance she'd made from her assailants. They were at least two hundred meters away. Sean ambled to the front of the ghostly division of foreign soldiers.

The forest grew thicker the farther she traveled, and the angled ground of the ravine began to give way to level ground. The sound of rushing water filled her ears. The warrior queen kept weaving between the trees and over the sticks and leaves. She labored to breathe. She ran hard. Survival instinct kicked in and propelled her forward. Her men had been wiped out. She had to make it back to Magnus and his small band of legionaries somehow. Some way.

The sound of water grew louder. She looked to the right. It must have been the same stream that bordered the sanctuary. She still couldn't see it. Only hear it.

Pain struck her left toe and shot up the rest of her leg.

Her utter shock seemed to soften the hard fall she suffered. The wet texture and smell of leaves blanketed her face.

Sean and the spirits must have gained on her.

"She is somewhere in these trees! Fan out! We will find her!"

Michaela stood up and limped forward. She quickly grabbed a low branch to prevent yet another nasty fall. Only she would have fallen much farther this time. Off a cliff and to the bottom of a rocky waterfall.

"Yeshua. Be with me." She looked behind her.

The pursuant ghost army neared.

CHAPTER NINETEEN

"Magnus, perhaps we should escort these children back to the safety of the village," Brayden suggested from his west-facing position among four other soldiers.

Magnus agreed. "We can move as one together. Two of you help guide the children."

"Look! Look!" A young boy of eight years or so pointed to the ground below him.

A rotted hand emerged from the dirt. The earth below them vibrated.

"Cassius, get the children out of there now!"

Cassius and three other legionaries broke the line and pulled the children back toward the great oak tree.

The dead Roman soldiers moved the soil that buried them and stood once more. Their eyes glowed. Some of their limbs indicated the force that had crushed them and drove them into the ground. The flattened and shattered body parts were encased by the blue ghostly spirts. They were a terrifying mix of corporeal, damaged flesh and a blue, supernatural form.

Their deathly, rotting smell sickened Magnus.

The blue spirits powered the dead Roman bodies. Other patches of straw burst into the air. Twenty living Roman soldiers were soon surrounded and confronted by many undead soldiers. Magnus was far too nervous and shocked to count. The priest had even risen from the impacted soil.

"Fight to the center first, men! We are stronger together!" Magnus crouched low. His shield protected him from his chin to his shins. He moved to clear the center of the sanctuary and former haphazard grave.

Together with his four men, he pushed forward. Eight undead soldiers armed with only swords and no shields threw caution to the wind and charged.

"Stop! Hold them, men! They can't be too powerful!" Magnus dug into a stationary position.

The men next to him did the same. The force of the charge hit their shielded position and caused them to shift only slightly.

"Let them have it."

The four Romans created a tiny space between each other, and together, they stabbed the enemy then pushed forward with their shields in concert. As one. A force of imperial nature.

Magnus could feel his sword push into the gut of his unholy enemy. He pulled back and thrust his sword forward once more. The undead soldiers fell to the ground. The centurion and legionaries stepped over them and took the center.

"Men! Form up! With me!"

The clanging of swords and the grunts of Magnus's living legionaries signaled the battle underway as the other fifteen legionaries fought their way to the center.

. . .

MICHAELA WEIGHED HER OPTIONS. Jump into the shallow rocky stream or stay crouched behind the last tree to take root on the top of the cliffside. Both options would likely lead to death.

She closed her eyes and prayed once more.

"Oh, my queen! There was a time when a collection of enemy heads would have pleased you and your royal family!" Sean yelled. He sounded as if he were close. Very, very close. Heavy steps crunched the leaves behind her.

Michaela opened her eyes. Hutch's pouch!

The sound of rustling leaves grew louder and louder. A stick broke on the other side of the tree she crouched behind.

Michaela held her breath.

She reached for the leather pouch attached to her right hip. She froze. Her lungs beckoned for relief. She moved her head slightly forward.

"A cliff! I wonder if my queen jumped off a cliff?" The possessed Sean spoke a few paces away to the right. Closer to the stream. Then he stomped away from the cliffside.

Michaela opened her mouth and took a deep breath. Her heart pounded. She stood up, opened the pouch, and applied the blue war paint to her face, arms, and legs. Every bit of exposed skin.

CHAPTER TWENTY

Magnus and his full charge of remaining legionaries took the center once more. This time the ground they stood on was clear of the crushed dead. The ten children were secured in the center once more. They comforted each other. The older ones held the younger. They displayed tenderness and compassion in the most horrific circumstances.

The battle ended for now. The dead bodies of Roman soldiers were felled once more, this time by their own countrymen, in an unholy simulation of civil war.

"Perhaps now it would be safe to get back to the village," Brayden said.

"Best to wait here for Michaela and the others. We risk being overtaken by this evil should we march," Magnus declared.

"Magnus, their eyes still glow." Romanus pointed his sword at a dead Roman bent over a Pict ceremonial stone.

"They do not remain dead men." Magnus readied his shield and sword.

The reanimated Romans stood again. Some of their

bodies lacked heads or limbs, yet they moved toward Magnus, the living legion, and the children. Their numbers were plenty enough to attack and severely stress all four sides of the Roman square that protected the children.

They stopped and stood still. Some groaned. Others gargled whatever blood or liquid was left in their bodies.

"How many of you still have your pila?" Magnus asked.

Three soldiers responded, "Yes."

"Everyone still have their daggers?"

All responded, "Yes."

"On my mark, throw your daggers and spears at them. We can thin them out before they inevitably charge."

"Baal wills his return!" The loud, distorted, deranged, raspy voice poured from the mouths of all the undead surrounding them.

Then it clicked. Magnus shook his head. "It can't be."

"Did they say Baal?" Romanus asked.

"They did. They sure did. It's the Carthaginians." Magnus gripped his dagger.

The children began to cry out.

The great oak behind them cracked loudly as if something wanted to tear the trunk in half from within.

"Thin them out!" Magnus threw his dagger.

The rest of the century's remaining soldiers followed suit. Magnus watched his dagger stick the throat of an undead soldier. It fell to the ground once more. Three spears cut down their targets easily. The rest of the daggers proved effective, but some undead still stood. At least twelve charged three sides of the Roman square.

"They won't stop, Magnus," Brayden said.

"We won't either. Let them come. Push them back and take their legs out." Magnus unsheathed his sword.

Six Carthaginians smashed into Magnus's line first. The

force was stronger this time. He nearly fell back onto the children. The soldiers next to him helped him into a stronger stance. He recovered his footing.

"Ah! You bastards." Magnus reversed the momentum of their charge and pushed back. He let his sword do its efficient, brutal work. He stabbed. He pulled back. He thrust. Pulled back. Each time, he felt the impact of the gladius tear through the thighs of the undead.

"With me, Romans!" He broke the square, and the four Romans decimated the Carthaginian legs.

The six enemy soldiers fell to their knees then began to crawl and grab at their ankles. Magnus drove his shield down. The force crushed the undead soldier's wrist and arm.

Magnus and his men returned to the square. The other six charging soldiers again fell to ground on the other sides of the square. The legionaries employed the same tactics.

"Let's see if they can attack with no legs." Magnus wiped sweat from his brow with his forearm.

"I want my mother. I want my mother," a little boy cried in the center of the square.

"We will get you to your mother, boy. I promise." Magnus turned, put his sword down, and patted the boy's head.

"Promise?" The boy sniffled.

"I promise."

"Magnus, the ones we felled with our daggers and pila." Cassius pointed.

The undead powered by the spirits of Carthaginian soldiers stood again and readied themselves for yet another attack.

CHAPTER TWENTY-ONE

Michaela could still hear the stomp of Sean's large feet. The crunch of the leaves and snap of sticks echoed and bounced off the trees in her vicinity. She had applied the traditional war paint. She needed to get to the sanctuary.

"Hutch...I hope this works," she whispered to herself.

Michaela turned around. She peeked around the trunk of the tree she'd previously took refuge behind and could see the blue glow of ancient soldiers looking high and low for her. Sean was off in the distance in the direction she'd come from. He kept putting his hand and mace up in the air. He seemed to grow impatient.

Michaela took a deep breath and walked out from behind the tree among the ghost-soldiers who headed towards Sean. She kept a steady pace behind one of them then bravely ran past the soldier. The soldier marched as if he hadn't noticed her.

Michaela smiled. She waved her arms in front of the soldier's sunken-in face. Nothing. He didn't notice her.

Hutch's paint worked. It shielded her from the spirit world. Gave her power of invisibility and worked to her advantage. She ran more swiftly between three more soldiers, then ten more, twenty. All fifty didn't notice her. The apparent leader spirit that controlled Sean's body didn't notice her either.

She grew bolder and ran as fast as she could away from the evil ghost army and to the sanctuary to warn Magnus of the impending doom. Up the ravine she went, and she made a sign of the cross as she passed her fallen warriors. Something she'd picked up on when the Roman priest had met with her. She now understood that the spirit world and Yeshua's world were inexplicably linked. Perhaps a mixture of the old traditions and the new would save her village and the children. She just didn't know exactly how quite yet. Her run helped clear her mind.

On her trek back to the sanctuary, she heard the all-too-familiar sounds of battle. The grunts of men, the heavy impacts, the cries of children.

"Oh dear. Oh dear, no!" Her heart beat faster in anticipation and fear of what she might see.

She could see the great oak's branches in the moonlight. The sounds of military engagement, and the louder cries of the children once more. She saw possessed Roman soldiers and ghosts combined swarm the center of the sanctuary.

Without hesitation, she grasped the crossbow, aimed, and shot into the fray. She missed the first shot at the undead horde. She kept moving. Loaded another bolt. She shot again. This time she didn't miss. The bolt tore through two undead Roman heads. She noticed that the Romans attacked the legs of the charging undead.

A good tactic to ensure they couldn't charge again with full strength. No legs. No charge.

More enemy soldiers fell to the ground, and the Roman position was almost successfully defended.

She fired yet another bolt. Another undead soldier fell to the ground in front of a familiar and very much living Roman soldier.

"Magnus!" She jumped over and tiptoed between the twitching and crawling undead.

"Michaela!" Magnus opened the square to her.

"More ghost soldiers come. At least fifty, and my strongest warrior is possessed by them. They are coming this way." Michaela breathed heavily.

"No matter how many times we repel their attacks, they keep coming back. There has to be another way we can defeat them," Magnus said.

"Thank you for protecting these children."

"They brought ten to the sanctuary, and all ten are alive, but I don't know for how much longer. I see you have your war paint on. It's a good look," Magnus said.

"This war paint helped me slip past them. They almost caught me."

"We can carve the husks that they possess, but the spirits do not die. These spirits are relentless. They said 'Baal wills his return,' which makes me think they are Carthaginian. Baal is a god in their religion," Magnus said.

"They come seeking vengeance for the Punic Wars." A familiar older man's voice sounded from next to the oak tree.

"Hutch!" Michaela was happy to see a familiar face of her own people. "How did the children get here, Magnus? Did you or your men find them?"

"They were brought here by the ghostly Carthaginians —" Magnus started.

"They want to sacrifice the children to unleash him," Hutch said.

The tree cracked again. Power pulsed through the roots and rattled in the trunk.

Hutch bowed his head. "Samhain has begun. The spirits beckon and call to be unleashed. I am afraid Magnus is right. It is not possible to defeat such evil with the current means at your disposal."

CHAPTER TWENTY-TWO

Michaela rubbed her forehead. "Who unleashed these spirits in the first place? They wouldn't just spew from the tree when the Romans and priest set foot on our soil."

"That is very likely the case. Someone had to have performed a ritual to alert these ancient spirits," Hutch said.

"We haven't time to ruminate or solve a mystery. I sent Romanus to get more help from the Iceni guarding the village. He should be back soon, and that should buy us more time to figure out how to combat this evil," Magnus said.

"The only suggestion I have is the power of Yeshua. Invoke him and perhaps that could be used as a defense and means to defeat Baal's army." Upon Hutch's suggestion, another vibrating pulse shot out from the roots and shook the ground they grew under.

Magnus lifted his sword. "I will take my chances with my sword over a poor dead carpenter."

Something rolled towards Magnus's feet. He readied his sword, assuming it was an undead crawler, when to his horror it was not an undead Carthaginian warrior but Romanus's head. Still bleeding and squirting blood from the mangled sinew of his shortened neck.

"Michaela. Hutch. You need to leave the sanctuary now. Give it up. Your efforts are fruitless." A voice emanated from the trees in the direction of the village.

"Conor?!" Michaela yelled.

"Who is Conor?" Magnus asked

The warrior queen answered, "I sent him to sue for peace with the Iceni after their men were killed in our village."

Conor walked into the sanctuary and wiped blood from a curved blade on his robes. "You mean to replace our tradition with these vile Roman intruders' religion. They will not rest until our culture is destroyed, Michaela. Hutch, you know I speak the truth."

"Yeshua brings a message of peace and selflessness, Conor. You would kill our own villagers in tribute to your gods," Michaela said.

"You are so quick to turn your back on what even you have known and practiced most of your life." Conor's brow furrowed. He lifted his arms up and spoke in a strange tongue.

The earth shook. It knocked the Romans, Michaela, Hutch, and the children to the ground.

Magnus looked up from his prone position. He looked to the trees surrounding the sanctuary. The spaces between the trees filled in with more reanimated dead. Now there was a mixture of Pict villagers, warriors, and his own men. He recognized some of their faces. Especially one, Tiberius. Conor had corrupted his dear friend's body.

The earth ceased to shake.

Magnus was the first to his feet. "To the center! All of us. Form a phalanx! Now!"

"Oh, you fools. Your tactics won't work. Which is fine. Baal and Danu won't mind more blood along with the children's," Conor warned.

Michaela and Hutch rolled into the center with the children.

Magnus lifted his shield and helped Brayden to his feet. "You will have to push in as far as you can to the center, Michaela. Hold the children if you have to."

The Romans formed a tighter, smaller square, except this time, the shields covered not only the ground attack but the air attack. The Romans in the interior of the square behind their fellow soldiers on the perimeter lifted their shields high over their heads. They formed a shell in the center of the sanctuary.

"Michaela, it is time to pray," Hutch suggested.

Michaela held the four-year-old girl who, at this point, had run out tears and nearly fell asleep on her shoulder. They were packed tight in the phalanx. The rest of the children hugged the backs and legs of the legionaries.

"Why don't they attack?" Cassius asked.

"They have us surrounded. They will. Be ready," Brayden said.

The ground rumbled again, this time in a rhythmic pattern. Like a drumbeat. Magnus, on the perimeter, peeked through a small crack in between his shield and Brayden's.

The rhythmic thumping grew in strength.

"Hutch, if I kill this bastard Conor, will it stop all this?"

"Don't break our phalanx, Magnus," Brayden warned.

"It may weaken their power, yes," Hutch answered.

The drumming grew louder and louder. Magnus looked through the phalanx once again. He saw the source of the earthquake, the cause of the village's destruction, the murderer who had stomped his men deep into the ground: one of Hannibal of Carthage's massive war elephants. It glowed blue like the other spirits, its tusks stretching at least six feet from each side of the long trunk. In but a few seconds, it would trample all of them.

Conor still stood in its path with his arms open.

"Michaela, it's time to pray. All of you, pray!" Magnus handed Michaela Tiberius's crucifix. Then he threw his shield down and charged Conor.

"Yeshua, defend us in battle," Michaela said. "Be our protection against the wickedness and snares of Baal. May Iehova **rebuke** him, we **humbly** pray..."

The war elephant breached the perimeter of the sanctuary.

Conor began to move from its path.

Magnus chased Conor, a mere meter between him and his enemy.

"And do **thou**, O Prince of the Heavenly Host, by the power of God, thrust into hell, Baal..."

The war elephant stomped three meters from the phalanx.

Magnus tackled Conor. They were somehow underneath the massive war elephant, having dodged its front feet.

"...and all evil spirits who wander through the world for the ruin of souls. Amen." Michaela began to cry.

The children screamed.

The elephant let out a tremendous, high-pitched, bloodthirsty roar.

Magnus drove his sword through the rib cage of Conor. The centurion didn't stop there. He angled the sword and drove it farther into his torso, thus piercing his heart.

A blinding light burst from the tree. Magnus rolled away and covered his eyes.

CHAPTER TWENTY-THREE

Magnus opened his eyes. Either Hutch's drink had worn off or Michaela's prayer had worked. The surrounding blue ghosts disappeared. The rampaging beast, gone. No corrupted dead bodies reanimated with the intent to kill. The feeling at present, miraculously, was peaceful.

A warm yellow glow emanated from the tree. Fireflies dotted the sanctuary. Magnus recalled the Picts referring to them as faeries.

The Romans threw off their shields, exhausted from their night of battle.

The children attached themselves to an adult or each other.

Michaela held the girl, who played with Tiberius's cross.

Hutch stood, walked over to Magnus, and hugged him.

"Druid, please. Let go of me. I am not certain it is I you should be embracing." Magnus nodded toward Michaela.

. . .

MAGNUS STOOD in front of Michaela at the entrance to the village. "I shall return with auxiliaries and more men to help rebuild and provide relief."

"We can handle the rebuild," Michaela insisted.

"I have no doubt you and your people are up to the task. I think Yeshua would approve of my offer to help." Magnus nodded.

"He would." Michaela smiled.

"We will be back. I have to return for Tiberius and the others." Magnus turned to his remaining nineteen men out of one hundred.

"It could have been a whole lot worse. The remaining children have been found in the caves in the valley. What will you tell your governor?" Michaela asked.

Magnus turned around. *"Veritas."*

"WHAT WILL you have me report to the emperor?" Governor Gricola asked.

Magnus stood with his helmet under his arm. "I suggest we form an Order to protect against these types of threats moving forward, especially if we intend to spread Yeshua's message even farther."

"You would have this woman lead this Order?"

"Her faith is unmatched, her leadership ever selfless, her demeanor ever humble. I think the emperor would approve of these traits as they echo that of Yeshua himself. I assure you, Yeshua favors this undertaking," Magnus said.

The governor took another swig of his wine. The story he was just told, frankly, frightened him. Made him nervous. Dreadfully uncomfortable. More horror stories from beyond the wall. One would think he would be used to them by now.

"Very well. This Order you speak of shall be proposed immediately."

AFTERWORD

ON "THE ANCIENT ORDER"

I hope you enjoyed the thrills and chills of "The Ancient Order!" This book was inspired by my fascination with history. I love learning of a bygone era to better make sense of the life I am living now. I was able to combine my passions for history, supernatural, and of course, thrillers to make something unique and that I feel further explores one of the more intriguing elements of the larger series: The Order of St. Michael's history.

The whole concept of a new religion subsuming old religions and customs is just eminently interesting to me. In the context of "The Ancient Order", Christianity has been adopted by the Roman Emperor and his sons thus, the evangelical spread of Christianity gives way to a more militant one. How do people respond to this new religion? Do some people willingly accept these new beliefs? Do some people stubbornly resist? How does the concept of religion play a role in the shaping of culture and identity?

I tried to properly communicate that the transition from

widespread and deeply entrenched pagan worship to Christianity was not exactly a smooth one and not without its protagonists, antagonists, and static characters that straddled that line of acting Christian but knowingly, in their heart are not willing to change that which they have known for the whole of their lives, which is giving tribute to the gods.

History is not to be oversimplified and given to gross generalizations as we tend to do in our modern era. History is messy and I very much wanted to show that chaos in "The Ancient Order." Of course, I do not portend that this book is exceedingly historically accurate. It is a fiction, yet one has to think that pagans struggled with the concept of monotheism and the God concept just as much as some of us do today.

In conclusion, I did more research for this short book than any other book I have written ever! I did take some inspiration from swords-and-sandals epics. I confess I do have familial origins in Roman Britain, Scotland, and Ireland so the ways of the Celtic people has been a lifelong personal journey of discovery. Again, I hope you enjoyed this book and will also delight in the continuing adventures of The Order of St. Michael.

Of course, you will have to get used to the eccentric Bud Hutchins to do that... please enjoy excerpts from the Bud Hutchins Supernatural Thrillers Series!

THE SERIES FEATURING THE ORDER OF ST. MICHAEL

AUTHOR'S NOTE ON "THE ORDER OF ST. MICHAEL" PLUS EXCERPT

The idea for Bud Hutchins came from a desire to create a contrasting main character in a dramatically different series. Bud is quite different from the honorable and lovable Captain Brendan in my Tannenbaum Tailors series. Captain Brendan is a natural leader with humor and genuine heart and Bud is an eccentric, self-absorbed genius. They are very different in many ways but also similar where it counts.

Bud speaks in a fake English accent and is a difficult person to be around, yet he is somehow magnetic, and I hope that you learn to root for him. My friend Tony suggested I write something completely different than the Christmas-themed action adventures of the Tailors. I took that suggestion to heart. I wanted to maintain the originality inherent in the Tailors series, so I brainstormed something off-beat that combined science fiction tech, ancient history, and supernatural thrills.

My love of Universal Studio's horror films also served as inspiration for the Order of St. Michael. You will find easter eggs and homages to those films with each subsequent book in the series. My grandparents were movie-lovers and introduced me to so many classic films and stories. I remember the day I graduated from kindergarten. My grandparents gave me action figures of the Wolf-Man, Dracula, and Frankenstein's Monster. Every October we would watch the old films on cassette tapes. I even remember what drawer they stored the movies in!

The gothic structures, the foggy atmosphere of the sets, and of course, the monsters continue to captivate me!

I can go on and on, but I won't.

Please enjoy three chapters of one of my early works:

1. MEET BUD

The bloodied corpse lay a few feet away from the broken trunk of an old oak tree. The ground vibrated, the wind howled, blowing the last leaves off the mangled, tattered branches of the New England forest.

"So terribly reminiscent of old horror films. And what is with these strange tremors? A minor earthquake, perhaps. I shall check geological data of the area. My work has been laid out for me, literally. Pun intended." Bud Hutchins knelt down, feeling the vibration of the earth steadily pulsing. He examined the victim.

The corpse was an older male wearing a dark grey robe with a hood. Streaked with blood and torn from the force of the multiple stab wounds and a sliced jugular vein, this person met Death in gruesome fashion.

"Stab wounds found near or in major arteries. Whoever stabbed this man, knows their way around a knife and human anatomy. Quite ostentatious. Judging from the amount of blood soaked into the robes and the ground, it is possible the murderer collected the blood. There should be a large amount pooled around the victim's neck."

Leaves rustled behind Bud. He turned quickly and saw a hooded figure weaving in between the dense brush. Bud gave chase. The autumn leaves, blanketing the forest floor, smelled dank. The faster Bud moved, the stronger the scent. The hooded figure weaved in and out between oak and maple trees. With each pounding foot, leaves kicked up into Bud's face. He put his hands up as a shield. His long Burberry trench coat flapping behind him, might actually have slowed him down. He refused to take it off. Not that he was naked underneath. He felt the coat was necessary to fit the part of his new job.

He gained on the hooded person. Bud took a flying leap and clipped the runaway's foot with his hand. Bud landed with a thud and lay sprawled on the forest floor. The hooded figure fell hard and narrowly missed a craggy fallen branch.

"Ack!" Bud spit leaves out. There are downsides to having a big mouth. Room for more stuff to enter. Plus, his verbal vomit problems. It worked both ways.

The hooded figure struggled to stand.

"Oh no you don't! It is clear that I have successfully impeded your progress. In my keen observation, those who try to run have a legitimate reason to." Bud pinned the hooded figure down with his knee.

"Let me go! Please! Please don't kill me!" A shrieking female voice burst forth.

"I believe we have a misunderstanding. I did not murder anyone. Perhaps you did!" Bud said.

"That was my uncle back there! I just called the cops.

Who are you? There is no way the cops could have made it here this fast."

"Ah yes, so you phoned it in." Bud turned the female over. Her face was pale and her eyes big and hazel. Striking.

Police sirens approached.

"Get off of me!"

"Get off the girl, young man. Let us have her." Squeaky, raspy, voices filled their ears with dread.

Bud looked up. Surrounding him as if they appeared from somewhere behind the trees were six haggard women, varying in age. Their tongues were hanging out. Their nails were craggy and overlong. One of the smaller figures giggled. The women closed in around Bud and the girl. Salivating and laughing.

2. BUD TIME

The girl struggled underneath Bud.

"I shall return!" Bud yelled. He closed his eyes and pressed the button on his wristband. When Bud opened his eyes, he was back in front of his parents' house. He scrambled in his trench coat for his keys and fumbled them. The keys descended toward the ground. He intercepted them at his knee. He found the right key and opened the door. He ran down the front hall to his bedroom.

Bud jumped towards his closet door and banged his head on the doorknob.

"Shit! This is not going well!" Bud recovered, opened the closet door, and secured a blue canister. Bud stood up and pushed his wristband again.

Bud was back in the forest. The haggard, partially bald, witches watched in amazement as Bud literally appeared in front of their eyes. They had closed in on the girl and Bud again.

"You left me here with them! You just disappeared!" The girl scolded Bud.

Bud didn't bother responding. He pulled a pin on the blue canister and threw it. Blue-grey smoke filled the air around them. He grabbed the girl's hand. The witches wretched hands clawed in blind desperation to capture the pair. Bud pushed one of the witches down with his free hand. This cleared the way out of the smoke and away from the horrid predators.

"Keep running! Trust me! I will find you! There were, at least, two younger witches fit enough to give chase. I will hold them off," Bud said.

"Okay!" The girl kept running.

Bud hoped that the smoke canister provided enough cover that the witches would not know where to look.

"Get your hands up!" A deep, gravelly, male voice sounded from behind Bud.

"Don't move!" Bud felt the pat of hands from his armpits to his hips and lower. Bud remembered the girl saying she called the police. Bud lowered his head and sighed.

3. ARRESTED PROCEDURE

Bud observed the wooden paneled Salem Police Station and smirked at how quaint and peaceful it seemed. It was the size of a roadside diner, and was cramped with desks. His home town, Chicago, had many police stations all of which were much more crowded, not with desks, but with perps and cops busy making phone calls, filling out paperwork, following leads.

Bud sat in a wooden chair. A beam of sunlight illuminated the dust in the air and created a spotlight on the desk in front of him. On the other side of the desk was Officer Hanks.

"Maeve, the victim's niece saw you over her uncle's dead body earlier this afternoon. Why were you there?" Officer Hanks asked. His voice was deep perfect for the voiceover in a truck commercial.

"Have you examined the contents of my wallet? I assure you. This will explain my presence over the corpse."

"Listen kid, a wallet with a hokey P.I. license in it, doesn't count as an alibi. Why were you there?" Hanks said.

"Hokey? I think not. My credentials are just as legitimate as the ones issued by your fine operation here in Salem."

"Oh, so now, you are a city kid comparing us to your big city department. I assure you, you punk kid, that we here in Salem, have just as much power as the law in Chicago."

Bud had played his hand wonderfully, preyed upon Hanks's insecurities. Rural vs Urban. Small town vs Big City sometimes worked in these situations. Bud knew he should stop toying with Officer Hanks and answer his question but he would not believe the truthful answer. Misdirection and non-answers seemed the right course of action.

"I never said anything of the sort, Officer. Have you determined the time the murder occurred? By my estimation, since some of the blood surrounding the body had soaked into the ground, the act of murder had to have occurred at least five to six hours before the niece saw me examining the body."

Officer Hanks knew who led the conversation. He had allowed his emotions to negate any power he had in the interrogation. Hanks slammed his hands down on the desk, pushed his chair back with his long arms, and left the room. Bud heard a muffled, "Keep that smarmy little shit in there overnight. What is with that fake British accent anyway?"

Bud got lucky. Hanks was in a bad mood or just didn't

feel like dealing with a murder investigation. There had been few murders here in Salem, since the Salem Witch Trials of 1692. Twenty people were killed in a matter of months over a terrible example of greed, theocratic principles, and hysteria. Since then this town had been peaceful.

The beam of light through the window had dimmed, the sun was going down. The fall evening's crisp wind bit the air and rattled the leaves of the maple tree's outside of the interrogation room. Three hours had passed since Hanks talked with Bud. Bud's behind ached. His boredom intensified. A young man of his intellect needed almost constant stimulation. Bud stayed strong knowing that 'freezing' the suspect was a classic technique. Boring the person into talking, or keeping them awake for long periods of time worked in many cases of those with weak minds. Bud's mind displayed no signs of weakness.

Three more hours dragged on in the police station. By now, whoever killed the niece's uncle was long gone. The evening set in. Bright fluorescent bulbs buzzed over Bud's head. Still no Hanks. Bud could easily leave at any given moment except his belongings were here. Hanks secured the handcuffs over Bud's wristband. Bud just needed to adjust the cuffs to press the button. Bud looked to see if any officers were coming when he heard the niece Maeve's voice.

"Please officer, let him go. He is my friend. He was helping me."

"I understand that but..." Hanks response was cut short by the lights going out. The computer monitors stayed on for a few seconds then sparked off.

"Everybody stay calm. Just a power outage is all," Hanks said.

A young beat officer looked through the blinds, "Uh, the street lights are on as well as every other building on Main."

Bud suspected that witches of Salem were on the hunt. He shook the hand cuffs and his wristband showed. Bud used his chin to press the wristband.

Hanks stood in the doorway. His head cocked to the side. He looked like a bird had possessed him. He could not believe his eyes. Bud Hutchins had disappeared. Vanished in front of his eyes. How could this be? There had to be an explanation. Whatever the case, he hoped Bud would come back to help to make sense of the situation. Hanks saw what he thought were witches break through the perimeter fence of the department parking lot. As much as Bud was a pain in the ass, his intelligence and wit were apparent.

A tinny, screeching rake from the roof signaled the witches presence. A cackling coven circled in for the kill.

Bud Hutchins scoured his closet for a weapon. Anything that might help in the situation. His old baseball bat leaned up against the back wall of his messy, funky-smelling closet. He grabbed it.

"This should make the jump with me as will this." He grabbed an old hockey stick

"Bert get me out of these cuffs," Bud said.

"Yes, sir." A teenager, similar to Bud, used a key to detach the cuffs.

"Thank you. Goodbye." Bud vanished from the closet.

Officer Hanks unlocked the gun cabinet in the locker room. He pulled a pump shotgun and loaded four rounds. He would have loaded more but his nerves were too rattled. Hanks stood in the next to the cage where they held the girl for interrogation. He pulled down the pump handle and readied a round in the barrel.

The tinny raking sound settled into a thumping bass. The witches trampled on the roof for fun to scare and intimidate the buildings occupants before entering. Hanks looked up with the butt of the shotgun pressed to his shoulder. Sweat beaded down his tired face.

"Make them stop!" Maeve covered her ears.

"I don't believe we can manage to make them cease, but we can make them shriek even moreso." Bud Hutchins appeared. He held his hockey stick and bat together to from a cross.

"How the hell did you get back here?" Hanks said, letting the shotgun rest.

"Never mind that. We had all better make it to an automobile on the double quick." Bud moved towards the front door of the police station, holding his makeshift cross up to eye level.

"Is your motorcar near the front of the building?" Bud asked.

"Yes, it is right outside. But how are we gonna make it out there with these crazy people attacking us? You planning on hitting them with your sports equipment?" Hanks asked.

"Not so savage as to hit but repel."

"Are they frickin' witch vampires or something?" Hanks asked.

The sound of glass shattering and smattering across the floor in the interrogation room behind them caused Hanks to flinch and fire two rounds. He shattered the door lock.

"It would have been wise not to help them." Bud motioned towards Maeve to follow him. Hanks brought up the rear as Maeve and Bud opened the front door. The street lights flickered. The brisk fall evening air caused Bud a slight shiver. He held his makeshift cross high in front of him. The witches were nowhere to be found. The cackling, thumping, scratching that resonated inside the police department now seemed imaginary.

"I got the keys right here." Hanks tossed them to Maeve. He held the shotgun steady.

"I just got my permit. I don't feel comfortable doing this!"

"Hutchins, you drive then. I am the only one who can shoot!" Hanks yelled.

"I don't drive motorcars. They are extremely inefficient and drain the world's resources."

"Holy hell! Seriously?"

A witch busted through the entrance and out onto the sidewalk. Hanks shot a round hitting the witch flush in the chest. She flew back inside the station like a rag doll.

"Your driving experience Maeve, though limited, might lend itself greatly to our escape," Bud said.

"Shit. Oh God!" Maeve made her way to the driver door of the squad car. The nearest light post flickered. A squeaking sound as if someone was sliding down it caused Maeve to fumble the keys. In between yellow flashes and mild darkness, Maeve searched for the keys on the street. She found them next to the front wheel. She stood up and glowing green eyes and frizzed hair met her gaze. A long tongue slithered from a mouth from which a foul odor emanated.

Bud pushed Maeve back towards the trunk of the car. He gripped his bat and stick displaying the cross. The witch cowered. Bud stepped forward. The witch contorted her elbow behind her head. Bud took another step. The witch ran, twitching.

"Now might be the opportune moment," Bud said.

Maeve opened the driver door, hopped in, and started the car.

Hanks took the back seat, unrolled the window, set the shotgun on the passenger window frame. Bud sat in the front.

"Where we going?" Maeve jerked the car out of park.

"County," Hanks answered.

"The emperor has requested that I formally query you for your opinion of this chronicle of our travels and experiences in the form of a book review. So please leave a review of The Ancient Order. We thank you very much.

-MAGNUS VICILLIUS, SPQR

USA TODAY BESTSELLING AUTHOR
JB MICHAELS

THE ORDER OF ST. MICHAEL

A BUD HUTCHINS THRILLER

PRAISE FOR THE ORDER OF ST. MICHAEL

"I started to smile as I listened to Bud's discourse on the condition of the corpse he encounters and kept smiling throughout this exciting, original and very entertaining book, which cunningly blends science with the supernatural. Michaels' plot is fast-paced and filled with the unexpected, and his characters are finely drawn and credible. I'll be watching for more Bud Hutchins Thrillers -- surely an inventor/investigator this prodigious deserves a few more adventures. The Order of St. Michael: A Bud Hutchins Thriller is grand fun for contemporary fantasy lovers of all ages and it's most highly recommended."

Reviewed by Jack Magnus for Readers' Favorite

1

MEET BUD

The bloodied corpse lay a few feet away from the broken trunk of an old oak tree. The ground vibrated, the wind howled, blowing the last leaves off the mangled, tattered branches of the New England forest.

"So terribly reminiscent of old horror films. And what is with these strange tremors? A minor earthquake, perhaps. I shall check geological data of the area. My work has been laid out for me, literally. Pun intended." Bud Hutchins knelt down, feeling the vibration of the earth steadily pulsing. He examined the victim.

The corpse was an older male wearing a dark grey robe with a hood. Streaked with blood and torn from the force of the multiple stab wounds and a sliced jugular vein, this person met Death in gruesome fashion.

"Stab wounds found near or in major arteries. Whoever stabbed this man, knows their way around a knife and human anatomy. Quite ostentatious. Judging from the amount of blood soaked into the robes and the ground, it is possible the murderer collected the blood. There should be a large amount pooled around the victim's neck."

Leaves rustled behind Bud. He turned quickly and saw a hooded figure weaving in between the dense brush. Bud gave chase. The autumn leaves, blanketing the forest floor, smelled dank. The faster Bud moved, the stronger the scent. The hooded figure weaved in and out between oak and maple trees. With each pounding foot, leaves kicked up into Bud's face. He put his hands up as a shield. His long Burberry trench coat flapping behind him, might actually have slowed him down. He refused to take it off. Not that he was naked underneath. He felt the coat was necessary to fit the part of his new job.

He gained on the hooded person. Bud took a flying leap and clipped the runaway's foot with his hand. Bud landed with a thud and lay sprawled on the forest floor. The hooded figure fell hard and narrowly missed a craggy fallen branch.

"Ack!" Bud spit leaves out. There are downsides to having a big mouth. Room for more stuff to enter. Plus, his verbal vomit problems. It worked both ways.

The hooded figure struggled to stand.

"Oh no you don't! It is clear that I have successfully impeded your progress. In my keen observation, those who try to run have a legitimate reason to." Bud pinned the hooded figure down with his knee.

"Let me go! Please! Please don't kill me!" A shrieking female voice burst forth.

"I believe we have a misunderstanding. I did not murder anyone. Perhaps you did!" Bud said.

"That was my uncle back there! I just called the cops. Who are you? There is no way the cops could have made it here this fast."

"Ah yes, so you phoned it in." Bud turned the female over. Her face was pale and her eyes big and hazel. Striking.

Police sirens approached.

"Get off of me!"

"Get off the girl, young man. Let us have her." Squeaky, raspy, voices filled their ears with dread.

Bud looked up. Surrounding him as if they appeared from somewhere behind the trees were six haggard women, varying in age. Their tongues were hanging out. Their nails were craggy and overlong. One of the smaller figures giggled. The women closed in around Bud and the girl. Salivating and laughing.

2

BUD TIME

The girl struggled underneath Bud.

"I shall return!" Bud yelled. He closed his eyes and pressed the button on his wristband. When Bud opened his eyes, he was back in front of his parents' house. He scrambled in his trench coat for his keys and fumbled them. The keys descended toward the ground. He intercepted them at his knee. He found the right key and opened the door. He ran down the front hall to his bedroom.

Bud jumped towards his closet door and banged his head on the doorknob.

"Shit! This is not going well!" Bud recovered, opened the closet door, and secured a blue canister. Bud stood up and pushed his wristband again.

Bud was back in the forest. The haggard, partially bald, witches watched in amazement as Bud literally appeared in front of their eyes. They had closed in on the girl and Bud again.

"You left me here with them! You just disappeared!" The girl scolded Bud.

Bud didn't bother responding. He pulled a pin on the

blue canister and threw it. Blue-grey smoke filled the air around them. He grabbed the girl's hand. The witches wretched hands clawed in blind desperation to capture the pair. Bud pushed one of the witches down with his free hand. This cleared the way out of the smoke and away from the horrid predators.

"Keep running! Trust me! I will find you! There were, at least, two younger witches fit enough to give chase. I will hold them off," Bud said.

"Okay!" The girl kept running.

Bud hoped that the smoke canister provided enough cover that the witches would not know where to look.

"Get your hands up!" A deep, gravelly, male voice sounded from behind Bud.

"Don't move!" Bud felt the pat of hands from his armpits to his hips and lower. Bud remembered the girl saying she called the police. Bud lowered his head and sighed.

3

ARRESTED PROCEDURE

Bud observed the wooden paneled Salem Police Station and smirked at how quaint and peaceful it seemed. It was the size of a roadside diner, and was cramped with desks. His home town, Chicago, had many police stations all of which were much more crowded, not with desks, but with perps and cops busy making phone calls, filling out paperwork, following leads.

Bud sat in a wooden chair. A beam of sunlight illuminated the dust in the air and created a spotlight on the desk in front of him. On the other side of the desk was Officer Hanks.

"Maeve, the victim's niece saw you over her uncle's dead body earlier this afternoon. Why were you there?" Officer Hanks asked. His voice was deep perfect for the voiceover in a truck commercial.

"Have you examined the contents of my wallet? I assure you. This will explain my presence over the corpse."

"Listen kid, a wallet with a hokey P.I. license in it, doesn't count as an alibi. Why were you there?" Hanks said.

"Hokey? I think not. My credentials are just as legitimate as the ones issued by your fine operation here in Salem."

"Oh, so now, you are a city kid comparing us to your big city department. I assure you, you punk kid, that we here in Salem, have just as much power as the law in Chicago."

Bud had played his hand wonderfully, preyed upon Hanks's insecurities. Rural vs Urban. Small town vs Big City sometimes worked in these situations. Bud knew he should stop toying with Officer Hanks and answer his question but he would not believe the truthful answer. Misdirection and non-answers seemed the right course of action.

"I never said anything of the sort, Officer. Have you determined the time the murder occurred? By my estimation, since some of the blood surrounding the body had soaked into the ground, the act of murder had to have occurred at least five to six hours before the niece saw me examining the body."

Officer Hanks knew who led the conversation. He had allowed his emotions to negate any power he had in the interrogation. Hanks slammed his hands down on the desk, pushed his chair back with his long arms, and left the room. Bud heard a muffled, "Keep that smarmy little shit in there overnight. What is with that fake British accent anyway?"

Bud got lucky. Hanks was in a bad mood or just didn't feel like dealing with a murder investigation. There had been few murders here in Salem, since the Salem Witch Trials of 1692. Twenty people were killed in a matter of months over a terrible example of greed, theocratic principles, and hysteria. Since then this town had been peaceful.

The beam of light through the window had dimmed, the sun was going down. The fall evening's crisp wind bit the air and rattled the leaves of the maple tree's outside of the interrogation room. Three hours had passed since

Hanks talked with Bud. Bud's behind ached. His boredom intensified. A young man of his intellect needed almost constant stimulation. Bud stayed strong knowing that 'freezing' the suspect was a classic technique. Boring the person into talking, or keeping them awake for long periods of time worked in many cases of those with weak minds. Bud's mind displayed no signs of weakness.

Three more hours dragged on in the police station. By now, whoever killed the niece's uncle was long gone. The evening set in. Bright fluorescent bulbs buzzed over Bud's head. Still no Hanks. Bud could easily leave at any given moment except his belongings were here. Hanks secured the handcuffs over Bud's wristband. Bud just needed to adjust the cuffs to press the button. Bud looked to see if any officers were coming when he heard the niece Maeve's voice.

"Please officer, let him go. He is my friend. He was helping me."

"I understand that but..." Hanks response was cut short by the lights going out. The computer monitors stayed on for a few seconds then sparked off.

"Everybody stay calm. Just a power outage is all," Hanks said.

A young beat officer looked through the blinds, "Uh, the street lights are on as well as every other building on Main."

Bud suspected that witches of Salem were on the hunt. He shook the hand cuffs and his wristband showed. Bud used his chin to press the wristband.

Hanks stood in the doorway. His head cocked to the side. He looked like a bird had possessed him. He could not believe his eyes. Bud Hutchins had disappeared. Vanished in front of his eyes. How could this be? There had to be an explanation. Whatever the case, he hoped Bud would come back to help to make sense of the situation. Hanks saw what he thought were witches break through the perimeter fence of the department parking lot. As much as Bud was a pain in the ass, his intelligence and wit were apparent.

A tinny, screeching rake from the roof signaled the witches presence. A cackling coven circled in for the kill.

Bud Hutchins scoured his closet for a weapon. Anything that might help in the situation. His old baseball bat leaned up against the back wall of his messy, funky-smelling closet. He grabbed it.

"This should make the jump with me as will this." He grabbed an old hockey stick

"Bert get me out of these cuffs," Bud said.

"Yes, sir." A teenager, similar to Bud, used a key to detach the cuffs.

"Thank you. Goodbye." Bud vanished from the closet.

Officer Hanks unlocked the gun cabinet in the locker room. He pulled a pump shotgun and loaded four rounds. He would have loaded more but his nerves were too rattled. Hanks stood in the next to the cage where they held the girl for interrogation. He pulled down the pump handle and readied a round in the barrel.

The tinny raking sound settled into a thumping bass. The witches trampled on the roof for fun to scare and intimidate the buildings occupants before entering. Hanks looked up with the butt of the shotgun pressed to his shoulder. Sweat beaded down his tired face.

"Make them stop!" Maeve covered her ears.

"I don't believe we can manage to make them cease, but we can make them shriek even moreso." Bud Hutchins appeared. He held his hockey stick and bat together to from a cross.

"How the hell did you get back here?" Hanks said, letting the shotgun rest.

"Never mind that. We had all better make it to an automobile on the double quick." Bud moved towards the front door of the police station, holding his makeshift cross up to eye level.

"Is your motorcar near the front of the building?" Bud asked.

"Yes, it is right outside. But how are we gonna make it out there with these crazy people attacking us? You planning on hitting them with your sports equipment?" Hanks asked.

"Not so savage as to hit but repel."

"Are they frickin' witch vampires or something?" Hanks asked.

The sound of glass shattering and smattering across the floor in the interrogation room behind them caused Hanks to flinch and fire two rounds. He shattered the door lock.

"It would have been wise not to help them." Bud motioned towards Maeve to follow him. Hanks brought up the rear as Maeve and Bud opened the front door. The street lights flickered. The brisk fall evening air caused Bud a slight shiver. He held his makeshift cross high in front of him. The witches were nowhere to be found. The cackling, thumping, scratching that resonated inside the police department now seemed imaginary.

"I got the keys right here." Hanks tossed them to Maeve. He held the shotgun steady.

"I just got my permit. I don't feel comfortable doing this!"

"Hutchins, you drive then. I am the only one who can shoot!" Hanks yelled.

"I don't drive motorcars. They are extremely inefficient and drain the world's resources."

"Holy hell! Seriously?"

A witch busted through the entrance and out onto the sidewalk. Hanks shot a round hitting the witch flush in the chest. She flew back inside the station like a rag doll.

"Your driving experience Maeve, though limited, might lend itself greatly to our escape," Bud said.

"Shit. Oh God!" Maeve made her way to the driver door of the squad car. The nearest light post flickered. A squeaking sound as if someone was sliding down it caused Maeve to fumble the keys. In between yellow flashes and mild darkness, Maeve searched for the keys on the street. She found them next to the front wheel. She stood up and glowing green eyes and frizzed hair met her gaze. A long tongue slithered from a mouth from which a foul odor emanated.

Bud pushed Maeve back towards the trunk of the car. He gripped his bat and stick displaying the cross. The witch cowered. Bud stepped forward. The witch contorted her elbow behind her head. Bud took another step. The witch ran, twitching.

"Now might be the opportune moment," Bud said.

Maeve opened the driver door, hopped in, and started the car.

Hanks took the back seat, unrolled the window, set the shotgun on the passenger window frame. Bud sat in the front.

"Where we going?" Maeve jerked the car out of park.

"County," Hanks answered.

4

BROOMS AND BRAKES

The squad car moved steadily down the tree-lined main street of Salem towards the state road that led to the County offices.

"I cannot believe your makeshift cross worked there Hutchins." Hanks said.

"I can believe it."

"How did you know?"

"The crucifix is a symbol of fear. Of death. The Romans used the cross as a form of punishment and execution. It was not until that Jesus fellow died on one, that it became a symbol of the divine. Those witches have been resurrected from the 1690s. Christianity was the cause of their demise. For them, the Christian symbol is still seen as a deathly symbol rather than a holy one."

"Wow. Now wait a minute you are telling me that those things that back there are witches from four centuries ago?" Hanks moved his head next to Bud's from the back seat.

"That is what I said. If you think me mistaken ask Maeve."

"How would she know?" Hanks asked.

"My Uncle died trying to prevent their return to the living world," Maeve said.

"So the dead guy in the robes was trying to stop the witches return."

Hanks sat back in the seat and sighed. Thump! Something hit the top of the car. Hanks grabbed the shotgun and looked out the rear window. Bristles from the bottom of a broom hovered in and out of Hank's field of vision.

"Well, Hutchins you were right. Brooms? Holy Shit! Witches are chasing us on flying brooms."

"Thanks for the keen observation Officer Hanks, but I assure you, I am in no need for your endorsement of that which is so painfully obvious. Maeve, I believe a heavier foot on the accelerator is in order," Bud said.

Thump! Thump!

"Shit! Shit! Shit! I can barely see on this crappy country road. It is so dark! I am scared to go any faster!" Maeve said.

"They are trying to scare you. Ignore their poor attempts at distraction and keep your eyes to the road and your pedal foot to the floor," Bud urged.

The rear window cracked from the force of the witch's pounding on the top of the car. Maeve pressed harder on the gas. 88 miles per hour. 90. 95. The thumping stopped. Their assailant gone. Maeve felt the rush of victory.

"Yes!" She yelled.

"Good job kid. I don't see them anywhere! County is just a few miles ahead!" Hanks said.

The rear window shattered. Before Hanks could raise the shotgun, the witch grabbed hold of him and pulled his collar with surprising force. She dragged him out onto the trunk of car.

"Maeve! Slow this infernal machine down!" Bud yelled.

Maeve slammed on the brakes. She lost control. The car spun then flipped off the road.

5
───

DITCH

Smoke billowed from the engine block. The crumpled hood showed jagged edges but the windshield bore only a few cracks. Bud yanked Maeve through the car's passenger door, which was more laborious than one would think. Bud rarely engaged in physical exercise.

"Maeve, is it possible that you could push with your legs? You having the consistency of a giant wet noodle is not helpful," Bud said.

Maeve, clearly in shock, shook with nerves.

"Maeve my dear, your left leg is pinned by the steering column. You have to push with all the might you can muster whilst I pull. Does this make sense?"

"What happened? Wha..." Maeve's pupils rolled back. The whites of her eyes shone brightly in the moonlight.

"Maeve! Don't lose consciousness!"

Her hazel pupils rolled back to the front of her head.

"Excellent. Peripheral vision restored," Bud said.

Maeve managed to push for Bud. She was wobbly when her feet hit the ground.

"We have to move. We better stick to the tree-line.

According to my phone, County is a half hour traversal from here."

"What happened to Hanks?" Maeve rubbed the back of her neck.

"Hanks was pulled from the backseat right before you lost control of the motor vehicle, which may have been to his advantage."

"Shouldn't we go back and find him?"

"I think it better to move forward. He is a resourceful man. He will expect us to go to County for more help, as he perspicaciously suggested earlier."

"Perspa...what?" Maeve looked confused not from the crash but from Bud's word usage.

Bud walked down the side of road towards County. Maeve followed suit.

"Bud we need to go back."

"Your resistance can be attributed to the head trauma you may have sustained in the accident. Let's traverse," Bud said, moving further ahead.

"I don't think you understand. I am the only one that can stop the witches. At least I think I can."

"You can barely drive a car. To what logic can you apply this claim?"

"My Uncle taught me. For years, he has been grooming me to take over for him. Now he's dead. I have to go back."

Bud's eyelids went wide. He mouthed the word "deranged" and slapped his forehead but turned around just the same.

6

COVEN

Bud walked back to Salem behind Maeve who maintained a speed a few paces ahead. He only turned around because Maeve's story made some sense. The witches gave chase for a reason. Maeve claims that reason is her, and she believes that she can stop them.

"May I inquire as to how you plan on stopping the coven?" Bud asked.

"My Uncle belonged to an ancient group known as the Order of St. Michael, a group that the Catholic Church formed to keep evil spirits contained to their realm."

Bud laughed, then coughed to cover it up.

"Laugh all you want Hutchins. You have done some far-fetched things already. I saw you disappear and reappear a couple times," Maeve said.

"I assure you there is a legitimate, scientific reason for my movement."

"Explain away." She turned around to face him.

"I have developed a technology to breakdown mass into molecular form and direct it at near quantum speeds to another location rather instantly."

"Stop with the fake British accent and speak damn English!"

"Teleportation. I have developed technology to teleport from one place to another. I am still in the beta stage of development, but it does work. As you have witnessed. Your turn."

Maeve now walked next to Bud. "That is amazing. Not really sure how it will help our situation. Why did you teleport here anyway? Why are you even here?"

"Someone stole my tech and used it to teleport here. That is when I saw your uncle. I am able to follow whoever is using my tech. As of now I have reason to believe that whoever stole my tech is still here."

The teenaged pair reached the curve in the road that led to the straight shot into town. There was no trace of Hanks anywhere. No shoes or blood trails. Nothing.

"We have to head back to where they killed my uncle," Maeve said.

"Shan't we head to the precinct. To fetch more help? Perhaps the morning shift is arriving early."

"No, it's only 3AM. The only cop on duty on the midnight shift is 350-lb Barney. He is useless."

"Perhaps his heft would help in the fight against the coven," Bud said.

"No, we can't afford to drag anyone else into this mess. The witches will take Hanks back to the area they spawned from."

"Why is that?"

"They need his blood."

7

BLOODLETTING

Bud Hutchins and Maeve picked up their pace and cut through the woods back to the original crime scene. The site where the witches first showed themselves.

"Are you implying that these witches are a hybrid of vampire and witch?"

"No. They need his blood as a sacrifice to summon more evil spirits. Come on Hutchins! Get with it! When you found my uncle he had no blood in his veins. It was all spilled around him."

"So I will operate under the assumption that the person who stole my tech killed your uncle? Since I traced the last teleportation to the exact spot he was killed, it is highly likely. How do I know you didn't subscribe to the ancient humor theory and bleed your uncle yourself?"

Maeve took a break leaned up against a tree.

"My uncle was like a father to me, you ass."

"A strong reaction like that implies you could be hiding something. Also given you haven't mentioned biological parents, perhaps your parents treated you horribly or one of them did and your uncle adopted you to save you from a life of mental illness and deprivation from unloving parent or parents. Alas you couldn't be saved and evil took root anyway and you killed the one person who actually cared for you," Bud rambled.

He saw Maeve eyes glisten and her brow furrow. "You are an idiot."

A cold gust of air carried a cackle to them. Maeve looked at Bud and brought a finger to her closed mouth, shushing him.

"You are sick!" It was Hanks yelling from the same direction as the cackle.

Maeve took a few steps toward the noise, careful not to break any branches. Bud followed. He tightened the waist strap on his Burberry trench coat to prevent snagging on the brush.

The place where her uncle died was a small clearing. Hanks was kneeling in front of and old oak tree. All around him were dead rabbits, which had been placed in a deliberate formation.

"They are going to sacrifice him," Maeve whispered.

Bud stood behind her. "Shall we step in to save the fellow or just observe?"

"We cannot just rush in there. We have no weapons and your makeshift cross is in the car."

"Very well then." Bud leisurely walked out into the clearing.

"Bud! What the hell are you doing?" Maeve yelped.

Bud reached Hanks. "I take it you need assistance."

"Hutchins! You walked right into their damn trap!"

Four witches on brooms hovered over Bud and Hanks. The monstrous, rotten-smelling monsters carried scythes, ready to reap.

8

FLOP

The first swipe missed. The second swipe missed too. Bud was sure the third would not miss.

He quickly fastened something around Hanks' wrist. He pulled a coin from his Burberry coat pocket and tossed it into the woods away from the clearing. Just as a witch took aim at the police officer's neck, Hanks vanished. Bud flopped to the ground on his belly to avoid severe injury from the reaping tool.

"Your blood will suffice!" The witches said in unison. They ignored the sudden disappearance of Officer Hanks.

"My blood is far too thick for sacrificial purposes. It truly has the consistency of maple syrup," Bud said.

Maeve grabbed the thistles of one of the witch's brooms and spun the witch away from Bud. "Bud! Run!"

He quickly jumped to his feet and scurried in the same direction he threw his coin.

The three remaining witches on brooms took notice. Two stayed to deal with Maeve while the other split off in pursuit of Bud.

Bud tightened the waist belt of his trench coat and

ran. The darkness of the forest crept in around him. Visibility was extremely low. He thought for sure that Hanks would be in this area somewhere. He heard a branch fall to the ground behind him, and another. Bud leaned back on a tree and crouched. The darkness, even for Bud, was unsettling. The moon beams in the sacrificial clearing seemed as bright as the sun compared to the sparing, feint glow on the ground around him now. Bud with his back on the trunk peeked over his shoulder towards the clearing.

He looked up and saw a witch slowly flying above. He followed the upper branches movements. He squinted to keep track of her. It was no use. The light was too dim. Bud decided to stay still. Perhaps she would miss him.

A branch cracked above, a few feet in front of Bud. She must have passed over him. He maintained a wooden pose, but there didn't seem to be any nasty old witches anywhere. A calm washed over him. He let out a sigh. Leg muscles straining from his crouch, he stood up.

Bud felt a tremendous weight on his shoulders and fell to his knees. The hot breath on his neck made him gag. The witch had jumped on him from above. Bud reeled from the sudden physical contact and then became overwhelmed with the awful smell of body odor and urine.

"Such a young man! Ooh! I just love young blood!" The witch cackled.

She piggybacked Bud. Her hand clawed at his eyes, and she choked him with her other arm. Bud was never known for his strength and she was able to push her bony hand towards his face. Her long middle finger grazed Bud's eyelashes.

"Oh, just one eye! I am just so hungry. You can keep the other one!" The witch pleaded.

"I prefer to keep both eyes intact," Bud said. Her smell threw Bud into a coughing fit.

Boom! Crack! He felt a warm liquid trickle down his neck. He flipped the dead witch from his back.

"Hutchins, you okay?" Hanks stood next to him, smoking gun in hand.

Bud and Hanks ran back to the clearing and watched Maeve. She displayed her cross as protection. Her uncle told her to always have it ready. The witch she spun away from Bud a few moments earlier fell from her broom. Maeve pointed the cross at the fallen witch to keep her grounded. Maeve grabbed the hovering broom and secured it between her legs.

The other two witches hovered. "Put away that cross little girl. Come play with us."

Maeve's feet left the ground. She took control of the broom and dipped forward, confidently flying and managing her first shot at broom flight. Her cross was still exposed. The witches could do nothing but watch. The symbol of the cross kept her safe. A force field from God.

Maeve flew over to the tree where her uncle died. She, at first, spoke with a tremor in her voice, but it soon transformed into a tone of authority. Of power...

"Saint Michael the Archangel, defend us in battle, be our protection against the malice and snares of the devil. May God rebuke him we humbly pray; and do thou, O Prince of the Heavenly host, by the power of God, thrust into hell Satan and all evil spirits who wander through the world for the ruin of souls. Amen!"

The tree below her burst into flame. The witches fell from their brooms. Explosions burst from the tree and covered the witches in bright blue flames. Maeve hovered above them holding her cross in her hand. She mourned for her uncle but her tears dried from the heat of the tree below. Her years under the tutelage of her uncle had paid off. She had the courage to face evil and smite the deadly witches.

Bud and Hanks yelled for her.

Maeve flew down to them.

"Run away! I am not sure how bad this fire will be!"

"Setting the forest alight with flame was your plan?" Bud asked.

The flames spread to the adjacent trees and made quick work of the dry leaves that were masking the ground.

Bud and Hanks tried to run out of the clearing to no avail. The flames surrounded them.

"May I please have my wristband back please?" Bud asked.

"Here you go." Hanks unfastened the band and returned it to Bud.

"Let Maeve give you a lift!" Bud said. He vanished.

"Hold on to me tight! I am new at this!" Maeve said.

Hanks hopped on. The broom drooped from their combined weight. Maeve moved forward quickly then pulled up and away from the flames that were spreading through the tops of trees.

9
―――――
CATCH UP

Maeve and Officer Hanks flew back over the road and followed the same direction to County.

"Where's Hutchins?" Officers Hanks asked.

"He probably teleported, or so he says." Maeve gripped the broomstick tightly. The brisk night air pushed the blood away from her fingers.

"So that is what happened to me? One second I was surrounded by dead rabbits. Next, I was about 30 feet away in the brush. He teleported me! Now I am on a broom with you! You kids are nuts."

"We may be nuts but we just saved your life Officer," Maeve said.

"Where are we going? Slow down!" Hanks said.

"We need to go to County, correct? It can't be that much further." Maeve had gotten the hang of broom flying rather quickly. A natural.

"Pardon! Pardon! Pardon!"

A familiar voice yelled from the wreckage of the overturned car below on the road to County.

"Oh, what does he want now?" Hanks said.

Bud waved his hands rather awkwardly. It was not a sweeping motion, but more of a quick, short motion as if he trying to rival a hummingbird's wing speed.

"What IS wrong with him?" Maeve landed the broom. Hanks quickly jumped off.

"What did you do to me back there, Hutchins?" Hanks asked.

"Saved your life I might add, which puts red on your ledger. You owe me and will assist me as I see fit," Bud said.

"Thank you Hutchins, but Maeve said you teleported me? Is that true? How the hell did you do that?"

Bud reached into the car, searching for something.

"I can explain it to you in greater depth of course. I found a way to externally dismantle cells on the molecular plane and transport and reconstruct the atoms, molecules, cells and so on and so forth into another place in space and time. The ability to start this process externally is both wonderful yet limiting as I need transpond...."

"Hutchins. For the love of God, you teleported me? Just say it."

"In a way, yes."

"Shouldn't we be headed to County to get more help? We really don't know how many more witches are out there?" Maeve said.

"We needn't worry about the coven anymore. I counted how many there were when we were initially surrounded by your uncle's body and cross checked it with how many witches were initially put to death during the Salem Witch Trials. The numbers matched. It is highly likely that they are all dead again. There is a greater threat in our midst. Hence, I need both of you to assist me."

"That seems rather weak there Hutchins," Hanks said.

"It is of no matter the strength of my argument. What matters is that you assist me," Bud said.

"I guess I owe ya one for bailing me outta there. What do you need? What greater threat?"

"I am not exactly sure who, but I do know what he or she stole. A version of my teleportation tech is missing and I tracked it here to Salem. I recently surveyed my tracking app and another blip shows that a destination marker was used in the bayous of Louisiana at a Beauregard plantation. Maeve and I will investigate that. You will go to my former high school in Chicago, Illinois to find out who stole the tech. Start with my Physics teacher and go from there. I've arranged transportation for you. You just have to make it to the County airport."

"Chicago? What? Illinois? Can you just slow down?" Hanks yelled.

"Slowing down may mean more lives lost to whatever evil menace is teleporting and dealing death with extreme prejudice to the vascular systems of he or she's next victim. We are off. Maeve put this on." Bud handed her a wristband.

Maeve secured it to her wrist. She and Bud vanished.

Hanks shook his head.

Bud returned, "Oh and when you arrive at the airport in Chicago you will be picked up by my friend Bert. Be kind to Bert. Tally ho." Bud vanished again.

Hanks shook his head, "Bert and Bud. Really. What the hell am I doing?" Hanks searched the car for his phone. He peeled from it between the backseat and a door resting against the ground. He called the station. "Barney! We need a team here and I need a lift to the airport asap."

10

BEAUREGARD

Bud noticed the expansive bowling green. A field of grass sprung forth from an old mansion up a small hill.

"Quite similar to Mt. Vernon and tended to," Bud said.

"Went there on a field trip before I went to live with my uncle. It does look like it," Maeve said.

"One would suppose that we have to go towards the rather unkempt mansion. The thief should still be here somewhere as my tracking app has yet to ping another location. Why come to a rundown old mansion in Louisiana?" Bud walked up the bowling green.

Maeve ran to catch up with him. The mansion loomed large. The paint on the two pillars marking the front door were chipped. The porch creaked with their footsteps.

"Stealth has failed us. The house is not properly maintained, but the grass is," Bud whispered. He opened the front door and walked in. The inside bore little light from the outside.

Maeve noted, "The windows have been boarded up."

A few beams of light hit the winding staircase ahead of

them. Cobwebs clung to the banister. The carpet was worn and stained.

"This keeps getting more and more pleasant, I say. Alas, we must carry on," Bud said.

"Any pings on your tracker?" Maeve asked.

"No, but we are most definitely not alone." Bud pointed to the dining room to the right of the foyer. Maeve gasped.

Someone sat at the head of the table facing away from the foyer. The person sat slumped, motionless. Bud moved towards the table. Bud approached the slumped figure with a curiosity mixed with foreboding. The figure smelled terribly. The closer he got the worse the smell--deathly, rotting.

"Do you really need to examine him? I am pretty sure he is a goner. He smells like it." Maeve waved air in front of her nose.

"One can never be too sure, given you just flew on a broom and banished evil witches back to the nether realms." Bud moved closer to the table until he could see that the face was wrinkled with age, and likely too much time in the sun. The rest of the body teemed with dirt as if he'd emerged from a coal mine. Thinning gray hair sprouted from a sun-spotted head, freckled and weathered.

"No breath is exhaling from his lungs. I would officially surmise that this fellow has passed away. Yet, his skin seems rather freshly burnt and the bowling green in front of the mansion was carefully trimmed." Bud moved away from the man, cocked his head, and examined the man, one more time.

"Yep, he's dead. Can we move on? There is probably a tree out back with blood spilled around it already. Do you even want to catch this so-called thief of your teleportation tech?" Maeve urged Bud to action.

"Oh yes, indeed. Tally ho." Bud walked from the dining

room to a sitting room likely used for tea and entertaining guests, Victorian chairs with high backs, ornate coffee tables, and a fireplace were carefully placed to properly maximize room.

Maeve ran ahead to the back of the mansion, hoping to find another tree that needed the protection of the Order of St. Michael.

Bud looked back in the dining room. The slumped figure no longer sat on the chair. The dead man no longer was in the room at all.

"I will absolutely not fall into the same traps as most teens in a horror film do, and look for this fellow. He certainly will find me." Bud quickened his pace and headed towards Maeve. He did not break into a full run, but moved at a faster pace than he usually employed.

Maeve ran towards a copse of trees lining the bank of the Mississippi River. Bud followed, yelling, "We have an interesting, developing, rather disconcerting situation!"

Maeve slowed her pace and allowed Bud to catch up. "What are you talking about? Do you always yell? That doesn't help the whole catch-a-killer mission we are on." She stopped at the tree line.

"The dead fellow at the dining room has since moved from that seemingly permanent seat."

"Oh great, that means we are too late. The next monk is probably dead already," Maeve said.

"It would appear so. The regional haunts in the Bayou consist of hoodoo and voodoo combinations and variations. This area features many stories, legends, and institutions deriving from Haiti and various other islands in the leeward and windward isles of the Caribbean. Slavery acted the vessel that carried the zombie legend to the bayous of Louisiana. One can deduce the spirits spewing forth from this copse of trees is indeed, the cause of the dead keeper of the plantation's reanimation."

"Here he comes now." Maeve pointed to the slow, ambling, dead man who carried a pair of bush trimmers.

"Perhaps we should retreat into these trees to surmise a plan." Bud backed into the copse of trees behind the mansion.

11

SURMISING THE DEAD

Bud and Maeve entered the forested area in a rushed walk. The ambling undead was not far behind.

"We have to find the monk. He has to be in here somewhere, lying in his own pool of blood." Maeve scanned the trees.

"Is it possible that the monk could have been reanimated by the same ephemeral spirits as our groundskeeper?" Bud asked.

"It is. It probably is. There is the tree. The one at the end of this bank here." Maeve ran over to it.

Fallen branches cracked behind them. The undead groundskeeper entered the copse of trees.

"There is the blood but no body. You are right Bud. The monk is around here somewhere too. I will seal this tree. We should assume these undead spirits are good at killing living things in order to ensure their transfer to our realm. Watch my back while I say the words," Maeve said.

Bud looked around for something to use as a weapon. He wished he could teleport back home for a proper weapon, but that would prove counterproductive given the fact that the undead were so close. All he could find was a craggy stick that could pass for a spear.

"So savage and rudimentary but it will do." Bud gripped his stick-spear and held it front of him and posed like a Spartan from Ancient Greece. The undead groundskeeper with the trimmers entered the copse of trees slowly. The smell of flesh, Bud noticed, caused the groundskeeper to shuffle just a bit faster.

"Maeve, as in the car, earlier. I urge you to step on it. Not quite sure why it is taking you quite so long to say that simple prayer." Bud turned towards the ancient tree Maeve needed to seal. She was gone. The groundskeeper shuffled faster. He was only ten feet away. Bud readied his stick-spear. Bush trimmers flew past his head before Bud even realized what happened.

"Quite grateful that you missed, should make my counter even easier to execute," Bud said.

"He didn't miss," a gargled voice said.

Bud turned around. The monk stood close opening and closing the bush trimmers. His arteries were cut and robes bloodied in the same fashion as Maeve's uncle. The monk's face bore no marks and his head twitched. The trimmers created an unsettling cacophony of steely danger. With the blades open, the monk lunged towards Bud.

"Oh dear me, you mustn't be serious. Your body is in the early stages of decay and your fighting rigor mortis. How can you possibly think you have a chance to win this match?" Bud jumped away with time to spare before the trimmer's blades met their target. "How are you even able to vocalize anyway? Or is it that your vocal chords have yet to stiffen?"

The rotting smell of the groundskeeper intensified. Bud swung the stick-spear wildly and struck the groundskeeper on the shoulder. He shrugged and groaned but was undeterred. Bud was able to put twenty feet between himself and both of the undead. The monk kept opening and closing the bush trimmers. The pair headed in Bud's direction.

"Relentless, though pitifully so," Bud thought.

"Bud! The cemetery! Hurry!" Maeve's voice was soft from the distance.

Bud followed the direction of her voice. He left the copse of the trees and ran south down the riverbank away from the plantation. He saw a few gravestones in the distance and Maeve running back towards him. "Back to the mansion now!"

Behind Maeve, a horde of the undead was giving chase. Their speed varied. Some moved swiftly and with vigor while others moped. Their appearances were mostly skeletal, and they wore gray military uniforms.

12

SOUTHERN DISCOMFORT

"Where exactly did you go? You told me you were going to say the prayer over the tree and the very next moment you vanished? I am certain only I can vanish that quickly." Bud managed to match her speed, but was out of breath.

"I wanted to be certain I knew which tree it was so I wandered and found the cemetery!" Maeve ran up the back porch and entered the mansion.

"There has to be a set of weapons somewhere. I mean there must be at least, a shotgun or a revolver or something!" Maeve rummaged through the desk in the sitting room.

"The situation really doesn't merit us staging a battle. We can just teleport and regroup. Grab my hand." Bud held his hand out. The undead groans sounded just outside the back door.

"You are right," Maeve said, grabbing Bud's hand.

Bud looked to his wristband to start the molecular breakdown and noticed that it was gone.

"Oh my!" Bud yelled.

The monk entered the mansion first, still wielding the

bush trimmers. The rest of the skeletal horde followed suit, bashing through the windows from the back porch.

"You lost your band?" Maeve ran from the sitting room back to the front hall. Bud followed.

"I still have the band you gave me. Couldn't we just teleport together with this wristband?" Maeve asked.

"My band is the only one that can trigger the teleportation process. I put strict security measures on the rest of the bands with a near-field communication unlock since I found my tech had been absconded. Now it appears to have worked against me and us, for that matter." Bud's shoulders slumped, much like the horde that followed close behind, "I suggest we flee."

"Ya think Bud!" Maeve opened the front door. More skeletal soldiers greeted her. Some of their faces still bore decaying skin. None had eyelids. Their eyeballs were either sunk in to their skulls or popping out.

Their military training had not failed them and they had successfully flanked the pair. The teenagers were now surrounded by undead, looking to satiate their need for living flesh. Maeve shut the door on the soldier's hand which separated from the rest of his body and fell to the hardwood floor. Maeve screamed and ran up the stairs in a panic.

Bud followed suit, even though he felt the move foolish.

"Is this really the best way to get out of this situation. How will we ever get down from here?" Bud asked.

"We can make a rope or something!" Bud and Maeve searched the first room at the top of the stairs for sheets. The room was filled with books. A library. No sheets, just books, but also a collection of antique firearms lining the wall.

"The undead Confederates are slowly making their way up the stairs. I suggest we fashion a rope quickly," Bud said.

"I have a better idea." Maeve grabbed a six-shooter pistol off the wall and handed a hunter's shotgun to Bud.

"Oh dear, I don't use guns."

"Fine I will take the shotgun," Maeve said, opening the barrel to see if it was loaded.

"Check the desk for more shells."

Bud walked to the mahogany desk. On the floor behind the desk was a dead man with a box of shotgun shells spilled next to him. The man looked emaciated not from decay but from starvation. Bud collected the shotgun shells, placed them in the box, and stood ready to provide ammo.

"Don't just stand there. Let's move the desk to the door so we can slow them some more!" Maeve grabbed an end of the desk. Bud shut the door and grabbed the other side of the desk.

"How long do you think this desk will hold them off?"

"Not very long at all. That is why I have the shotgun."

Bud handed her two shells when the first thump on the door rattled the bookshelves of the old library. Bud's heartbeat quickened.

THUMP. The second pound knocked some books off the shelves. The dust billowed as the books hit the hardwood floor.

"Is the gun even operational?"

Maeve loaded two shells into the double barrel and waited.

THUMP. The third impact showed a crack in the door.

"How, might I inquire, did you learn how to load, handle, and presumably shoot a gun that size?" Bud asked.

"My uncle took me hunting." Maeve lifted the shotgun to shoulder height.

A crack in the door grew larger with each successive pounding. The undead soldiers were relentless. Bud and Maeve couldn't tell if the audible cracking was wood or frail bones. The space in the door spread into a fissure. A deathly arm burst through. Another arm pulled at the opening and the fissure grew into a chasm.

Maeve readied the shotgun.

"You are planning to use the shotgun?" Bud asked.

BOOM. Maeve squeezed off the first shot. Three undead soldier's heads blew off their shoulders. Bone splinters and rotted flesh sprayed the doorway.

The second line moved forward with many more intact heads and shoulders. One soldier's eye dangled from his skull. Another's jaw detached and fell to the ground.

BOOM.

Another shot rattled Bud's ears. Maeve stood three feet behind the blockade desk calm as can be. She put her hand toward Bud for more shells which he happily provided. The second shell had blown back three more soldiers.

"There are only six shells left in this box. We can't employ the shotgun, no matter how effective presently, as a long term tactical solution to our ungainly and undead problem," Bud said.

Maeve loaded two more shells. The undead soldiers were still clambering toward the cracked door. The desk moved ever so slightly towards Bud and Maeve. The decapitated undead soldier's bodies provided a temporary obstacle.

"Why would that guy on the floor hole himself up here. There has to be a reason?" Maeve loosed another shell from the barrel of the shotgun. This time bone matter and gray flesh sprayed into the room like a cloud of dust.

Bud searched around for a reason other than the collectible weapons adorning the walls. He started throwing books on the ground as if to trigger a secret chamber like the ones in old movies set in dusty old mansions.

"Certainly there must be butler's pantry or stairway if this were actually used as a workspace. There must be something, a dumbwaiter perhaps?" Bud threw more books around.

BOOM. Maeve shot again. More undead sinew filled the air. The desk moved again. The collective weight of the crowd of undead forced the door open. None had figured out how to crawl over the desk through the large crack in the upper part of the door. They pushed with their combined weight. The desk moved yet again.

"Bud, we have an exit yet? I think I might be able to shoot a couple more shells before they pile in here and then into our guts." Maeve loaded two more shells Bud had left for her on the floor. He was still flinging books around.

"Try moving the entire bookshelf dummy. Maybe the dumbwaiter is behind it," Maeve said.

"Oh right. That might be a more efficient use of all my energies." Bud pulled the case down on top of the corpse.

"Sorry chap." Bud saw a small golden knob on the wall. The dumbwaiter door.

BOOM. Another shot sprayed the undead entry line but had no effect. They continued to march into the room towards warm, living flesh.

"We can take our leave Maeve." Bud opened the dumbwaiter door.

"Shit! We have to go now!"

The desk now tumbled over on its side, the drawers crashing just as the bookcase did. The undead soldiers poured into the room, some dove for the corpse underneath the bookcase while others ambled towards Bud and Maeve.

Maeve gripped the shotgun and squeezed into the shaft

of the dumbwaiter feet first. "Whaaaaa!" Maeve's yell softened the further down the shaft she fell.

Bud stopped to tighten the belt of his precious Burberry trench. An undead soldier gripped his collar. Bud nearly lost his balance as the soldier pulled him away from the dumbwaiter. He had no choice but to untie his jacket. Bud's eyes teared up, but he had to let his favorite coat go. This allowed him to slip the grip of the undead and jump into the shaft. The darkness overwhelmed him and the thrill of falling terrified him.

13

PROHIBITED EXIT

Bud's elbows and shoes scraped the sides of the dumbwaiter shaft as he descended towards what he hoped was a basement with a soft landing. The rubber soles of his shoes he hoped would help cushion the impact of gravity's pull. The shoes helped slow his descent a little but the stop at the bottom of the shaft proved painful anyways.

"That was not a thrill I wish to partake in again ever. Maeve I do hope that you are down here as well." Bud pulled himself out of the dumbwaiter shaft.

"I think I found a way for us to leave and make sure those zombies don't follow us," Maeve said, pointing to barrels around the basement.

"Are we planning to play Donkey Kong in reverse? How would the barrels be of any use?" Bud asked.

"The barrels are filled with alcohol."

"This place does smack of the prohibition era. This is where the drinks would be sent up the dumbwaiter shaft. Also if you notice there are tubs near the barrels as well, indicating they prepared the alcohol here," Bud said.

"So who wants to lure them down here?" Maeve waited for Bud to say he would be the bait.

"I assume from your tone that it will be me. Why are we attracting those who we were just repelling?"

"I can get us out of this mess by setting these barrels on fire but we should make some of them come down."

BOOM. SNAP.

"I don't think they need any goading." Bud pointed at the dumbwaiter shaft. The first soldier had fallen and contorted into a mangled mess when he hit bottom. The rest of the undead horde caved in his brittle skull then used him as a step to pour into the basement.

Bud ran towards the stairs at the opposite side of the room. Maeve shot through two wooden barrels with one shell. Alcohol poured forth and hit the floor in a rush. She fired again then quickly dropped the shotgun and gripped the crucifix hanging from her neck. She recited the same words that set the forest alight with fire. The creed of the Order of St. Michael.

Bud felt intense heat on his backside. He turned around to see the basement erupt into flames. Maeve held her crucifix tight at the bottom of the stairs with her eyes closed. Bud ran to her and grabbed her under the shoulders.

"You have succeeded. We must take our leave of this inferno!" Bud had to pull her up the stairs. His arms and back strained to help her. Flaming undead soldiers fell towards her feet. Bud pulled her up just quick enough before the stairs caught fire. More undead piled up towards them. Bud struggled. Maeve lost any semblance of consciousness. She was a 110 pound dead weight and he was a young man who had never picked up a dumbbell in his life, let alone a whole human.

The summit of the basement stairs was two steps away.

The smoke billowed upward into the stairway. Bud saw more and more fiery soldiers piling up on each other. The bottom of the stairs gave way to the insatiable fire. Maeve's leg dangled and danced over the flames.

Bud fell into the door at the top of the stairs and knocked it open. When the stairs gave way he lost his grip under her shoulders. The sweat glistened his brow. The roar of the undead horde pounded his ear. The smoke crippled his lungs. He still held her left arm and pulled her up with all his might. Bud and Maeve were now on the main floor.

The fire leapt to the basement door frame as the undead regiment maintained their pursuit by piling on top of each other. The fire now spread to the main level of the mansion.

Bud shook his head and continued to drag Maeve to the front door. The fire gave chase. Bud noticed a hooded figure's outline ahead. The undead monk waited in the doorway blocking their only exit.

14

SEALING SCARED

The monk lurched forward from the front door. His grey hood was draped over his head. His arms shook and his shoulders twitched. The singular monk's slow speed caused more fear in Bud than the horde's faster pursuit. Bud faced his fear and dropped Maeve's arms. He rushed at the monk. Bud's best impression of a linebacker proved accurate. The monk easily fell from the impact of Bud's tackle.

"Take this," a raspy, labored voice said.

Bud scrambled to his feet. Sweat dripped down his face from the heat of the fire.

"So you have the ability to speak? What exactly did you say?"

The monk lay flat on the floor with an arm raised.

"Take this. Seal the tree. Llanwelly. The Talbot castle. Hurry..." The monk's back lifted from the floor. His bones cracked. His arm was raised. His hand held Bud's teleport wristband. Bud grabbed for the band when the monk pulled him down to him. The monk's voice now sounded like the rest of the undead horde. His battle against turning into a zombie, though valiant, was ending in defeat.

"Raaaar!" The monk writhed in agony and chomped at Bud's face.

Bud pulled away and ripped the band from the monk's grip. He turned and saw burning undead soldiers falling towards Maeve who was still unconscious on the floor. Bud fastened the wristband on and leapt towards Maeve. He reached her and initiated teleportation just before a soldier landed on her.

On the bowling green, a football field away from the mansion Bud started to revive Maeve to consciousness. He shook her. She did not move.

"Oh please don't force me into performing cardiopulmonary resuscitation!" Bud lowered his head to her chest to check for a heartbeat.

"What the hell are you doing? What the hell happened?" Maeve wiped the dust from her face.

Bud eyes went wide and he quickly raised his head off her chest. "I was checking for a heartbeat. You managed to lose consciousness after you spoke your piece about St. Michael and set the mansion on fire." Bud pointed at the mansion covered in flames. The majority of the undead horde was trapped within the burning home, but a few stragglers had managed to find their way onto the bowling green.

"I must say these walking dead are relentless," Bud observed.

"We still have to seal the tree. And stop this zombie voodoo curse from spreading too far." Maeve lifted herself from the grass and headed back towards the copse of trees.

"We must hurry. Your representative of the Order, the undead monk, proved to be a help. He did not want to eat me. He wanted to direct me where to go next. He also knew to give me the wristband. Perhaps he saw our thief use it.

Llanwelly mean anything to you?" Bud followed Maeve whose pace quickened. When she reached the copse of trees, two undead soldiers greeted her.

"Sick of this shit." Maeve punched one of the soldiers so hard his head came right off his shoulders. The other undead soldier slowly turned away.

"Do we recall the location of the tree?" Bud laughed at the fleeing undead soldier.

"Yes, right where the monk found us earlier," Maeve said. She reached the tree in the back of the copse near the riverbank. The sun was setting and the light from the flaming mansion flickered on the tree. She once again grasped the crucifix and said the prayer of the Order of St. Michael. She almost fell unconscious once more from the toll of the prayer and her power, but forced herself to stay awake.

"Why am I standing here? That prayer starts conflagrations. Do you have an unhealthy obsession with fire? I am off to the bowling green!" Bud ran from the tree, which exploded into bright, scalding blue flame then spread and changed to orange and yellow. Maeve followed him. They reached the bowling green.

Bud pulled his cellphone from his pants pocket.

"Where we headed to next Bud? Llanwelly?" Maeve's shoulders relaxed now that the current horror had been contained.

Bud looked up from his phone. "I have no data pointing towards a location called Llanwelly. I do however think we should head back home in Chicago to regroup. Shall we head to the Second City?" Bud asked.

"Sounds good. Let's go. Always wanted to go to Chicago."

Bud grasped her wrist and they vanished.

15

HANKS MEETS BERT

The landing at Chicago's Midway Airport jarred Hanks from his half-conscious slumber. The short length of the runway requires a forceful application of the brakes on every landing. The plane arrived at the gate and many passengers crowded the middle of the narrow walkway waiting for the door to open. Hanks waited and did not stand up. He was still reeling from the experience of witches almost sacrificing him. He wondered how the hell Bud convinced him to come to Chicago. When the door finally opened, Hanks grabbed his bag from the compartment above and made his way out of the plane, down the moving walkways, and to the street for pick up. He looked for Bert.

An old red Pontiac Grand Am pulled up. Hanks shook his head.

"Officer Hanks. Hello," a voice sounded from the car.

"You must be Bert." Hanks bent down to see a pasty-faced teenager who weighed ninety pounds.

"I am Bert. Bud sent me. Welcome to Chicago. Enter the vehicle," Bert said.

Hanks had already gotten in done so before Bert issued the command.

"Shall we begin the investigation now?" Bert asked.

"I would like to get some breakfast actually. I just got off the plane."

"Bud said to start the investigation right away, as time is of the essence."

"Can we just get some drive thru then? Are you just as difficult as Bud?"

"I don't understand what you mean by difficult." Bert cocked his head when the Midway traffic guard hit the windshield signaling Bert to drive.

"IS THERE an insect I missed upon my last washing?" Bert examined the windshield.

"She means fricking drive Bert! Jeez!" Hanks yelled.

"Understood," Bert said. The Pontiac billowed with smoke yet managed to leave the airport in one piece.

Bud and Maeve arrived in Bud's room in his parent's home. This was where he earlier grabbed the smoke canisters to save Maeve from the witches of Salem.

The room's messiness surprised Maeve.

"I had you pegged a neat freak there Hutchins. This is better. Way better. Makes me think you are actually human."

"The tidiness of my living quarters is not a priority,

especially now, or mind you not really ever. That is what Bert is for." Bud searched around his room, lifting piles of clothes to find his credit card.

"So your best friend Bert actually is your housekeeper as well?" Maeve asked.

"No, he really is just my assistant. I don't believe he considers me a friend. That is another story altogether."

"Where are your parents?" Maeve asked.

"Ah. Excellent! I found it." Bud ignored her question.

"What?"

"The credit card we will use to fly to Llanwelly or at least some airport close to it. Speaking of, Hanks should commence his investigation soon. He just departed Midway and we will soon enter Midway."

"Why can't we just teleport to Llanwelly?" Maeve asked.

"I left no destination marker there. The DMs guide us to any location we choose. But I would have to travel to the location by normal travel methods first to place the marker before I can teleport there. Whoever stole my tech has been planting and using the markers but not destroying them afterwards. This may mean they have no idea I know they stole from me. This is how I have been able to trace the tech. The DM acts as a GPS for teleportation. It is safe to say that whoever stole my tech has yet to put one in Llanwelly. If and when they do, we can follow him or her like I did to Salem and we to Beauregard plantation," Bud explained.

"Now that I think about it. Llanwelly is another location for the Order of St. Michael. My uncle spoke highly of the Order there, saying they were one of the original monasteries and had a history of success keeping Wales safe. That must be where the murderer is headed next." Maeve looked visibly upset.

"We will bring this murderer to task, Maeve. I can promise you that. Perhaps the afflicted monk at Beauregard warned his colleague at Llanwelly of the murderer's possible arrival. Let us catch a plane, shall we?"

16

INVESTIGATE AND PROGNOSTICATE

Hanks scarfed down his burger and fries. He and Bert were heading directly to Bud's High School to investigate as to who may have had knowledge of Bud's teleportation tech. The brown brick of Brother Edmund High School on the city's Southside, was neither inviting or repelling. It was just boring. A typical Catholic high school built in the mid-20th century. Hanks shook his head. He had attended a high school similar to this one just outside of Boston. The leaves still clung to a few trees on the campus as October wound to a close and Halloween quickly approached.

"Now Bud has messaged me to inform you that the only person that could have possibly known about his tech was his Physics teacher, Mr. Hurley," Bert informed.

"Hurley, okay. Now how does he 'possibly' know anything?" Hanks asked.

"Bud used his teleportation tech mathematical equations for a final examination at the end of his junior year. Hurley was impressed with it. So impressed that he asked to work with Bud to further develop the tech." Bert braked and the red beater car sputtered to a stop next to the curb near the main entrance.

"So Hurley definitely knows about it and at the very least, should be able to help us. You think this guy is capable of theft and murder?" Hanks slurped the last drops of his soft drink.

Bert shook his head, "Highly improbable that Hurley would enact such atrocity."

"Highly improbable you say. Jeez, Bert ya sound like a damn robot."

Hanks checked his watch that read 10:30AM. He hoped to be done with this investigation in time to catch a red eye back to Massachusetts.

Hanks opened the car door and exited the car. "Back to school I go."

Bud and Maeve teleported to Chicago Midway, a hundred yards from the departure drop off lane.

"You keep a destination marker at the airport?" Maeve asked.

"Of course I do. The Airfield gives me a base of operations to drop off other markers at whatever destination I deem worthy of travel."

Bud carried a backpack with him. He sorely missed his trench coat. Maeve had nothing with her except her cross and the clothes on her back. Security should prove easy.

"We will have to find passage either to New York then

to London or Dublin then connect to Cardiff then find a way to Llanwelly," Bud said.

Bud and Maeve entered the airport and approached the ticket counter for Southeasy Airlines. An alert sounded from Bud's phone.

"Hopefully we aren't too late again." Bud checked his phone and it was just a message from Bert confirming Hank's arrival at Brother Edmund High School.

"The long way it is. Two tickets to New York with connection to London please," Bud said.

Within the hour, Maeve and Bud were aboard a plane to New York.

"Tell me more of the Order of St. Michael and your fire abilities," Bud said.

Bud looked nervous and sweat beaded from the pores of scalp down his forehead. Maeve laughed.

"Bud, the nerdy kid who can teleport is afraid of flying?"

"It is not the means of travel. It is the people and threat of disease that gives me cause for anxiety. Tell me more of the Order of St. Michael. Please. We should corroborate our knowledge to further determine our presumably common enemy."

"Okay, whatever you need me to do to. It must be pretty rough dropping off destination markers if this is what you go through each time."

"I mostly travel by rail, but understand the benefits of air travel. Corroboration please."

The passenger in front of Bud let out a huge sneeze.

"Oh, oh dear." Bud reached for collar of his missing trench coat and had to settle for the collar of his shirt to cover his nose and mouth.

"You are worse than I thought," Maeve said.

"Teleportation's safety far surpasses the so-called

friendly skies," Bud mumbled. Half of his face was still covered with his shirt.

Maeve shook her head, "Anyway, the Order is a secret society beset with the task of protecting mankind from evil spirits and ancient maladies that permeate then take form in the real world. The Druids who converted to Christianity worshipped trees. They must have known that old trees act as an entrance into the world for evil spirits. The Order of St. Michael was formed to seal the trees every evening to keep evil contained. My power to set things on fire is an ability I trained to master. It is summoning the fire used by the Holy Spirit. Fire is a most powerful cleanser, a symbol of purity and power."

"You will have to show me how you trained to do that. You say the spirits are inherently evil? Is this an assumption emanating from the Order's experience or just Christian prejudice of spiritual activity not resembling or originating from Jesus Christ?" Bud asked, with shirt over mouth.

"You saw what came out of the tree in Salem and the Beauregard's backyard. I understand your question but these spirits aren't holy, in fact, they are the opposite of holy. They want to dominate the world there is no pleasing these spirits."

"What are we to expect in Llanwelly?"

"We can hope that the monk was able to warn the Order's members in Wales. Llanwelly is a logical place for your thief to go. It was the site of a Druid forest and is where the first tree was used to capture and seal any pagan or evil spirits from earth. Imagine all of the gods, goddesses, demons, of all ancient civilizations packed into one tree. Llanwelly could be ground zero."

"So Christianity is the reason for the spirit's banishment. The Order of St. Michael moniker makes sense now. St.

Michael, according to your religion, is the archangel who fought Lucifer and banished him and his minions to hell. Same concept, except in a much more practical context," Bud said.

"So let's pray that whoever stole your tech has not killed the monks at Llanwelly castle."

"If they are dead, then our thief must have used traditional transportation since there is no trace of my tech in Llanwelly as of now."

Bud passed out asleep with his mouth open soon after he finished his sentence. The journey had just begun. Llanwelly still two planes and many hours away.

17

BACK TO SCHOOL

Officer Hanks smoothed his tie and pulled his jacket together to button it after just filling himself with fast food. Hanks noticed the stone marking the founding year read 1956. Hanks went to Catholic school for a year then transferred. He was a typical Protestant non-denominational type. He believed in God and celebrated Christmas but his years of hard police work tested his faith and trust in Jesus, although his new experiences with the Order of St. Michael and Salem witches may have caused him to pray a bit more than he usually did. More than ever actually.

"I should go to church." Hanks thought as he entered Edmund High.

There was an older man sitting at a desk at the entrance. Hanks flashed his badge, "Hi, I am Officer Hanks all the way from the Salem Police department. I was wondering if you could help me."

The older man had the whitest eyebrows in stark contrast with his dark brown eyes. He was older. He examined the badge closely. "How do I know this badge isn't fake?"

Hanks laughed. "What do you want from me? If it said New York PD on it would that make it more legit? I have to follow a lead. A man was murdered in Salem and a former student of yours has reason to believe there might be a connection to your faculty. I can call in CPD if you want and have them roll up in squads and cause a scene or you can just cooperate with me. Judging from the fact that you rely on tuition and reputation that might not be the best idea."

"Let me call your department to get confirmation," the older man said. He put a paper and pen on the desk for Hanks to grab. Hanks shook his head and scribbled the number down.

"Jesus Christ."

The older man shot him a look.

Hanks snarled. Hanks walked back and forth in the foyer and examined the culture of the school from the walls. The mission statement had the words "Act Manfully" in it. Hanks assumed acting "manfully" meant something noble and proud, a definition that he disagreed with. Being a cop tests your perception of humanity.

"Okay Officer Hanks. Let's head to principal's office. We will help in any way we can, of course."

"Thanks for acting manfully," Hanks said.

"I am Ed Kelly, by the way. It is my job to make sure people don't just have fun and fancy free access to da building ya know."

"I understand. I was annoyed that my badge wasn't enough. It used to be." Hanks noted the other man's thick Chicago accent.

"Different times. Different times. We have a lot of young men to take care of here."

The pair walked down a corridor. To their right was the

school's swimming pool. The people swimming in the pool were not male, however.

"I thought this was an all-male school?" Hanks asked.

"Oh those are the students from the all-female school on the same campus as our school. The largest all-female school in the country, actually."

"I am sure that is a reprieve for your student population," Hanks said.

"They use our pool and we use their facilities as well. So it works out. We keep them separated during school hours," Ed said.

Ed and Hanks walked down another hallway at the end was an office area.

"Principal Dan Green." Hanks read the sign on the door.

Ed walked into the office first.

"Hey Danny, we have a cop here from Salem, Massachusetts. Has a request to spend a couple hours here to ask a few questions and what not."

The principal took his reading glasses off laid his paper on his desk, and stood to greet Hanks.

"Please have a seat." Dan Green extended his hand.

Hanks shook the hand, "Sorry to bother you Mr. Green. Was sent here by a former student of yours, a Bud Hutchins."

Dan Green's smile turned to a frown at the mention of Bud's name.

"Ah yes, Mr. Hutchins. This is not surprising," Dan said.

"Oh I get it. I know he is a pain in the ass and I have only spent a few hours with him. You spent four years with him. Listen, he sent me here because he thinks someone in this building may have stolen an invention of his and there is strong evidence to suggest that whoever stole that invention of his is also murdering people." Hanks released Dan's hand.

"I see so this is pretty serious. What do you need from me? Hutchins was difficult but still a good kid."

"I just need to see his former schedules and he mentioned his Physics teacher, said I should start with him or her."

"Mr. Hurley was his Physics teacher. I am sorry Officer Hanks but Mr. Hurley died a few days ago."

18

HURLED

Hanks could not believe his luck. "A coincidental death? This could be a home run," he thought.

"Do we know how Hurley died?" Hanks asked out loud.

"He had a heart attack in the faculty lounge. So, it has been a rough few days for the staff and students here. He was a beloved teacher who held the kids to high standards. He was getting older, but still had great rapport with the students," Dan said.

"I am sorry for your loss. Any insight into Hurley and Hutchins's relationship?" Hanks asked.

"Bob, Hurley's first name, would come talk to me about challenging Bud, since he aced everything he could throw at him. So he began to give Bud special projects in quantum physics, theoretical type-stuff. You know futurist ideas and what not."

"That explains Bud's tech. He probably developed it from one of Hurley's special projects. Did Hurley have any friends, members of the faculty I can talk with?"

"You can start with Ms. Eren; she is the Science department chair. I can show you to her room," Dan said.

"What about all of Hurley's belongings? They still in his classroom?" Hanks asked.

"Actually I think Ms. Eren made sure to clean his room out for the substitute. She will know where everything is. Hurley was a bachelor. Lived here for the most part."

Principal Green led Hanks to another long hallway. This one was adorned with a Faculty Hall of Fame, pictures of past teachers who were mostly Christian brothers and admin who contributed to the school's rich history. The science labs were in the same hallway. Ms. Eren's room was empty of students.

"Ms. Eren, I would like you to meet Officer Hanks. He just has a few questions to ask you about Bob. I will be in my office if you need anything, Officer."

"Thanks for all your help, Mr. Green," Hanks said.

Ms. Eren was in her 30s, well-dressed and her room full of boards and group projects, her whiteboard full of agendas and equations.

"I am sorry to bother you and am sorry for your loss. I just have a few questions to ask you about Bob Hurley," Hanks said.

"Oh absolutely, come on in Officer. Yes, I was in the room when Bob died," she said.

"Can you describe what happened?"

"He put the coffee pot down, took a few drinks of his coffee, handed me a cup, and sat down. He did not let out his usual 'ah' after he finishes his first cup. Then he grabbed his chest and fell over."

"You said he took a few drinks of his coffee, he grabbed his chest, and then he died?" Hanks asked.

"Yes, that is what happened." Her eyes glistened slightly.

"Was there anyone else in the room?"

"No just him and me. He always made the coffee for everyone. He was always here the earliest."

"You also drank the coffee as well, correct?"

"Yes I said that I did. He made it fresh every morning."

"What about his cup? Did he always use the same cup?"

"He did. I have it over here in one of the boxes of his stuff. I gathered it a couple days after he passed. Are you suggesting that Bob may have been murdered?" Ms. Eren asked.

"I am suggesting that he may have been poisoned, yes." Hanks helped her lift the box onto the table.

Ms. Eren shuffled a few items in box around and reached for the mug. The mug's lime green color stood out more than any of the other items in the box.

"Do you have plastic bag I can put this mug in? Also I will need the rest of this stuff. His notes in here?" Hanks asked.

"Sure. No problem. Please take it. If you think there is foul play. I will help in any way I can." Ms. Eren handed him a plastic bag.

Hanks deposited the lime green mug into the bag and grabbed the box.

"Anything else I should know? Hurley have any rival teachers or disgruntled students I should know about?"

"Hurley had to deal with a lot of disgruntled parents over the years because he demanded a lot of his students, but those who stepped up learned a lot from him. There was one student whose father was a bit overbearing and demanding. I think the kid's name was McGann. The father didn't understand why his kid was doing so much worse in his class than his other classes. Bob had a lot of emails from Mr. McGann and was on the phone with him almost every week," Ms. Eren said.

"I would say that is a disgruntled parent. I will check it out. Any faculty that didn't like him?" Hanks asked.

"No, he got along with everyone. Let me get you McGann's information." Ms. Eren typed into her computer and gave Hanks McGann's address.

"Thanks for your cooperation. I will be in touch."

19

BERT BRINGS IT

Hanks checked out of Edmund High with Hurley's box and informed Dan and Ed that he would be in touch. They were cooperative and wanted to keep things quiet until there was something substantial to report. Bert pulled the beater car up to curb of the main entrance. Hanks opened the back door and put the box in the backseat then proceeded to the passenger seat.

"Well, Bert can you help me with this box of evidence? I don't want to bring this to CPD if I don't have to. Although I don't have the equipment to check everything out. I am assuming Bud has lab stuff we can use from what I just learned about him from his teachers," Hanks said.

"Ah yes, we can retreat to Bud's home. We can examine the contents of the box. Absolutely." Bert said, robotically.

A few minutes they arrived at Bud's parent's home. It was a small bungalow in a Catholic parish on the South Side of Chicago, with tan brick, a big wooden porch, and a green awning.

"Here we are." Bert hit the curb, rattling the box and causing the contents to spill out.

"Great, Bert. Just great." Hanks hopped out, opened the back door, and started gathering Hurley's items.

"We can enter through the front door. Bud's parents are on vacation." Bert exited the car and walked slowly to the porch.

"Thanks for your help, Bert. I got everything. Don't worry."

"No problem." Bert opened the front door of the modest home.

Hanks shook his head and adjusted his grip on the box. Hanks entered Bud's house and noticed a front room with a big, old wooden entertainment center. A bedroom was to the left and a hallway was on the right that led to a bathroom and two more bedrooms. Bud's room lay directly ahead.

"Bud has a microscope and a computer that scans and identifies immediately the contents of whatever we're looking at under the microscope."

Hanks looked at Bud's room. He still had Star Wars bedding on his twin bed and video game systems on the floor. Books were everywhere. His closet lay open with good-as-new sporting equipment falling out of it.

"How do we find the microscope in this mess?" Hanks asked.

"It is right here." Bert lifted a coat off a small desk.

"Okay good, we gotta check out this mug." Hanks removed it from the bag and examined it. He reached into the mug and noticed a slimy substance on the bottom.

"This is slimy. Coffee doesn't leave a slimy film on the bottom of the mug. Let's start here. Can you take a sample of this slimy bottom, Bert?"

"Let me see it. A peculiar color for a coffee mug. Neon green." Bert broke the mug over the desk.

"What the hell was that for?" Hanks said.

"To obtain a true sample, I will have to chip the bottom of the mug. The best way to do so is to fracture the mug's overall structure." Bert peeled a chip from the cup's bottom, placed it under the microscope, and booted up the computer that was next to it.

"Maybe a little warning before you tamper with evidence, Bert!"

"What exactly are we looking for?"

"Any traces of poison in the cup. Ms. Eren drank from the same brew of coffee and was fine. If Hurley was poisoned then it would be from his cup."

"There seems to be a filmic substance on the inside of the mug." Bert rubbed his fingertips together and waited for the computer to gather the data from the microscope.

"I already told you that it felt slimy, Bert." Hanks stood up and stared at the computer screen, impatiently. A beep resounded from the mono speaker in the monitor.

"Calcium oxide crystalline form and fructose," Hanks read.

"I shall run a search of what lime green colored substances contain calcium oxide." Bert typed on the keyboard next to the microscope. "It appears to be commonly found in internal combustion engines to keep the parts therein from freezing."

"Bert, you mean anti-freeze. Hurley was poisoned with anti-freeze. I suppose the fructose was used to sweeten or mask the taste. How could he die so suddenly from a coated mug?" Hanks asked.

"Judging from the search I just completed about anti-freeze poisoning it accelerates the heart rate. Hurley was an older man. He may have had heart disease already and the poison may have caused his cardiopulmonary system to suffer a massive episode of cardiac arrest," Bert added.

"Poisoning that brought on a heart attack. Okay, now who would want to do such a thing? Can you do a search on this kid's dad? Name's McGann."

"I can run a local search for McGann in the database."

"Just google it," Hanks said.

Bert did a simple search, "McGann Chicago". Hanks couldn't believe his luck, "This is too good to be true. The first thing that pops up is the local McGann Auto Parts store? Let's go Bert!"

20

MCGANNED

Bert and Hanks parked the car in space the closest to the shamrock-adorned McGann Auto Parts store, which boasted to be the number one auto parts store in Chicago. Bert stayed back on Hank's orders.

Officer Hanks walked into the store and noticed the usual row upon row of shelving and more shamrock-adorned signs marked what each aisle offered.

Hanks did not concern himself with the shelving and looked around for a managerial office which he assumed would be in the back of the store. He made his way through the interior accessories section towards the door that most likely led to a stockroom and an office.

Hanks entered without batting an eye. His Salem badge ready, he surveilled the back room.

It was full of boxes, and roughly the same size as the retail space in the front of the building. No one bothered him. No one seemed to be around. A door marked 'Store Manager' was cracked. Hanks knocked on the door but his knock also forced the door open. This room was empty too.

"This store is open for business right?" Hanks wondered.

"Who da hell are you? What da hell a'ya doin' back here?" a man with a thick Chicago accent yelled.

Hanks looked towards an open loading door. A truck just pulled away. A large man with silver hair walked towards him.

"Mr. McGann? I am Officer Hanks." Hanks flashed his badge quickly, hoping to avoid the Salem legitimacy issue.

"Oh shit, what da hell happened? Was it my idiot son? What'd he do? Jack McGann." The man held his hand out for Hanks to shake.

Hanks shook his hand, "Just had a few questions to ask you about your son's teacher. As far as I know your son is innocent of any wrongdoing."

"Which one? Dat idiot physics teacher?" McGann walked into his office where he offered Hanks a seat.

Hanks noted McGann's frankness about his feelings towards Hurley.

"I did hear from fellow teachers that you and Hurley had a contentious relationship."

"Not contentious from his side. I will admit I was da one pissed off most a'da time. Robbie gets straight As his whole frick'n life until dat class wit Hurley. I may have tried to pull my weight a bit since I donate a lot to the Dad's club and da school's booster club. What happened ta Hurley dat your here?"

"Mr. Hurley was murdered."

McGann's jaw dropped. "And you think I had somethin' to do wit' it? I may have a hot temper but I don't kill people."

Hanks knew from McGann's reaction that the business owner did not murder Hurley. Hanks also knew he had to pursue leads quickly and didn't want the hassle of involving the Chicago PD.

Hanks knew Hurley was poisoned with anti-freeze. It seemed all too cute for the begrudged parent to go to such great lengths to murder a teacher with their own product but the kid might overlook those details.

"Where is Robbie if I may ask? He still at school?" Hanks pressed.

"He just left last night for a school trip actually to Europe and North Africa, a Roman Empire tour with his history teacher."

"Where does he fly into?"

"He flies inta London first. Stays there for da night then heads to Rome. I want to let ya know. I will help in any way I can. Just let me know. I am sorry for being so upset Officer."

"Thanks for your help. I may be in touch," Hanks left the store and checked the time on his watch. Bud and Maeve should be in London soon. Bert pulled the car up.

"Thanks for the service there Bert. We have to do some regular police work. Dust for prints, etc." Hanks hopped in the car.

"I have already done so, sir. While you were in the store, I gathered evidential data and the like with the materials in the victim's box. Now we just have to scan the evidence into Bud's computer and run it through the usual databases. What news have you?" Bert said, as he drove the car.

"The kid's Dad ain't a killer. He didn't even know Hurley had passed away. My intuition tells me he is telling the truth. He was honest about being upset with Hurley and your natural inclination would be to play that down if you murdered the man. The kid is who we need to get more info about. We gotta go back to school. Also this may be just a coincidence but the kid is on a trip with his History teacher and they are flying into England and staying the night. Bud and Maeve are headed to UK right now as well. Right now this kid is a major person of interest."

21

ROBBIE

Robbie McGann sat huddled in the tour bus that headed to the Westminster portion of London, England. He kept to himself usually. He didn't ruffle any feathers and never crossed a teacher. He preferred heavy metal and aggressive Wagner orchestral music. Robbie stood about 5'10" with a wiry frame. He felt comfortable in large flannel shirts and band t-shirts from concerts he never attended. He had looked forward to this trip since his history teacher put a sign up at the end of last year. Brother Mike is a student favorite because of his sense of humor and rapport with his students.

The other chaperone, Ms. Jenner, was not as well-liked. She was a younger, demanding English teacher who probably overcompensated on the toughness because she taught in an all boy's high school. There was a total of twelve students on the trip and they were growing on Robbie.

The tour bus stopped at the Westminster Inn, a smaller hotel that they would only be staying in for one night.

"Robbie, you ready to go?" Brother Mike asked.

Robbie took his earbuds out of his ear. "Yeah."

"Okay everyone hang out in the lobby while Ms. Jenner gets us checked in," Brother Mike announced. Ms. Jenner took to the logistical tasks well. She counted the students as they disembarked the bus and entered the hotel.

Robbie reached the lobby and noticed how small it was compared to the other hotels he had been used to on trips with his parents. The bell hops grabbed the luggage from storage space under the cabin of the bus. Robbie watched from the lobby as his bag ripped open and his sketchbooks fell out. He ran out to procure them and save himself embarrassment.

"I can get those. Those are mine."

"We got them Robbie. No worries." Brother Mike picked up a sketchbook while Robbie scrambled to pick up the other two. The book had fallen open to cartoonish sketches of Mr. Hurley with bullet holes in him. Brother Mike hesitated while he looked at the picture then gave the sketchbook back to Robbie.

"Interesting artwork there Robbie," Brother Mike said.

"I am sorry. I- it was before he passed away."

"It's okay Robbie. You know that you can talk to me or Ms. Jenner anytime if you need to." Brother Mike put his hand on his chest then pointed to Ms. Jenner, only a couple feet away.

"Okay thanks." Robbie put the sketchbooks in his bag and walked back into the lobby. His face was red with embarrassment which turned to anger.

Two hours later, Robbie napped to rid himself of the immediate effects of jet lag. He looked over to his roommate, Brent, who still snored the afternoon away. Robbie flipped through one of his sketchbooks. He felt like he needed to talk to Brother Mike.

Robbie walked into the hallway, Ms. Jenner sat at the

end of the hallway as monitor. Brother Mike's room was at the other end of the hallway. Robbie signaled to her that he headed towards Brother Mike's room. He knocked on the door. Again, he knocked. No answer. Robbie figured he may be sleeping. He sighed and looked down. He saw a piece of paper on the floor, a piece of an airline ticket stub, that probably fell from Brother Mike's pocket. He slipped it under the door. He knocked again and the door came open. Robbie peeked inside. The bed was made. No Brother Mike, but his luggage lay open. Robbie entered the room and let the door shut behind him.

22

BUDDED INN

Maeve struggled to get sufficient sleep. Bud, on the other hand, slept with his shirt still over his mouth. Maeve could see wetness from his drool peppering his shirt collar. The aircraft landed at Heathrow after a few bumps of the landing gear touching the ground.

Maeve shook Bud's shoulder. He awoke with a clatter, smacking his hand against the window. Maeve giggled adding to the cacophony of audible notifications spewing from Bud's phone he just powered on.

"Oh dear, we have landed safely I presume?" Bud asked.

"Yes and how can you sleep that entire time?" Maeve asked.

"I feel that the depth of my sleep has, for lack of better term in my current mental state, deepened since I developed my teleportation technology."

"Ah, I see. You might want to check your phone. Maybe Hanks, has some news." Maeve watched as everyone in the plane stood in the walkway opening the luggage compartments overhead.

Bud reached for his phone in his pocket.

"Indeed there are a few messages from Officer Hanks and Bert. Bert of course excessively sends messages all the time. I appreciate the attention to detail, but even me with my loquacious tendencies thinks 28 messages borders on problematic. Hanks only sent a few and his were pointed. Looks like we will have to miss our connecting flight for now. We have to head to the Westminster Inn when we depart this germ-infested tube."

"What's at the Westminster Inn? Isn't Llanwelly priority?"

"It is not what but who. A kid I came to know, Robbie McGann is a person of interest in the murder of one of my favorite teachers. I thought his death was deemed a cardiac arrest. Although his murder makes sense since that teacher, Hurley, helped inspire me to develop my experimental tech. Hurley was tough for most students, Robbie was no exception I presume. Bert correctly identified the cause of death as an anti-freeze coating of Hurley's coffee cup."

"How does that link Robbie?" Maeve asked.

"McGann's family owns auto parts stores all over Chicagoland. Seems a bit too on the nose for me but we have to investigate this boy further. Perhaps we can use your good looks to loosen his lips, as it were, and tell us information we need."

Maeve blushed. Not many boys complimented her looks.

"Oh please don't take my cold observation skills to heart. Your physical appearance is merely useful in this instance."

Maeve frowned. "Glad I can be of assistance Hutchins. You ass."

Maeve rushed into the line moving out of the plane. Bud was stuck a few people behind her.

She waited for Bud inside the airport terminal with her arms crossed.

Bud approached like normal. "Shall we hail a taxi?"

Maeve waited for an apology. Nothing.

The cab pulled up to the Westminster Inn. Evening had supplanted the light of day a couple hours ago in the capital city.

"Now as I relayed to you earlier, perhaps you should approach him first. He will recognize me, most likely as I only graduated last spring," Bud said.

"Whatever you say Bud. I have no idea what he looks like." Maeve exited the cab.

He will most likely be dressed in black. He has messy hair and a wiry frame. He will be brooding around in a miserable existence with earbuds spewing from his shaggy hair." Bud paid the cabbie with a credit card then followed Maeve.

"That him?" Maeve pointed at a teenage boy on a red Victorian chair in the small lobby of the inn.

"Yes, yes, it is."

"I don't understand what you want me to do. Ask him if he is a murderer?" Maeve said.

"Spark conversation with him as we discussed in the plane and lure him outside where I will take it from there. If we hurry, we may make our connecting flight."

Maeve entered the inn and approached Robbie.

"Hi, I was wondering if you could help me with my

bags? I over packed. My name is Mindy by the way?" Maeve held her hand out for Robbie to shake.

Robbie pulled the earbuds out of his ear and fumbled to turn his music down. He shook Maeve's hand weakly.

"I am Robbie. What exactly did you need?"

"Oh gosh. I am sorry, you had your earbuds in. I was just wondering if you could help me with my bags? This place doesn't seem to have any bellhops," Maeve repeated.

"Oh yeah, yeah. I can do that." Robbie stood up straight and ran his fingers through his hair. He carried his sketchbook with him.

"Just around the corner by the roundabout actually." Maeve aka Mindy said.

Robbie followed Maeve. Interacting with teenage girls was rare for Robbie, especially at an all boy's school.

Maeve walked around to the corner.

Bud grabbed Robbie and attempted to push him up against the stone wall of the inn but slipped and fell. Robbie dropped the sketchbook.

Robbie pulled away from Bud's grip and tried to run. Maeve grabbed the chain hanging from Robbie's wallet and pulled him back to the wall then helped Bud to his feet.

"Your incompetence baffles me," Maeve said to Bud. He quickly secured a grip on Robbie's shirt.

"Robbie. Why did you end Hurley's life?"

"What the hell are you talking about? I swear I drew the pictures because I was upset. I would never murder Hurley!" Robbie said, terrified, voice cracking.

"Convenient that you made an anti-freeze cocktail for his morning coffee. Get that from your father's shop?" Bud pressed.

"I would never do that. I swear. Hurley was a jerk. My

Dad would never kill him. I didn't even know he was murdered I swear. I swear to God."

Bud loosened his grip.

Maeve picked up the sketchbook and examined the pictures therein.

"Um, Bud. You might want to take a look at this."

23

CLASS DISMISSED

Hanks and Bert returned to Brother Edmund High after dismissal of the students to get into Hurley's classroom. This entrance was much easier than the last. Ed let them right in. Bert followed Hanks awkwardly, almost touching Hanks's shoulder with his shoulder every couple paces.

"Bert, cut it out. Gimme some room here pal?" Hanks said.

The pair walked back into the science classroom corridor. Hurley's door was open and they entered.

"I will check his desk for any clues that might connect Robbie." Bert rifled through drawers.

"Sounds good. I will look in this office nook back here." Hanks walked into the small office with supplies stacked in various piles all over the place. He picked some piles up and set them down, checked a cabinet drawer that was blocked by some calculators. The drawer was locked but had a flimsy lock. Hanks pulled hard and the lock gave way.

A small moleskin notebook was the only item in the drawer. Hanks flipped through ideas for lessons and some comments on classroom management. Dated, but not always, showing the non-linear nature of Hurley's mind. Hanks noticed a series of pages whose content looked familiar.

"Bert come over here. Check this out," Hanks said.

"Right away." Bert robotically walked towards the office.

"Anything of interest in the desk?" Hanks asked.

"Nothing of value. What do you have? Oh and look this office connects to another classroom."

Hanks looked through the window of a connecting door. The connected classroom had World Maps adorning the walls and various lines drawn throughout the maps.

"Hmm thought this was a science hallway only. Random History classroom thrown into the mix. Whatever, look at this." Hanks handed Bert the notebook.

Bert quickly scanned the pages Hanks marked.

"Yes, indeed this is Bud's technology that he developed with Hurley's guidance. Yes, see we have the destination markers and the wristband prototype sketches and the appropriate power levels needed to pass molecular information to and fro."

"Why would Hurley lock this up in this office? Didn't seem like a paranoid person."

"Perhaps sharing this office caused him to take necessary precaution," Bert said.

"I suppose so but this stuff is so far advanced people might not take it seriously. Teleportation is a bit far-fetched. Don't you think?" Hanks looked through the connected door's glass pane into the History classroom.

"Not if you knew Bud. His genius is not to be underestimated."

Hanks kept staring through the glass pane.

"Oh shit. Bert. We have to get a hold of Hutchins now."

Bud held Robbie to the wall with one hand and examined a piece of paper that had fallen out of the sketchbook.

"Did you travel from New Orleans to London?" Bud asked.

"No, no, I found that ticket on the floor in front of Brother Mike's door. I swear. I kept it to give back to him," Robbie answered quickly.

Bud looked at Maeve, who showed Bud some more sketches including the one of Hurley being killed.

"Why would you draw this?" Bud asked.

"I told you before I was upset with him but would never kill him! I feel bad enough already that he died and we were not on good terms," Robbie said.

Bud's phone sounded in his pants pocket. "Yes Officer Hanks."

The loudness of the phone's receiving speaker made their conversation audible to Maeve and Robbie.

"Hutchins, think we might have a more solid lead than Robbie. Hurley shared a classroom with a History teacher. The maps on the walls in this classroom show the route of Robbie's trip. Chicago to London, then London to Rome then North Africa. We found a notebook of Hurley's locked in a cabinet in this office that detailed all of your tech. Hurley may have suspected this History teacher was snooping around."

"Brother Mike did share a room with Hurley. He always hovered around our conversations, shamelessly eavesdropping. We also found an airline boarding pass that Robbie procured from the floor near Brother Mike's inn room door. New Orleans, not far from the Beauregard Mansion, to London. Robbie, was Brother Mike with you on your flight from Chicago?"

"No, he met us at Heathrow." Robbie said.

Hanks voice bellowed through the phone, "Brother Mike is now our prime suspect."

24

MYSTERY BOX

"I can help. After I found the ticket stub. Brother Mike's room was open and I saw some strange things. I walked out quickly so I wouldn't get caught," Robbie said.

"Take us up there on the double quick," Bud said.

Robbie adjusted his shirt that Bud stretched out with his grip.

Maeve still held Robbie's sketchbook as the three young adults walked back into the lobby and up the stairs.

"Ms. Jenner will be monitoring the hallway. I can distract her for you," Robbie walked down the hallway towards the English teacher's station. Bud and Maeve waited for Robbie to get close enough to obscure her vision.

Bud and Maeve opened the already ajar door and entered the room. Brother Mike's luggage lay open on the bed. Bud scanned the clothing.

"Nothing out of the ordinary here. Clothing, toiletries, etc. Nothing begets guilt."

Maeve checked the miniature fridge. Inside was a black box with gold symbols etched into it.

"Bud," Maeve said. She pulled the box out of the fridge and opened it.

"We must handle this with care," Bud said.

"Okay this is strange," Maeve said.

Two vials of blood with a spot for a third.

"He collects the blood but to what end?" Bud asked.

"This blood is most likely from the monks of the Order. He is collecting blood probably for some sort of sacrifice. My uncle warned me about ancient blood cults," Maeve said.

"Yes, makes sense, blood sacrifice proved to be a very common sacrifice in many pagan religious traditions. Why would he bring this here?"

"He is obviously planning to use this blood soon. Keeping it fresh in the fridge. He's killed two monks already and we can safely assume the missing third vial is for the monk in Llanwelly," Maeve said.

"Put the box back in the fridge. We don't want to arouse suspicion and have him do anything daft. He still hasn't a clue we are following him. He must have left in a hurry to get to Llanwelly before the school trip resumed. No destination markers have been activated. He used two to travel quickly from Salem then to Beauregard. Those he could have planted easily with a dedicated weekend trip. He didn't have time or resources to plant a Llanwelly marker, across an ocean. I shall scan the room for any markers he may have left here." Bud pulled out his phone and opened the camera app and scanned the room for another of his stolen markers.

"Do you know how many of those markers he stole from you?"

"Well, Hurley would help me make them in his classroom lab. I would procure new ones from him on a weekly basis. Hurley would be able to make about three a week, sometimes extra. Brother Mike could have stolen a few over time being right next door to Hurley's lab. So no way to be absolutely certain. As far as the wristband, he stole Hurley's. I left him one to try but he never did, sadly. He was a good man. I miss him. The news of his murder is so awful, devastating really." Bud looked upset.

Maeve put her hand on his shoulder. "Bud, I understand. We both lost someone close to us but we have to focus. We have a chance to spare others our pain. Any destination markers here? If not, we should hurry to Llanwelly. He already has a head start. We may have a chance to stop another monk from getting viciously murdered."

"No, but it is possible he could have left one on the perimeter of the building. No bother we can leave one in this room and if he uses one close to here we can just teleport and give chase. To Llanwelly we go! If we make haste, we may be able to catch our flight!"

Maeve left the room. Bud quickly messaged Hanks the contents of Brother Mike's room and asked for him to research why he might be using blood.

Bud ran out of the room disregarding the hall monitor and Robbie.

He found a stairwell and turned around to see if Maeve followed. She didn't. He stomped back up the stairs. She appeared with a broom in her hand.

"I have a way that will get us there faster."

25

ANCIENT HISTORY

Hanks checked his phone, "Brother Mike has been collecting blood and Bud needs us to find out why exactly, Bert." The partners converged on Brother Mike's classroom like children to candy fallen from a piñata.

"There has to be an explanation for why this guy is doing this." Hanks rummaged through his desk.

Bert looked around to the walls and the poster for the Roman History Tour brochure hung on the walls of the classroom.

"Perhaps there is historical significance that we must research in regards to this tour, like where he might use the blood. Let's examine the tour stops."

Hanks walked over to Bert who held the brochure in his hand.

"Rome is obviously a stop then some stops in other parts of Italy. What's with North Africa? I can't remember from my history class. It was a long time ago. I know it was part of the Empire."

Bert took to the teacher's edition of an AP World History textbook and flipped to Ancient Rome.

"The significance should bare itself in this book, one would think."

Hanks spotted the section first, "There the 'Rome and North Africa' section."

Bert scanned the pages quickly like a robotic speed reader.

"Punic Wars between Roman armies and Hannibal, the great Carthaginian commander, have major significance in the history of Rome and North Africa."

"So will he use the blood on an old battlefield or something?" Hanks asked.

"Says here Carthage's strange religious customs would limit its growth and popularity in the Ancient World. It then explains..." Bert stopped when the door to the classroom opened. Principal Dan Green entered the room.

"Hey Officer Hanks, just locking up for the day. Was wondering how much more time you needed. Also what are you doing in Brother Mike's room?"

"Only a few more minutes. We just wanted to check this room out since it shared an office with Hurley's room. Routine," Hanks said.

"Sounds good. Keep me updated. The janitor will let you out when you are done. Have a good night." Principal Green left the room.

"You were saying Bert," Hanks said.

"The Carthaginian religion demanded sacrifices to Baal Hammon, their central deity," Bert said.

"Okay, so blood sacrifices to ancient pagan god are not uncommon. So the blood will be used at the North African stop of the tour."

"Yes that is a likely scenario. Alas, there is something more troubling. The Carthaginians would sacrifice children for their gods."

Hanks mouth dropped.

Bert flipped the next couple pages. "There is more here. Annotations, rather illegible. Symbols that resemble trees and a polaroid picture of students on a trip with a desert ruin in the background."

"Shit. Take that book with us. Brother Mike is on trip with a bunch of kids. This just gets weirder and weirder. I better tell Hutchins and Maeve."

Bud reluctantly put his arms around Maeve's waist. Travel by broom wasn't ideal but it was better than the germ-ridden tube of airplanes.

"Now how exactly did you learn this skill, flight by broom?" Bud asked.

"I don't know after the witches attacked me I felt something come over me, just like in the basement at Beauregard when I passed out. Once the spirits leave the tree and permeate the area they are in. I suppose I absorb some of the energy."

"Conclusively, you are a witch as of now. Are you concerned that you may become a member of the walking dead?"

"That I am not so sure about. I feel very much alive now." Maeve pushed from the ground and the pair took flight over the River Thames and north by northwest to Wales.

Bud gripped her waist and hugged her backside. His head rested on her shoulder blade. Maeve felt his warmth.

Despite his annoying tendencies, she was happy to have met Bud Hutchins. The mutual and tragic losses of loved ones strengthened their partnership.

"How long might it take us to get there?" Bud asked. The cool air smacked the side of his face. He looked down but regretted it. The whole of London became smaller and smaller as they gained more altitude. He shut his eyes.

"I can go faster I think." Maeve lowered her head slightly and pushed her nose forward over the handle of the broom. Their speed increased.

Bud wished he had his jacket with him and hoped Brother Mike took a slow beater car to Wales.

26

WALES

Upon entry into Wales proper, Maeve and Bud landed the broom in an open field near the Welsh city of Worcester to briefly rest and input the GPS to determine the location of Llanwelly.

"Let's hope that my phone maintains signal clarity in Wales." Bud examined his phone and saw a message from Hanks.

"Turns out a trip to ancient site of Carthage, aka North Africa, calls for child sacrifices. Could it be that Brother Mike will slaughter the students on his trip? That would be so messy. Interesting theory, Hanks and Bert derived from the Brother's classroom. Brother Mike was on a student trip similar to the one he is chaperoning now, when he was a teen. They found an old picture in his textbook Bert matched a ruin in the background to Israel, very close to North Africa."

Maeve looked surprised, yet keenly interested, "The Order of St. Michael originated from the Druids of the Celtic people who had close ties religiously with Carthaginian religious rulers. The two pagan religions share similar deities and customs. The Druids, who broke away from the pagan traditions, became the first Christian monks of the Order of St. Michael. The remaining pagan Druids along with Carthaginian migrants in the British Isles sought to kill these former Druids turned Christians and a great battle took place. Obviously, the Christian monks defeated the pagans under the banner of the St. Michael, the archangel who smote the demons of hell and banished Lucifer forever into the realm of Hell. It is very possible Bud, that Brother Mike wants to revive these pagan traditions and gods."

Bud's jaw dropped. For the first time, he was more than impressed with Maeve.

"So Brother Mike is now killing members of the Order of St. Michael to finish the job or take vengeance upon them?"

"Think bigger Hutchins. He is collecting their blood as part of the sacrifice to Baal Hammon, the big bad Carthaginian deity who demands children's blood and apparently, blood of the betrayers. Killing the monks is part of a greater goal to unleash a powerful evil menace onto the Earth. He is headed to North Africa to Carthage, to unleash Baal."

"You talk of blood of the betrayers? The monk's blood?" Bud asked.

"Yes and it looks like he needs three vials to represent the Holy Trinity of the Catholic tradition. Spilling the blood of Christians was common in the early days of Christianity. The pagans and blood cults would collect blood from three different Christians and pour the blood into a stone cross at the foot of whatever god they worshipped. We have to stop Brother Mike at Llanwelly before he can even think about making it to North Africa."

Bud typed in Llanwelly and its location pinged perfectly.

"Before we go I shall text Bert to phone Robbie at the inn to take the box of blood in Brother Mike's room to Scotland Yard." Bud sent the text quickly.

The pair hopped on the broom and into the moonlit night.

27

TALBOT CASTLE

The town of Llanwelly was dimly lit. Only a few street lamps had been converted from gas to electric lit the cobblestone streets. There were a few two story buildings made from stone and a small cottage with a straw roof. The rest of the buildings were pubs and a small grocery store which was at the end of the street. Bud and Maeve landed safely with no one seeing them. With the exception of music playing from Johnson's pub, the town seemed empty. At the end of the street, there was a smaller dirt road that split off from the main drag. Bud and Maeve noticed fresh tire tracks in the dirt. They hopped back on the broom and followed the dirt road, by the light of the moon.

"The freshness of the tire's imprints would imply that our Christian brother-turned-Pagan worshipper beat us to the Talbots," Bud said.

"We will find out soon enough. We have to stop him here or we may have to call in for some help which will be difficult considering how outlandish the whole thing is." Maeve lowered the broom as she noticed Talbot castle ahead. A car was parked inside the gates. The castle looked like a structure straight out of Oxford, gothic, with sharp spires, brownstone instead of grey, a tall tower and a long rectangular main building with turrets and more sharp spires.

"Let's tread carefully. Who knows what sort of malady may very well spring from the grounds of this decrepit structure." Bud hopped off the broom and his face grimaced from the soreness of a three-hour ride.

"Looks like around the back are trees. Let's hope we made it to the monk before Brother Mike did. I wish there was a way to get a hold of other monks. The Order hasn't really updated to modern technology," Maeve said.

"It is presumably better to maintain a low profile, dear Maeve. The Internet is still very much the wild, Wild West with many ways to hack information that one would otherwise deem secure. My question is, why is Brother Mike going to these specific locations, Salem, Beauregard, and now Llanwelly? What significance do these specific locations have?" Bud entered through a rusty gate. It bore marks of damage from Brother Mike's rental vehicle.

"Brother Mike seems to be picking areas where great evils existed. The Order only has monks stationed at trees in these certain areas of high need." Maeve followed Bud and noticed the gate's damage and a blue BMW with a crushed grill and scraped paint.

"I understand Salem, the witch trials. Beauregard, I assume so close to New Orleans, once the biggest slave market in North America, but Llanwelly? What evil befell this hamlet?" Bud said.

"Bud, get down now," Maeve commanded. The main door to the castle flew open, cracking the side of the entrance. Two men fell to the ground embroiled in a life and death struggle. Bud and Maeve watched from behind the damaged BMW. One man was dressed in regular clothes the other in traditional robes. Brother Mike and a monk of the Order battled. Brother Mike held a scimitar, a sharply curved blade perfect for slicing arteries, in his left hand, the monk pushed Mike's hand away from his throat. Brother Mike was in a mounted position forcing his weight down through his hand to stab the monk.

"Let us offer assistance." Bud ran out from behind the vehicle and lunged towards Brother Mike's torso. Bud tackled the middle-aged man and relieved the monk of the dutiful task of self-defense.

Maeve ran to the monk still lying flat on the ground. "Are you okay? I am Maeve of the Order. Salem diocese. We are here to help."

The monk's face showed his age, early 70s, gray beard and tired eyes.

"The tree in the greenhouse. I didn't seal. He prevented me from saying the words, you must go there. The moon is...the moon is full. I am afraid it is too LAAAAAAAAATE!" The monk convulsed. His back arched. His bones cracked. His beard grew at such a rate that it covered his torso in seconds. The monk's nose pushed forward into a snout his fingers curled then extended into haggard claws. The malady of Llanwelly: Werewolves.

28

THE BEAST OF LLANWELLY

The monk turned into a wolf man in a gruesome, violent manner before Maeve's eyes. She ran into the castle hoping to get some distance between her and the latest victim of Brother Mike's dastardly scheme. He was turning monks of the Order of St. Michael into ravenous beasts and hideous monsters.

Bud's tackle had knocked Mike unconscious. Bud quickly snatched the short scimitar and tried to stand, but the werewolf leapt over his head and knocked him down again. He looked through the castle entrance and saw Maeve running down a long corridor filled with armor and shields from medieval times. The werewolf darted toward the corridor as well. Torn grey robes dragged on the floor, partially draped on the white haired beast's waist. Bud took the scimitar with him and gave chase down the hall.

Maeve searched deeper into the castle for the greenhouse. The armored corridor gave way to a hallway that offered a choice of right or left. She chose to go right in the hope the moonbeams she saw gleaming on the floor would lead to the greenhouse. The gargled breaths, scratching claws, and pounding steps of the werewolf ravaged her senses. He moved fast, faster than she could move without having a broom. She ran down the hallway and to her left she saw a glass encased room.

"The greenhouse!" Maeve entered the room and slammed the door behind her. The door buckled and bent from the force of the werewolf's push. Maeve backed away from the door. The werewolf's growl grew louder and louder. She gripped her crucifix tightly. The moonbeams cutting through the darkness accentuated her white knuckles. The sound of claws tearing and splintering the door shocked her into finding the tree more quickly than she thought possible. Maeve noticed potted plants strewn about the room and in the center of the room was a great tree, old and stout. The greenhouse must have been built around it.

GRRRR! CRACK! The werewolf's arm pulled away wood with the efficiency of a properly utilized axe. Maeve focused on the tree and lifted the cross around her neck.

"Saint Michael the Archangel, defend us in battle. Be our protection against wickedness..."

BUD HEARD the incessant panting and growls of the werewolf salivating in anticipation of eating Maeve. Hutchins ran with bravery gained by the terrible thought of losing his friend. He didn't usually stick his neck out for anyone. Then again he didn't really have many friends.

He gripped Brother Mike's murder weapon, the scimitar, with blistering pressure.

"Halt! You feral beast!" He closed the distance between him and the werewolf who was surrounded by splinters of wood flying through the air. Bud hoped to catch him before the door completely gave way.

The splinters of wood settled and the growls became muffled once again. The werewolf burst into the greenhouse. Bud heard a scream that ended in a gargled cough. Bud hopped over what remained of the door and into the center of the greenhouse. A moonbeam lit the white hair of the werewolf's back. Bud stood only a few feet away. The werewolf smelled Bud's presence and slowly turned his head towards Bud. The black eyes stared into Bud's soul. Its mouth dripped with blood. Its snout gave way to curled snarl that twitched above huge fangs covered in bits of flesh. Bud saw Maeve's limp body with her throat ripped from her neck. Her right hand clutched the crucifix. Maeve was dead.

29

BUD HUTCHINS VS THE WOLFMAN

Bud fought back tears. Another friend dead. First, Hurley, then Maeve. His time to grieve would be postponed as the werewolf swiped at Bud's face. Bud struck back with the scimitar. The werewolf dodged underneath the swing by getting down on all fours.

"Shit. This is a most dubious situation. Surely somewhere underneath all the fur there is the monk of the Order, sworn to protect the world from such demons!" Bud exercised futility and tried to talk to the beast.

The werewolf cocked his head then swiped again, which sent shards of a pot towards Bud's face. Bud shielded with his arms. He recovered quickly and grabbed a pot of his own with one hand and hurled it towards the werewolf's head. The pot struck the beast in the snout causing it to shake its head violently and stand up. Bud saw a chance to strike with the scimitar. The height of the beast was intimidating, but also gave Bud an opportunity to get it in close to his torso. He used the short sword and stabbed the werewolf through the rib cage.

"AWOOOOOOOO!" The werewolf howled from the blow.

Bud pushed the sword through the beast's ribs until the blade disappeared. The werewolf buckled then grabbed Bud by the shirt and threw him through a glass pane of the greenhouse. Bud could barely breathe as he reeled from the vicious throw through a glass wall. His neck twitched and intense pain enveloped his back. He saw the werewolf jump over him and heard the volume of pounding footfalls decrease the further away the werewolf ran.

"Going to lick your wounds, I see." Bud had no choice but to pursue. The murder weapon that would link Brother Mike to the death of two monks of the Order was lodged in the ribs of that werewolf. Not to mention, vengeance fueled Bud as well and the general safety of Llanwelly. Bud suffered a few bruises and scratches but shook off the pain to hunt the werewolf. He looked back towards Maeve but would not pause long.

"I shall finish this Maeve. I promise." She died trying to seal the tree. With the werewolf still at large, she must not have finished the prayer. Bud had no choice but to put down the werewolf using natural not supernatural means.

"One could add Werewolf Hunter to my already impressive list of accomplishments," Bud said aloud to himself as he followed the beaten path of the beast.

30

COLLECTION

A thrust of cool night air helped bring Brother Mike to consciousness. His neck ached. He pulled himself up to his knees and panicked. He searched for his scimitar at the foot of the entrance to Talbot castle. It was nowhere to be found. He checked his pockets for the glass vial. It somehow survived the violent altercation with the monk and his former student. The Brother knew Hutchins would eventually be a problem as he figured his former student would have a way to track his stolen tech. Brother Mike prepared for the inevitability and would be ready for the next confrontation with Hutchins.

    He got to his feet and examined the area at the entrance of the castle then headed in. Tattered clothes and scratches on the floor led down a corridor filled with armor. He followed the path to the hall and turned towards the greenhouse. The silence beckoned the Brother to keep going. The castle was silent and empty. He saw the remnants of the door that lay in tatters. The sacred tree, he knew, was in this greenhouse. He hoped to find the monk's body somewhere to collect the blood. Brother Mike's gratitude for not being severely injured gave way to dread. The monk's blood was the last blood sample he needed.

"Just one more! No! No! No!" His dread gave way to rage as he rushed towards the tree in the greenhouse. He knocked over pots and plants dirt spread over the floor. When the smell of dirt dissipated he smelled blood and his dread gave way to hope. He approached the tree and noticed a teenage girl's body in front of the tree. Brother Mike examined her and noticed she held a crucifix of the Order of St. Michael in her right hand.

"Who are you? Are you a member of the Order?" Brother Mike looked for any other indication of a monk of the Order. He knew that part of the initiation of the Order was scourging. He knelt, flipped the girl over, and pulled the back of her shirt up.

"There it is. Yes! There it is." On the dead girl's back, was a singular scar from the lash of a whip. Brother Mike enthusiastically popped open the cap of the vial then flipped her back over and collected the blood pooled in the wound on her neck.

"Your blood will do." He stood up and kicked the dead body.

He walked away pleased, secured the vial to his pocket. He was so close. So close to the end.

"Baal I will summon you soon! Yes, soon!" Brother Mike practically skipped back to his car.

"The lie of the Christian brotherhood would be wiped away from existence. The lies of Christianity will be exposed. The hypocrisy of the Roman Catholic Church, all of monotheism will suffer the wrath of the gods. It is the only way. Nearly two thousand years of holy wars will cease with your resurrection Baal. Your pantheon will be restored.

Hannibal's armies will conquer the Earth." Brother Mike spouted aloud.

Back outside of the castle, he saw that the BMW's front grill had suffered damage but it didn't matter. He opened the passenger door and reached into the glove box and pulled out a wristband. He fastened the band to his wrist and vanished from Talbot castle's grounds.

31

A PINT OF BLOOD AND A SHOT OF SILVER

Bud followed the werewolf's blood trail in the direction of the heart of Llanwelly.

"Oh this may-" Bud labored in pursuit. "'This may turn into a particularly problematic debacle."

Bud saw the werewolf reach the dimly lit cobblestone streets. The werewolf stopped next to a street lamp, removed the scimitar from his side. The beast let out a loud howl, "AWOOOOOO!"

The werewolf's break spurred Bud to move faster, but the creature heard him and ran towards the raucous noise of Johnson's Pub.

"Hence, the heightened difficulty of this ridiculous encounter," Bud said. He almost ran past the bloodied scimitar. "How can I be so ill of mind?" Bud picked the blade up and disregarded the awful smell and sinewy film that covered it.

The werewolf burst into Johnson's Pub, hungry, hurt, and ready to feast. Bud jumped over the remains of the doorway, similar to the castle. The patrons yelled and panicked. Some ran to the bathrooms. Others had jumped behind the bar.

Bud scanned the room for anyone that might be of sound mind and fit body to help him push the beast down. The patrons of Johnson's pub ranged in age from 55 to 18. A communal pub for the drinkers of Llanwelly. The old trusty dive bar.

One older man in a golf cap took a swig of his beer and turned away from the bar.

"Alright, me son. What the fuck do we have 'ere?"

The werewolf was bleeding all over the floor of the pub. He slipped on his own mess but recovered quickly and launched towards a group of six younger patrons at the bar. The group scattered.

"It's bleeding true it is!" a younger man, not much older than Bud yelled.

"It's the Beast of Llanwelly!" a woman yelled.

Most of the patrons bolted for the exit. The werewolf clawed a middle aged man. Blood spattered against a card table. The rest of the patrons made a clean exit.

The man in the golf cap still sat in his stool observing the chaos. "Fuck it. Ang," the man said to the barkeep, "Give me my shotgun."

Bud grabbed a chair in his left hand and held it up like a lion tamer. He raised the scimitar with his right hand. He would try to corner the Beast then stab it to death. The werewolf grunted and pounced towards the man on the floor. Bud lunged at the beast with the chair. The werewolf bit a leg off the makeshift shield and Bud struggled to keep a grip on it.

The werewolf clamped on another leg of the chair with its jaws. Beads of sweat spewed from Bud's brow. He shook violently from the might of the werewolf's bite. His hands blistered. His grip weakened. His energy waned.

BOOM.

The werewolf's body jolted and crashed through a card table. The man in the golf cap confidently stood over the shocked werewolf with a double barreled shotgun and emptied the second barrel into its head.

BOOM.

"Aye, that'll fuckin' do me son."

Bud stood dumbfounded, amazed, and grateful.

"Thank you, kind sir." Bud said.

"Don't thank me, me son. I been waitin' foreva to kill the Beast of Llanwelly. Took my brother's life he did. And don't worry. The shells were filled with silver shards from my grandmother's fine dinin' collection. Hahahahaha! This wolf ain't recoverin' from that me son."

Bud shook the man's hand. "Your heeding the call of duty will be forever emblazoned in the steel of my heart, sir."

"Ah, don't even worry bout it me son."

Bud ran out of the pub, but he could still hear the man.

"Hey Ang, what the fuck accent was that?"

The barkeep was tending to his injured patron's wounds. "Sounded like fucking fake English to me, Brian."

32

THE TROPES OF TELEPORTATION

Bud hurried back to the grounds of Talbot castle. He hadn't run so much since his sophomore year of high school, when he had to in order to pass physical education. Bud preferred gentler exercises like walking. He reached for his phone, which still carried a suitable charge, thanks to his own tinkering which produced a week of battery life. He checked the display. His heart dropped. He stopped at the broken gate of Talbot castle.

"Oh bother. You awoke and used a marker you bastard. I am coming for you."

The marker Brother Mike pinged was two blocks away from the Westminster Inn at a car rental station. Bud opened his GPS app and zeroed in on the marker he left in Brother Mike's room in the hopes he still had time to catch Brother Mike collecting his luggage. He hesitated and looked at the castle. Llanwelly's troubles were far from over. The malevolent spirits let loose from the sacred tree were still at large. Maeve died trying to seal the tree. He didn't want to leave her at Talbot castle.

A wave of sadness struck his chest. His eyes watered. He dropped his last destination marker at the gates of Talbot castle.

"I will come back for you. I promise." Bud vanished from Llanwelly.

Bud teleported into Brother Mike's room at the Westminster Inn. The luggage still lay open.

Bud checked the fridge. The black box of collected blood was gone. He'd hoped Bert phoned Robbie to give the blood to Scotland yard. Bud ran into the hallway to see if he could find Brother Mike, perhaps rounding a corner in an attempt to escape.

"He shan't be too many paces ahead!" Bud yelled.

He called Bert. "Bert, tell me you reached Robbie on the blower and instructed him to give the blood to the authorities."

"Yes I did. He told me he would do it straight away."

"Thanks Bert." Bud ended the call.

Bud ran to the stairwell. Checked every floor with an awkward run and probably woke up all the occupants. Nothing. He stopped for a breather then his phone vibrated in his pocket. Another destination marker was activated. Bud waited for the signal to subside then honed in on its destination. He readied his wristband and grimaced. He teleported from the Westminster Inn.

The darkness, the bumps, the discomfort of being in a confined space, and the sound of tires rolling on the ground led Bud to the conclusion that he'd teleported into the trunk of a motor car. He hadn't much luck with motor cars. Salem was fresh in his memory.

"Don't have to be here long. I will simply teleport out of here." Bud contorted his body and waggled his wrist. The

LED strip in his wristband didn't illuminate. His phone lit up but showed no signal.

"Unceremonious defeat. I am trapped. Bloody hell."

33

JENNER

Ms. Jenner awoke from her slumber after repeated attempts to keep her head up for Westminster Inn hall monitoring duty. She had waited for Brother Mike to relieve her but he hadn't come. It was almost 6AM and time to wake the students to prepare for the flight to Rome. She stomped down to Brother Mike's room, more than a little upset. The room was empty except for his luggage on the bed. He was nowhere to be found. She grabbed the hotel room phone and dialed his number. The phone rang twice.

"Hello?" Brother Mike answered.

"Mike, where are you? You haven't been back all night and your room was open," Ms. Jenner asked.

"I will have to meet you at the airport. You can rally the troops by yourself, right?"

Jenner rolled her eyes. "Yes, I of course, can handle it. Where are you anyway?"

"I told you. I have cousins from here. I am sorry! I should have just come back!"

"Don't worry about it. You don't get to see them very

often. What about your bags?"Ms. Jenner rolled her eyes again.

"I can swing back real quick and get them then check out. Don't worry about it."

"Your door was left open too, by the way."

"My mistake. Please lock it for me. I have my key! Listen, gotta go. Driving on the wrong side of the road while on the phone is rough," Brother Mike said.

"Drive safe. See you at Heathrow." Ms. Jenner hung up the phone and shook her head. First, he met the group in London and only spent a few hours with the students. Then he disappeared the whole night. Ms. Jenner also worried that a student would tell that one of the chaperones was absent for the first part of the itinerary.

She checked the time on her phone. It was time to start knocking on doors to make sure the students were up.

She had six doors to knock on with two students in each room. A few minutes later, five out of six rooms complied with the early morning wake up call. Students opened the doors quickly.

She knocked and knocked on Robbie and Brent's room. She called a bellhop to open the door. Similar to Brother Mike's room, the bags were in there, but not Robbie and Brent.

"Where the hell are those two?" Ms. Jenner barely held back the panic building in her stomach. She must have missed them leave the room when she struggled to stay awake on her extended hall monitoring duty. She blamed Brother Mike.

34

THE UNDERGROUND

Bud surmised that the muffled voice he heard talking had been Brother Mike's which made sense, Bud remembered Brother Mike using a signal jammer in his classroom to keep students off their cellphones hence why Bud's cell and band didn't work. Although this jammer must have a very short range since someone just ended a phone conversation. He'd hoped the jammer and voice was not Brother Mike's. He hoped it was a random cab on the way to the English countryside. It wasn't.

The car stopped. Bud rolled a bit. The car accelerated on bumpy ground. Bud rolled more then stopped. He heard the driver door open and close. The passenger backdoor opened. A few moments passed. The back door closed. Bud still had the scimitar from Llanwelly on him, tucked in his pants. He didn't have enough room to ready it.

"Oh, you poor fool. Just let me out of here this most preposterous position. End this tomfoolery."

The trunk opened. Robbie McGann stood over Bud.

Bud's eyes' widened, "You driveling idiot. You are helping him! You actually did kill Hurley. You little shi-"

Bud's rant was stopped short by the sensation of a hypodermic needle to his neck. The sharp pain gave way to a tingling sensation that started in his fingers and toes and slowly spread to the rest of his body. Bud was awake but barely able to move.

"We have to walk it from here. I got Brent. You get Bud. You can handle him, right?" Brother Mike asked.

"I can handle Hutchins for sure." Robbie punched Bud in the face then removed his wristband, his phone, and the scimitar.

"My sword! Excellent! Hutchins, thanks for keeping it safe. Leave that stuff in the trunk. Easy, we need his body."

Bud barely felt Robbie's punch due to the drug that numbed his nerve receptors.

Bud saw they were on Liverpool Street as Robbie pulled him from the trunk and began to drag him by his armpits. Bud's legs were limp on the craggy street that was under construction. Work had not started for the day. After a couple minutes, Robbie headed down an incline. They were going underground.

Bud noticed a boy, Robbie's age, pulled by Brother Mike into the depths of London.

"This was Londinium down here, Robbie. The Roman settlement, right here. They of course, chased the Druids out of the area, but there is a site of a particular sect of Druids that..." Brother Mike huffed as he pulled Brent. "A sect of Druids that had close ties to Carthaginian rituals and gods had a site down here. Romans had no sympathy for anything remotely Carthaginian, due to the Punic Wars, and summarily wiped them out. To try to save themselves, the Carthaginian Druids attempted to summon Baal to defend them. Seven children were sacrificed. Burned alive.

Stolen from their mothers on the night of Samhain or Halloween."

Bud wished he could shut Brother Mike up. The drug held his tongue.

"We're they successful in summoning Baal?" Robbie asked.

"No, no, but we will be." Brother Mike dropped Brent's arms. He grabbed for his pocket, pulled out his phone, and turned the flashlight on. They came to the bottom of the incline and were met by a decrepit brick wall. They had arrived at their destination. Brother Mike pushed through the weak wall. The light from his phone showed a site dedicated to human sacrifice, an ancient pagan altar to Baal Hammon.

35

BIG BERT IS WATCHING

Bert sat straight up in Bud's bedroom desk chair. It was a little after midnight in Chicago. Hanks snored on Bud's twin bed. Bert rarely tired. He could stay up as long as he was charged with some task helping out Bud. The computer screen showed various windows all running tasks. Bert sought a different way to communicate with Bud since he lost signal to both his phone and wristband a few moments ago. Bert furiously typed on the keyboard. All his efforts proved futile. He shook Hanks to wake him up.

"Aww Christ Bert. I need to sleep. I haven't slept in two days," Hanks barked, his head buried in the pillow.

"I have lost connection to Bud's signal and I have tried every frequency, bandwidth, emergency band. Everything."

Hanks lifted his head then pulled himself up to sitting on the bed. "Okay what was his last location."

"He was in the Westminster Inn then another marker activated in what looked like a moving vehicle traveling down a Liverpool Street. We can safely assume, Bud teleported to that beacon, although I am not sure he survived.

We hadn't tested teleporting to a moving marker yet. Hence, we lost signal after he activated his band from the Inn."

"Can't you hack into London's CCTV systems and track the vehicle through the cameras?"

"This did not occur to me. That could work." Bert brought up a City of London database which he easily accessed. He loaded a surveillance interface on one side of the screen then on the opposite side of the screen, the GPS tag from the activated marker on the other.

The cameras showed a yellow cab. Bert zoomed and saw Brother Mike in the driver's seat. An unconscious man was in the front passenger seat, his head leaned against the side window.

"Brother Mike is driving the car. Same face as the yearbook pictures," Bert said.

"Cabs should be lojacked or have some sorta tracking on them. Get the plate and ping the GPS, that should be faster than checking all the cameras, right?" Hanks said.

Bert had already finished the task before Hanks stopped talking.

"I can't ping the car. Brother Mike must have blocked all digital and satellite communication in the car. That is why Bud's signal is lost. The cameras will have to suffice."

Bert scanned and typed the camera numbers and views exceptionally fast. Hanks could not keep up.

"How the hell are you doing this so fast Bert?"

"The cab stopped on Liverpool Street near what looks a like a construction site. I shall now cross-reference the Liverpool street with associations to the occult. A John Aubrey and John Toland wrote of this site in their Druid Revival works. This is the site of Londinium. There are connections to Druids and Carthaginian deities. This could be the place where Brother Mike plans to use the plasma he collected and NOT North Africa. I shall notify Scotland Yard."

Bert typed even faster. He put on a headset with a microphone and called Scotland Yard, using a number he cloned remotely from a cellphone dealer near Liverpool Street.

"Help me please! have reason to believe a murderer is at large at the Underground construction site on Liverpool Street. Please send any and all units."

Bert's voice mimicked a teenage boy's crackling voice in peril.

Hanks shook his head, "The first part was convincing Bert but the last part was hokey. Are they sending units? How the hell did you change your voice like that?"

"Yes, please. Hurry! The taxi-driver is unconscious and I am hiding in the site!" Bert finished his conversation with the emergency dispatcher. His voice back to normal, "They are sending units as soon as possible."

"How the hell did you do all that so damn fast?" Hanks said, bewildered.

"It is part of my programming."

"What?"

"Officer Hanks, look." Bert pointed under the desk.

Hanks couldn't believe his eyes. There were several cords attached to Bert's leg and left foot.

"I am an artificial intelligence android created by Bud. Right now I am charging."

"You are a robot!"

"Yes. Now let's hope my main mission to help Bud is accomplished." Bert turned his head back to computer screen.

Hanks stared in awe. "Witches, a teleporting teenage genius, a young woman who could fly and set forests on fire, a pagan worshipper obsessed with blood, and now a robot!" He fell back on the bed exhausted.

36

RITUAL

The secret chamber in the London Underground looked like a miniature temple, it had an altar with ceremonial fonts for sacred rituals.

In the center of the chamber, Bud was laying on ground at the foot of a statue that looked like a man with a large hat on sitting on a throne and flanked on each side by two small sphinxes.

"Baal, I presume," Bud thought.

He heard rustling next to him. Brother Mike and Robbie were moving Brent's unconscious body onto one of the ceremonial fonts that was raised a few feet from the floor.

"Robbie, run back to the cab and grab my backpack, will ya buddy?"

"I got it." Robbie made his way through the broken brick wall and up the incline.

"Yes, master. Igor will do it. Yes." Bud thought to himself. If only he could have smiled.

"Well, Hutchins. I must say that your genius made my mission possible."

Bud used his mind to will himself to overcome the diazepam that flooded into his nervous system. It didn't work, it only caused a furrowed brow.

"Looking constipated Hutchins. Relax. That is why I drugged you. Turns out your brains and body will be perfect for Baal's spirit to possess. Then he can singlehandedly wipe away monotheistic religion and restore order. Too many keep dying in the name of a single God, Hutchins. I always told you in History class that the number one cause of death in the world is religion. Baal will stop the bloodshed."

"It is just a fucking, inanimate statue." Bud thought to himself. He willed his adrenal glands to secrete the endorphins needed to perform miraculous feats like overcome drug-induced paralysis. His eyes darted to Brother Mike. Bud could feel his toes. He battled to gain more feeling back to the rest of his body.

Robbie returned with the backpack. Brother Mike removed the black box with gold inlay on the sides. He opened the box, revealing the three vials of blood taken from the monks of the Order.

"Hutchins, your cute girlfriend's blood will hopefully suffice. She suffered a nasty wound from a member of her own Order I presume. Ouch. I really am sorry." Brother Mike brushed away a spot right in front of the statue of Baal near Bud's head.

"Perfect." He emptied the vials one by one making a sign of the cross. The ground vibrated. The statue cracked.

"The Christian sacrifice. The blood of the betrayers," Bud thought as he struggled to twitch his leg.

"Robbie, it is time for Brent. See Robbie, I was about your age and on a trip just like this, except on the way to the Holy Land, the age old conflict between the Arabs and

Israelis caused a few of my classmates to die in an attack. I was injured with head contusions but survived. Still, two monotheistic religions caused my friends to die just like they killed the people who believed in the gods and goddesses. So I did a lot of soul searching. Even joined the Christian brotherhood thinking that might help restore my faith. It didn't. In my education training, I studied the ancients. The gods and goddesses were feared, more palpable, and the founders of religion itself. Why place all your faith in one god when you can place it in many?" Brother Mike sprayed lighter fluid all over Brent who remained unconscious atop the raised ceremonial font.

"The child sacrifice," Bud thought in despair. He could now feel his fingertips.

Robbie looked nervous and unsure. Bud hoped the boy would come to his senses and stop the madness. Robbie held a Zippo lighter in his hand.

"Robbie, the lighter, please." Brother Mike commanded.

"The lighter Robbie." Brother Mike held his hand out.

Robbie gripped the lighter.

"Robbie!" Brother Mike grabbed Robbie's arm and pried the lighter from his hand.

Brother Mike let him go. He turned his attention to Brent.

Bud struggled to vibrate his vocal chords and move his mouth, "Don't."

Brother Mike turned to Hutchins. "Impressive you are able to talk. I will have to give you more Valium."

He grabbed Brent's arms and folded them. The boy's eyes were open. The smell of lighter fluid permeated the small chamber.

Brother Mike stood with his back toward the broken bricks of the entry point. He had nearly accomplished his mission. He smiled. The white light of his flashlight spotlighted preparations for a ritual sacrifice that had not performed in almost two millennia. Brent was on the font. Hutchins lay at the feet of the statue ready to receive the spirit of Baal. The time had come. He ignited the small flame of the Zippo lighter.

37

THE SUMMONING

The lighter flew through the air and fell to the ground near the backpack.

Bud heard a voice say, "Don't move!"

He was able to move his head to the voice.

The officer knelt on Brother Mike's back and readied the handcuffs. He struggled and pushed up with all his might. The police officer fell back, and the Brother vanished into thin air.

"What the shit?!" the police officer yelled. His partner entered the room, a female.

The nylon backpack burst into flames from the ignited Zippo. The fluid bottle was a few inches away at the base of the ceremonial font Brent laid on.

"We must evacuate these two now. Get up!" She helped her partner to his feet. The backpack fire created intense heat and the flames began to jump.

Bud grimaced. He could feel one arm and leg and reached for the bottle. The back pack fell to its side and the flames drew closer to Brent. Bud's fingertips scraped the bottle when a foot kicked it away.

"Time to leave." The female police officer helped Bud to his feet.

"Can you walk?" She asked.

"With one leg it appears." Bud hopped with the aid of the police officer at his side.

The male police officer secured and carried Brent on his shoulders and they left the secret chamber. The flames wrapped around the ceremonial font. The ground vibrated again. The statue of Baal Hammon cracked and began to crumble.

The group reached the cab at the top of the incline on street level.

"Thank you officers for the help. I am afraid the murderer and mastermind of this dastardly situation you found yourselves summoned to is still at large. Would you be so kind as to take the sword in the trunk of the cab as evidence of two dead monks in the United States? Also there should be a phone and a wristband in there as well. Could you procure it for me? I must then get a few paces away to avoid his scrambler that the culprit planted in the cab and thus pursue said culprit."

The officers examined the trunk, "Slow your speech young man. We shall sort this through."

The female officer handed Bud his wristband and phone.

"Thank you. How did you know to come to our aid?" Bud hopped away from the cab.

"He helped us." The officer pointed to Robbie who sat near the front bumper of the cab.

"No matter his attempts at redemption. He is an accessory to murder. Arrest him."

The officers were taken aback at Bud's aggressive and wordy approach.

The mouthy American with the terrible fake British accent disappeared.

38

RERUN

Morning had settled in at Llanwelly. Bud found himself back at the gate of Talbot castle. With the tree unsealed, he wondered what evils had been unleashed. Brother Mike must have detected the marker Bud planted.

The marker also looked damaged as if Brother Mike tried to damage to stop Bud from pursuing him. Thankfully, Hurley made tough, nearly unbreakable, markers. Bud looked around for the BMW rental. It was gone. On the ground near the tire tracks, was the stolen wristband. Bud put in his pocket. Brother Mike had ditched the wristband and now tried to escape through more conventional means. Bud heard the roar of the engine in the distance.

Bud dialed Bert.

"Bert, I need you to access any and all London car rental company's databases and search for a blue BMW sedan that had been rented in the last 24 hours. Then track it."

"Nice to hear your voice Bud. I am running a check now. There have been three BMW sedans rented from London proper in the last 24 hours. Two are located in Scotland. One in Wales and it is heading west out of Llanwelly, the location that just pinged from the activated destination marker. Shall I contact the authorities? Since you refuse to drive motor cars."

"Very funny. Yes, contact them. I am rather useless at the moment."

Bud heard a slow rustling behind him. "Werewolves don't come out in the daylight!" Bud hoped aloud.

He turned to see Maeve standing there with a broom in her hand.

"You're alive! How?" Bud said.

She pointed to her throat, shook her head, then pointed to the broom.

Bud approached and noticed the paleness of her skin. He vocal chords had been ripped away, blood had soaked into her hoodie.

"You can't speak. Oh Beauregard! You absorbed the undead spirits! You are now a zombie! This is absolute madness."

She nodded and began to hover.

"Let's finish this. Tally Ho!"

Bud hopped aboard and grasped Maeve's cold undead body. He was surprised she hadn't started to smell or perhaps the fresh air and wind masked it.

"I am surprised you don't wreak of rotting flesh!" Bud said.

She turned her head and gave him a dirty look then dipped the broom and flew faster. Bud reeled and grasped her tighter.

"Head west Wicked Witch!" Bud said.

They followed the road and soon caught up to a blue BMW sedan that sped along a country road.

"That is him Maeve! Get in close. Perhaps we should

use the method the Salem witches used on us and bump the roof."

Bud stomach dropped as Maeve dove to the sedan's roof. The wind battered them as they descended.

Brother Mike drove the sedan up a rolling hill. Maeve adjusted accordingly. BOOM! Her forearms and elbows dropped on the roof of the BMW. Brother Mike swerved but then gained control and continued the ascent up the hill.

Maeve and Bud dove again. BOOM! The impact was harder this time. Bud almost lost his grip. The car didn't swerve. The sedan reached the top of the hill and began to speed up.

Maeve dipped the broom and tried to close the gap created by the downhill speed of the sedan.

"Sheep! A shitload of sheep!" Bud yelled. Down the bottom of the hill, a sheep herder brought over forty sheep across the road. Brother Mike did not slow down.

A large black and white Shetland sheepdog stood in the center of the road and barked at the sedan. The dog protected the flock at his own peril.

"Not the dog!" Bud observed from above.

The sedan drew within fifty meters of the dog and flock.

Maeve flew closer to the sedan but couldn't close the distance.

Thirty meters.

Maeve flew as fast as she could. Bud shut his eyes.

Fifteen meters.

The dog barked and stood his ground.

The flock of sheep moved across the road but not fast enough.

Maeve dropped onto the roof of the sedan and let go of the broom. She grabbed the edge of the roof by the driver side door. Bud lost his grip on the broom then regained it on Maeve's legs. The lower half of his body flailed over the rear window.

Maeve smashed the driver side window. Her arm suffered major damage, but she grabbed the wheel. Brother Mike hit the brakes in a panic. The sedan's tires screeched. He tried to pull the wheel back to the center. Maeve overpowered him and pulled the wheel to the right off the road and onto the grass. Bud lost his grip and rolled off. The sedan narrowly missed the dog and ran into three sheep before it hit a castle ruin.

39

RUIN

Bud laid flat, arms spread, face planted in green, lush grass. The sheepdog came over to Bud and barked. Bud lifted his head.

"I am okay poufy friend. I am delighted to see you are too."

Bud stood up and patted the dog on the head. The majority of the flock were safe.

"You did your best buddy." Bud limped to the sedan and the castle ruin. The car steamed from its location at the base of castle ruin's tower. The ajar driver side door indicated Brother Mike had escaped the car. Bud limped further into the ruin and saw Maeve and Brother Mike engaged in a brawl.

Bud limped faster. Brother Mike had pinned Maeve and held a large rock over her head. Bud gritted his teeth, absorbed the pain in his leg, and ran toward them.

Maeve slashed at Brother Mike's neck then grabbed it. Blood dripped over her fingers from the force of her iron grip.

Brother Mike lowered the rock to his chest but then lifted it back up over his head in a fit of blind rage.

Bud tackled him. The rock fell to the side of Maeve. Mike and Bud rolled around on the ruin's rocky ground. The phone and stolen wristband fell from Bud's pocket. Brother Mike managed to punch Bud in the face then kneed his genitals. Bud buckled. Brother Mike grabbed the band that fell from the teenager's pocket. Bud grabbed for the stolen wristband that was now secured to Brother Mike's wrist.

Brother Mike stood up and laughed, "I will make sure you can't follow me this time you snide son of a bitch." Brother Mike vanished.

Maeve ambled over to Bud. She looked more and more like the walking dead. The car crash and struggle with Brother Mike had inflicted more damage to her body.

"Maeve, would you be so kind as to hand me my phone?"

The task took Maeve longer than a normal person with a beating heart.

"Make hast..." Bud stopped himself. He felt bad for her.

She handed him the phone.

40

REMOTE TRANSACTION

"Bert, is the remote client finally up and running?"

"Yes Bud. Alas we have not tested it on humans quite yet. We are only on the seventieth inanimate object trial."

"Bert. Lord, I have to work on your sub routines for being thorough. I need to you to tell Hanks to ready his sidearm and shackles."

Brother Mike teleported safely to the Beauregard mansion. He looked around at the undead Confederate soldiers spread over the field in poses similar to all the Brady photos he collected in his classroom of devastated battlefields. The mansion lay in ruins from a fire. He grabbed the destination marker. Quickly, he used his shoelaces to tie the marker to a heavy stone and threw it into the Mississippi River.

He let out a sigh of relief. Bud didn't pursue and if he did now, he may drown or worse.

Brother Mike noticed his wristband's LED blink. He hadn't started the sequence. He panicked and reached for the band but not before he felt the rush of teleportation.

He found himself on the front lawn of the Hutchins' Chicago home.

"Hands up! Don't move!" Hanks aimed his sidearm at Brother Mike's chest.

Brother Mike held his hands up. Bert approached Brother Mike and removed the wristband. Hanks pulled his arms down and handcuffed him.

"Looks like you ain't' goin' anywhere but to jail," Hanks said.

The Chicago Police Department rolled up in a squad.

Hanks joined Brother Mike for a ride to the station. Hanks didn't know how to explain everything but he would have to. He would have to bend the truth.

"Very good, Bert," Bud pressed the red icon of his touchscreen that ended the call.

"We did it, Maeve. We got him. Bert and I have been working on remote activation of wristbands for a couple months now but we were unsure it would work yet. I don't know why I doubted myself. I am more than capable. I did it!"

Maeve grimaced at his ignorance.

"As did you. You are more than capable as well."

Maeve nodded her head and pointed towards the castle. "Oh yes we have to seal the tree. How do we do that?" Maeve smirked.

41

INITIATION

Becoming a monk of the Order of St. Michael hurt.

Maeve lashed Bud in the back very hard. So hard, Bud cried.

She laid out the book she found in the monk's quarters in Talbot castle which outlined the initiation ceremony. Bud read aloud the scripture in front of the greenhouse tree.

Maeve checked that the lash's wound was deep enough to leave a prominent scar.

Bud put his shirt back on.

"This is a most undesirable way to heed a prestigious and solemn call of duty."

She handed Bud her crucifix then pointed to the tree.

Bud read, "Saint Michael Archangel, defend us in battle, be our protection against the wickedness and snares of the devil; may God rebuke him, we humbly pray; and do thou, O Prince of the heavenly host, by the power of God, cast into hell Satan and all the evil spirits who prowl through the world seeking the ruin of souls. Amen."

The ground vibrated.

Bud turned to Maeve, "That mean it's sealed?"

Maeve nodded.

"We don't know what else was released from here do we?"

Maeve shook her head.

"We shan't worry about it until more beasts show up. Let's patch you up."

Bud took her hand and Maeve hugged him. The relief washed over him. Maeve was alive and he could help her. He already had ideas to run by Bert. They vanished from Talbot castle.

A few hours later, Hanks returned to Bud's home. Bud sat on a chair and Maeve laid down on a couch in the front room.

"I fudged the timelines but gave them all that Bert and I gathered on Brother Mike and Hurley. Bert working with Scotland Yard?" Hanks said.

"Of course. The Roman History Tour has been canceled. Ms. Jenner and students will be on their way home later. Robbie McGann has been arrested. The murder weapon will be on its way, shortly," Bud said.

"Robbie a part of it? She okay?" Hanks asked. Maeve lay on the couch.

"He actually was helping Brother Mike but then had second thoughts and tried to redeem himself. Maeve will be okay. I am confident I can help her. She may be able to restart her heart with the next full moon, of course."

"Of course," Hanks didn't want to know why or how.

Awkward silence.

"One more thing, Hutchins. Mike drew a tree symbol all over his textbook."

"Makes sense, given the Druid connection."

"No, there is more to it. Bert and I did some research and we think that Brother Mike may have been involved with a big organization. A giant cult of sorts. Bert can tell you more," Hanks said.

"I am sure Bert will tell me absolutely everything, annoyingly so. Officer Hanks, I wanted to say thank you for all your help." Bud put his hand out.

"No problem Hutchins. It's been a wild ride. Say why did you develop this technology anyway? Because you could?" Hanks shook Bud's hand.

Bud looked at a picture on the wall of an older man in Burberry trench coat holding a young Bud while walking on a downtown Chicago street.

"I developed it to find my Grandfather who went missing some time ago. I will find him."

THE END

If you enjoyed The Order please consider leaving a review!
LINK FOR REVIEW!

"THE ELIXIR"

AUTHOR'S NOTE ON "THE ELIXIR"

The sequel to the Order, is both a love letter to Chicago and archaeology. The actual plot of the Elixir was not supposed to be attached to Bud Hutchins at all. For a year, I worked with a prominent museum in Chicago and pitched the idea for a book set in the museum. The pitch worked but the terms of the deal were not favorable, so it fell through. Alas, the idea for an Elixir of the Ancients remained thus, "The Elixir: A Bud Hutchins Supernatural Thriller" was written.

The adage to write what you know works here. I wanted to set the events of the book in Bud and I's hometown of Chicago. There are many landmarks, neighborhoods, and icons of the city used within the pages of the book. I then looked at what supernatural and historical legends I could use as well. Some famous legends include, Al Capone-the notorious king of Prohibition, Resurrection Mary-Chicago's own hitchhiking ghost, and mummies from the world-class museums the city has to offer.

There are also the threaded connections to "The

Order" with Universal and Victorian horror in the book as well. Bud, Bert, and Maeve go through even more intense trials this time around. The new characters of Ivy Zheng and Padre Martinez further deepen the lore and also diversify the characters. The series starts to come into its own with this entry I feel.

Here is an excerpt of "The Elixir":

GHOULISH GALLERY

"I shall go into the gallery first then I will activate your wristband."

Bud pulled back his black leather sleeve to reveal a similar band to the one Bud had just given Ivy. He suddenly disappeared. She was listening to the guards clearing the various offices upstairs when she realized that she was no longer in the lobby but in the gallery. She turned around to see the lights of the lobby through the glass double doors of the interior of the Babylonian gallery. Her nerves were rattled. She was shaking from the sudden shift through space she had experienced. Adrenaline pumped through her veins at a quickening pace and her heart pounded.

"You are officially the first student of Chicago Met to have teleported. Certainly, there must be no equal to that distinction in the annals of this great institution. Now gather yourself. We must find Ms. Tricia Pazinski's murderer."

Bud brought up the camera on his phone. He activated the flashlight and a list of different filters for three-dimensional space. A thermal camera, a motion detector, and fingerprint scanner-- the very same tech he used to enter Ivy's dormitory.

"How? Is this possible?" Ivy asked looking towards Bud's face softly illuminated by the phone's flashlight.

"Certainly you can surmise various theories on how I was able to accomplish teleportation but I will spare you the details. We must press our advantage and figure out where this hooded figure is."

"I mean I understand how you are able to break down your molecular mass but how do you transport and rebuild it in a different space? How did you do this?" Ivy's innate curiosity sparked. She became ravenous for answers.

"Ivy, if I tell you then the novelty would wear off. I cannot reveal too much especially to someone of your intellect. It will not be contained, nor would my patent for it be my own. I hope you understand my need for safeguarding my technology. Now we must stick to the sides of the gallery behind the cabinets so as to not arouse the guards' suspicion upon their return to the lobby."

Bud moved off the main walkway and in between two large show cabinets. He scanned the area for the culprit.

Ivy followed Bud shaking her head in disbelief. Respect for Bud began to grow. Perhaps he was not a typical private investigator who chased adulterers and people who stole credit card numbers from gas stations.

"I don't think her murderer would be hiding in this corner of pottery shards and demon figurines," Ivy said.

Bud scanned the glass cabinet. Ivy was not wrong. Shards and small figurines. One figure of which had a human body, a dog's head, and two pairs of large wings.

"Oh, dear, that is Pazuzu. Is it not?" Bud asked.

"Yes. A Babylonian demon associated with rain and drought. Inherently evil but also a champion against other evil spirits and the nemesis of Lamashtu, the demon that attacks pregnant woman," Ivy said.

"Hmm, keeps evil spirits at bay not unlike the Order of St. Michael..." Bud said.

"What's that? Anyway, Pazuzu is associated with horror films and people don't focus on the good efforts of the demon. Pregnant women would keep a figurine of Pazuzu in their home to keep away Lamashtu."

"Sounds perfectly logical..." Bud couldn't believe he had said that. His experiences with Maeve and the Order had been slowly turning him away from always thinking there is a scientific, practical reason for everything.

"...yet ludicrous." Bud finished. He still had a way to go even after all he had gone through. He moved on to the next section of the gallery and perhaps the most impressive.

"We are heading towards the giant Assyrian King Sargon relief. The one thing that might be of note is that the relief is not flush to the wall. There is a backside to it. Be careful. It is a pretty good hiding spot especially given how careless the cops were on their initial search," Ivy said.

Bud shined his cell light on the large stone raised relief section of a palace wall. The relief depicted King Sargon combined with a beast that had five legs and hooves for feet. Bud was impressed with the craftsmanship. He stepped closer to the ancient stone grey wall and slowly moved to the side to light the back of the wall.

Ivy followed Bud. She kept both hands on his back and peeked over his shoulder. Bud lifted his phone to eye level and initiated a thermal scan. The space behind the relief, which was only about a three-feet wide, showed a slight reading.

Bud and Ivy moved closer to the space. He looked at the screen of his phone. Ivy looked at what the phone's flashlight showed.

"There is no one there Bud," Ivy whispered.

Bud looked up from the screen of his thermal imaging app. "It appears to be so, yet someone may have rested here. I am still seeing a slight thermal signature."

POP!

Ivy jumped on Bud's back. He nearly lost his balance. One of the track lights that illuminated the writing above the rear of the relief had broken.

"A faulty light bulb! Even with the lights off, a loose wire can still carry a charge. It could have merely loosened from a poor job at screwing the bulb in. The wiring in this old building must not be to code. Anyway, what does this writing say?" Bud asked.

Ivy slid off Bud's back.

"Sorry about that. It is just the typical boasting of the king's greatness. His biography and achievements are written here but not necessarily for the purpose of being read. Knowing that it has been recorded is what mattered to the Assyrians. They would write on keystones implanted into the ground. It was not important that anyone knew the writing was there," Ivy said.

"How strange the ancient customs were." Bud turned away from the Assyrian gallery and headed to the next section. They had to make a right turn as the layout of the entire gallery was a U shape.

They heard the sound of something heavy, like a large piece of furniture, being dragged on the marble floor. It came from somewhere ahead of Ivy and Bud.

"One can assume the custodial staff does not respond that quickly to broken light vessels. What is the content of the next gallery?"

"The Egyptian mummies," Ivy said.

USA TODAY BESTSELLING AUTHOR

JB MICHAELS

THE ELIXIR

A BUD HUTCHINS THRILLER

Copyright 2017 Harrison and James Publishing

ALL RIGHTS RESERVED

ISBN: 1974014479

ISBN 13: 9781974014477

❦ Created with Vellum

CHAPTER ONE

CONCENTRATED RAGE

The glass beakers shattered, victims of the man's frustration. So close, but the elixir still needed more work. Probably different ingredients. He would have to start from square one. The year of research had failed him. He rested on the chair next to the long table of glass tubing, microscopes, petri dishes. He wanted to destroy the rest of his workspace, but that would set him back further. There was something missing, even the world's libraries bore nothing new for his research. He had considered a sabbatical many times, but the time was past for that. The board's decision would be final within weeks.

He stood up and looked at broken glass on the floor. He sighed and grabbed the broom that hung on the wall. The single light bulb cast just enough light to catch the glass shards strewn across the floor. He methodically swept in a controlled manner that belied his earlier rage. His outbursts were becoming more and more frequent. Many people had told him to perhaps seek anger management. He had no time for it. Too much to do.

He wanted to avoid going to the Institute. His relationship with the Institute was strained after the last incident, yet he knew that the contents of the Institute would be the only way forward. He finished shuffling the broken bits of glass into the dustpan, emptied it into a small blue recycling bin, and pulled the string of the singular light bulb. There was no way to see in the room when the light was off. No ambient light from the outside. He secured his phone and lit the flashlight, then walked over to a grey steel door. He pulled down a large handle that released the hatch. Still no light.

CHAPTER TWO

BUD P.I.

"Bert. I think it dreadfully silly, downright superfluous, that I am in this position." Bud lay on branch in a tree high above a residential street in the Lakeview neighborhood of Chicago.

"Sir, if you want this new technique to work than you must help activate it," Bert responded through Bud's earbud.

"Why do we always develop remote activation last? We should make it a priority before we even test any other aspect of any new contraption. For the love of all that's heavenly," Bud said, exasperated at how high he was from the street.

Bud pushed a mirrored button on the drone that he and Bert were field testing. The drone's quad-copter propellers spun, pushing away the smaller leaves attached to fig-like branches. It hovered in place. Bud gripped his mobile phone tight while still prone on the branch. He searched for the right app.

"Bert, I thought you said you would finish the app icon. I hope this is the bloody right one!"

"Sir, I think you should prep the piloting controls on your mobile. The couple is arriving," Bert said.

"Great. Just wonderful. Ready the remote teleportation program if I fall from this blooming tree as I will not be able to initiate it whilst fearing for my life."

A black Audi rolled up the residential street. Bud could see two people in the front cabin of the car. No hands on the wheel. The car's self-drive program had been initiated.

"Bert you may be obsolete. This Audi is driving independent of external manipulation," Bud said.

"I really believe you should learn how to drive Bud. Reliance on technology was almost your undoing with Brother Mike," Bert fired back.

"You saved me. So your point is quite ironic my android friend."

The Audi parked in front of a large new two-flat, red brick apartment building. A blue 'W' flag waived from the porch. The Cubs fans of the vehicle disembarked. One was a young blond woman with glasses and a short, shapely figure. The other person was an older man with a pipe jutting from his mouth and patches on the elbows of his tweed jacket.

Bert's robotic voice startled Bud. "That should be Dr. Covington."

"Yes, and as Mrs. Covington suggested, the other person is a teacher's assistant at Chicago Met University, Tricia Pazinski. I am starting the drone's camera operation now Bert."

"You should have done so already Bud."

"I am trying not to fall from this giant tree Bert to my inevitable death."

"I would have started the camera when informed the car was on approach. Just saying."

"Again, remote activation would have been welcome. Now shut it. I am attempting to concentrate." Bud piloted the drone off the branch and it hovered high above the couple, who opened the gate to a porch walkway. The drone's quad-copter design worked to limit the noise. Two propellers alternate operation so that all four do not fire at the same time. Bud moved the drone a good 25 feet above the couple.

"We need more evidence to convince Mrs. Covington of her husband's infidelity Bert. I am going to have to make the drone follow them in."

"I agree with you sir. There are no windows, curtains, or blinds open. Initiate the cloaking tech when you see fit. It drains too much battery and does not last long."

"I know that Bert. We designed it together. Are you getting the recording?"

Bud moved the drone high above the front door and waited while Tricia, the teacher's assistant held the storm door open, and Covington turned the key in the lock. Bud looked at his mobile phone's screen. He touched the settings icon and the screen showed invisibility was an option. He pushed it. A warning popped up on the screen: 'This feature will significantly drain the drone's battery. Dismiss. Never Show again.' Bud shook his head and dismissed the alert.

The drone disappeared. To anyone who didn't know what to look for it was invisible. To those who did, a distortion of light, similar to the effect of a floating mirror, gave it away.

"I am receiving the drone's feed Bud. You are good to go. You might want to hurry."

The couple moved to enter the two-flat. The storm door was closing. Bud fumbled the phone and the drone flew up instead of down. With one hand he saved the phone from its crash on the gravel below, only his other hand and leg still gripped the branch. He pulled himself up and flew the drone down to the doorway, but the storm door closed. Bud failed.

"Shit. Shit. Shitty shits." Bud swore profusely.

"Not good sir, perhaps we can wait 'til they come back out."

The storm door opened again. Tricia Pazinski had left her book bag on the porch.

"Oh yes yes!" Bud yelled from the tree. She stopped and looked up towards the tree. The teacher's assistant shook her head then looked away.

Bud piloted the drone into the house. Then shut his mouth.

"Sir, you don't have much battery left with the cloak initiated."

The low battery icon blinked in the drone app. Bud needed to rely on the app and the camera feed to pilot the drone. The drone itself hugged the ceiling in the front hall of the Covington's home. Mr. Covington entered the doorway and grabbed Tricia and pulled her for a passionate kiss. She pulled away to stop her bag from getting caught in the storm door. Covington grabbed her bag and threw it in the house. He pulled her close and resumed kissing her. She kissed him back this time. Coats hit the floor. The drone's camera, positioned on the bottom of the drone, caught the footage with a bird's eye view. The drone began to drop. Bud saw the battery was only 10 percent.

"Bert you are getting this?"

"Yes sir. We should have enough evidence to convince

Mrs. Covington of her husband's foul behavior. How on earth will you get the drone out of the house Bud?"

The couple had left the front hall and were well away from the drone. The drone's microphone did pick up faint moaning from somewhere in the interior.

"Let's hope they left the door open with their passionate ignorance Bert."

Bud pushed the button of his teleportation wristband. He was out of the tree and now on the street next to the Audi. Bud hurried to the front door. He turned off the invisibility feature of the drone; the battery was down to five percent. A crash would certainly alarm the couple no matter how intense their love-making session.

Bud reached the storm door. It was open. He reached for front door. Open. The drone fell from the ceiling. Bud reached out with his gangly arms and caught the drone.

"Time to go."

Bud hit his wristband and disappeared.

CHAPTER THREE

PARENTAL OBSTRUCTION OBSTRUCTED

Bud walked past a "For Sale" sign post on the front lawn of an old ranch home with brown brick. It was different than his smaller home he grew up in. He had taken up residence in his grandfather's vacant home. The house smelled like smoke from years of his grandmother smoking. She had passed away ten years prior. Lung cancer. Bud was merely ten years old, yet he had fond memories of her. She'd been a very strong-willed opinionated woman who would have made a great columnist. Bud often thought she could have even won a Pulitzer Prize had she pursued a career in journalism, yet the generation she grew up was not accepting of working women.

His grandfather went missing about a year ago, but Bud believed him to be alive. Bud had spent most of the previous year teleporting to places his grandfather had already been according to the photos around the house. Bert had set up shop in the back office. His entire computer console and charging station sat near the cat 5 cable box that connected to the internet and into any database Bud and Bert needed to hack.

The furniture had not been moved for years. The walls were stained from the smoke and carpet was original to the house. Bud relived his fondest memories of his childhood in this home every time he entered. His parents wanted to sell it. Bud refused to move out. He walked to Bert's office.

"Bud! Glad you made it back with the drone intact! I shall charge it for you. Your parents have arranged a showing of the house this evening at 7pm. There will be a full moon tonight. We should be able to scare them off fairly easily."

"Oh jolly good, Bert. Jolly good." Bud handed Bert the drone then headed to the kitchen for a bottle of water. A note was on the fridge. "Bud, this is your mother. There is a showing tonight. Please leave the house. Mom."

He shook his head. Her redundancy was insulting. Why she insisted on telling him it was her twice? Made no sense. There was no postscript that said love you. Bud's relationship with his parents was strained, indeed.

Bud sighed and threw the note into the garbage. He grabbed some leftover Chinese food and spread it over the floor. He chuckled. That might even deter someone from buying the home before they even got to the basement.

Bud walked down the steps. In one corner was the washer and dryer and a pile of clothes, and in the other there was a door with an open padlock. Bud removed it and walked in. It was quite cold in the room. The entire room was a freezer. He found her sitting on the floor of the freezer room. Bud, for years, refused to wear anything save his trench-coat but since the Beauregard zombies destroyed it, he now wore a leather jacket in an attempt to look like a tough mobster.

"How are you feeling today Maeve?"

"Okay. Looking forward to tonight. It is a full moon isn't it?" Maeve's voice was similar to Bert's. It was the best they could do with the artificial voice box they implanted to replace Maeve's undead throat that was ripped away by a monk-turned-werewolf of the Order of St. Michael, a sect of the Catholic Church stationed at trees around the world to stave off evil spirits.

"Yes, I shall lock you up as usual. Any more decay or has the freezer done well to slow it?"

"I think I look pretty good given the circumstances." She pointed to the mirror in the freezer. Her hazel eyes and face were in a perpetual scowl. The nerves in her face were fried. When she talked, the sound came from her throat. Maeve, a gifted monk of the Order of St. Michael, was made undead by zombie Confederate veterans at the Beauregard plantation a few months ago. Her ability to absorb supernatural abilities had saved her life...in a way.

"Any progress on achieving my reanimation?" Maeve asked.

"We just closed another adultery case so we should be able to fund more of the equipment needed to help sustain your heartbeat after you transform," Bud said.

"Oh good. I don't know how much longer I can sit in this freezer. This is no way to not live, hahaha." Maeve's voice was robotic and could not really convey any inflection.

Bud smiled at her. "Well, it is nearly time. Remember you can be as noisy as you like."

Bud walked out of the room. He placed the padlock back on the bracket, but forgot to lock it.

CHAPTER FOUR

SHOWING OFF

Bud and Bert watched a young couple walk up to the front door of Bud's grandfather's home. The possible buyers were greeted by an older woman who wore fancy, flashy clothes; a silver blouse, long dangly earrings and lots of makeup-- which Bud knew matched the veteran realtor's personality. She smiled and shook the couple's hands with a flourish. Her charismatic salesperson skills would be no match for Maeve.

"Do you think it wise that we sit here in the car?" Bert stared at the party about to enter the home.

"It matters not what I think. We have to do this for the sake of my Grandfather. He needs his home when we find him. Also, it makes for a good bit of fun to watch them scurry out of the house like fools." Bud leaned forward in the passenger seat of their red beater car.

The showing began. The interested couple and realtor entered the home. The kitchen would be a mess of Chinese leftovers and in the basement they would be met by Maeve's guttural growls.

Bud looked up at the full moon.

Maeve convulsed and tore down the shelf that Bert fastened to freezer wall for her just a day ago. Her undead heart began to beat. Her hair follicles suddenly came alive, and she grew more hair on her head. A silver streak flowed like a river from scalp to stomach. Her nerves began to fire with pain. Comfortable pain. The pain of being alive satiated Maeve during her transformation, but soon that pleasure would give way to her hunger. In the freezer lay meat that Bud bought for her transformations. She bounded over to a new package of steak and tore it open. Maeve ate like the feral beast she was. She bit into the meat with sharp, drooling canines. A light in the basement turned on. She could see it through a crack between the door and the jamb.

She threw down the meat and bounded toward the open door. She smashed through it on all fours. Her hair covered her face. A silver streaked monster rushed towards the realtor.

'"Aaaaaaah! What in god's name?!" The realtor fell to the floor. Her cellphone flew through the air. The couple who had been behind her on the house tour ran up the stairs.

Maeve pinned the realtor to the floor and smelled the realtor's neck. Her perfume pleased Maeve's rejuvenated sense of smell. The werewolf opened her mouth wide and with her newly restored vocal chords, growled in the realtor's face.

Bud and Bert saw the couple emerge from the house screaming and flailing their arms. The man fumbled for his keys. The woman grabbed them from him and unlocked the door to their white SUV. They sped off down the dimly lit residential street.

"I take it our resident she-wolf succeeded in quelling our real estate issues for now," Bud said, smiling.

"On the contrary sir, three people entered the house. Only two exited." Bert gave Bud a blank stare.

"The realtor. Oh shit." Bud opened the passenger door and ran to the house.

CHAPTER FIVE

UNLEASHED

A growling, feral Maeve burst through the front door just as Bud reached the walkway. The storm door's hinges bent from the force of a beast unleashed. The door was now broken and partially off the frame. Bud stopped and put his hands forward as if to tame Maeve. The long white streak of her hair was the most visible to Bud until she stood up and showed her hairy face. Pearly white canines dripped with drool, not blood, Bud noted.

"Maeve, my dear, it is effusively imperative that you cease, desist, and mar--, well, bound back down to the basement. You are a danger to your fellow man and you are a sworn monk of the Order of St. Michael."

Maeve cocked her head and howled. Her foul breath blew Bud's hair back. He pinched his nose. His ears ached. Bert approached from behind Bud. Maeve bolted away from them and headed south down Fairfield Avenue.

"Bert, you dolt. You scared her off."

"I seriously doubt I scared her Bud. She probably knew I could help you stop her."

"That is exactly what you will do. Let's get in the car and give chase. We must save her from murdering some unfortunate person or persons." Bud and Bert ran to their red Pontiac.

"What about the realtor, sir?"

The fancily dressed realtor fixed her hair as she emerged from the home fumbling for her keys. She checked around to see if the coast was clear.

"There she is now." Bud pointed then yelled to the realtor, "Not to worry, the beast is quite clear of this locale!"

"Let's hope the vehicle can match Maeve's speed," Bert said. He entered the car in his stiff, robotic fashion.

"She is heading south. Whatever for...I wonder." Bud sat in the passenger seat. He preferred to sit in the back, but this instance required a wider field-of-view. The car rumbled to a start.

Maeve tore down the street towards 87th street on the southside of Chicago. Bud tracked her location from his mobile device. She showed up as an orange blip on his map application. She moved steadily and with impressive, sustained speed.

"We can cut her off if we head, with great haste, down California Avenue then make a left."

"Sir, my protocols only allow me to go 5 mph over the speed limit," Bert, Bud's android assistant stated.

"Bert...Damnit. I programmed you that way for safety reasons. Undo your damn programming at this critical juncture."

"You have yet to implant me with voice commands to implement modifications to my vehicular protocol." Bert drove down California avenue at about 25 mph.

Bud slapped his forehead. He looked at Maeve's location. She was moving at a faster pace than Bert could drive the car, she was getting faster. Her speed was up to 35 mph. Her comfort with her newfound agility was progressing quickly. This was the first time she was able to stretch her legs in wolf form. She was supposed to be in the basement. Bud remembered that he may have left the room unlocked.

Maeve burned past 87th Street on her way to 95th Street. Bud and Bert were stopped at the light on 87th.

"Maeve is moving with purpose. But to where? Bert, what is south of here that would be of interest Maeve?"

"Sir, the southern tip of Chicago is known for its burial grounds. There is a monk of the Order of St. Michael stationed at Mt. Olivet cemetery on 111th Street and California Avenue, near Alternate Reality, the best comics shop in town."

"You mention the comics shop now! I need to update you. Let's keep heading south. If she stops before the cemetery, then I will press your right foot with my left foot to increase pressure on the accelerator. Her only reason to stop would be most likely to puncture someone's jugular vein. There are only residential neighborhoods and Catholic elementary schools between here and there." Bud furrowed his brow and looked at Maeve's location, willing her to keep moving.

Bert followed protocol and pursued her at the speed of 30 mph as they approached 95th Street. Maeve neared 107th Street, a few blocks from Mt. Olivet.

CHAPTER SIX

DISINTERRED

The full moon loomed large in the sky above Mt. Olivet Cemetery. Maeve stretched her back and arms as she stood up. Her long black hair with white streak fell over her back and partially spilled over the front of her shoulders. Her black hoodie and jeans were intact, mostly. There were tears at the extremities by her large clawed hands and feet. Her skin was covered with dark brown fur. Her jaw jutted slightly, caused by the growth of her canines. Her heart beat fast. Maeve breathed deeply. The chill air was a comfort. Any feeling she experienced was a comfort. In wolf form, she was alive again. When she had emerged from Bud's Grandfather's home, she had followed a strong scent. She smelled it every time she was locked in the basement and in wolf form. She finally was able to follow it tonight. The smell was coming from this cemetery.

She entered the cemetery with a single leap. The moonlight showed old gravestones, mostly dating from the 19th century. They were large and expensive--marble and stone with symbols adorning the tops. There were gothic mausoleums perched at the top of the hill. Down the hill were rows and rows of graves. Maeve moved to the interior of the cemetery. Trees lined the paths. One of the trees was, assuredly, a gateway that a monk of the Order was assigned to protect. Perhaps that was the source of the smell.

Maeve moved further into the cemetery and ascended the hilltop towards the mausoleums at the crest. There were trees up there. The scent grew stronger. She reached the top of the hill and down the path saw a police squad car. Parked. No lights were on. Maeve quickly dropped on all fours, bounded off the path and used the tombstones for cover as she approached. The squad car's passenger door and rear passenger side door were open. Maeve stood back up and examined the car closely. There was an unconscious police officer inside, leaning on the passenger door. Another officer's head rested on the steering wheel. Maeve noticed their sidearms were missing. Normal chatter and codes burst forth from the radio. The rack that usually held a bigger weapon was bent and broken. The shotgun missing.

The source of the odor had to have been here. It was strongest in this area.

A piercing, booming, sound resonated in the cemetery and rattled Maeve's sensitive ear drums. A bullet smacked up against the front passenger door, which Maeve stood behind. Another shot hit the window. It cracked. Maeve ducked behind the cover of the door. She waited to see if another shot would ring out. Nothing. She surmised that the gunman was near the mausoleum closer to the entrance. She bounded back to the tombstones for cover. Then she saw him--a man dressed in a cream trench coat and a suit that matched the jacket. He wore a fedora cocked to the left. The man's face bore a large scar. Al Capone had risen from the dead. ***The notorious world-famous gangster and king of Prohibition lived again.***

CHAPTER SEVEN

CAPONE

Bud and Bert stopped at the gate of Mt. Olivet Cemetery. They heard a gunshot. Bud emerged from the car quickly. He bonked his head on the door frame.

"It is most upsetting that we hear a shot at where Maeve stopped." Bud rubbed his head. He threw a destination marker over the gate and initiated teleportation. Without the marker in an open area, Bud could teleport into a gravestone mixing his molecules with the stone, thus death would ensue.

He vanished from outside the gate and appeared on the other side.

"Sir, couldn't you have just climbed the gate?" Bert said. His head hung out the driver window.

"Bert, another lecture from you and I may have to shut you down completely. Stay in the bloody car."

Bud shuffled towards Maeve's signal. He looked at his phone and saw that she had stopped in the center of the cemetery near the top of the hill. Another shot rang out.

Bud moved faster. His goal was to find Maeve and have them both teleport back home.

Maeve moved closer to Capone. Her hand and footfalls were silent with her padded feet. Capone scanned the area, she could see his short, stout silhouette in the moonlight, guns held waist-high. He scanned the area. Maeve noticed a bluish glow emanating from him. The moonlight was not capable of this illumination. He was corporeal, which meant he was able to inflict physical damage. He grimaced in frustration at not finding his prey, but kept to the path and walked towards the squad car.

Maeve hid behind a Celtic cross tombstone, right alongside him. She leapt out from her hiding spot and attacked his arms. Capone reeled and fell to the ground, dropping the guns but somehow his fedora stayed on his head. Maeve slashed at his face. The scar opened. His blood was blue. Capone pushed Maeve away and stood up. He stuck his chin out and bit his bottom lip. He grabbed her by the hoodie and landed two hard hitting bombs with his ring laden-right fist. Maeve growled and bit his left arm. Capone's brow furrowed and he threw her off his arm with incredible strength. She flew into the front grill of the squad car. Maeve's back felt like it was on fire. The pain blanketed her entire body. She almost wished to be in zombie form again.

Capone examined the bite wound. Then from his trench coat, he pulled the police shot gun. He pumped it and prepared to deal more damage to Maeve.

Bud heard the fighting, the howling, the pained verbal exclamations. He reached the top of the cemetery's one rolling hill. He didn't have time to process what he saw. Al Capone was alive and well. Bud was sure that his body had been moved from Mt. Olivet Cemetery to a place on the north side of town.

"Was that merely a ruse to divert people away from his actual grave that is still safely hidden here at Mt. Olivet?" Bud spoke out loud, but his words were interrupted by his heavy breathing. He wasn't used to running. He saw Maeve crouched near the front of a squad car. He saw Capone moving closer to her, prepping a death blow. Maeve jumped towards Capone and pinned him to the gravel. She unleashed a flurry of claws. A ferocious mauling.

Bud thought, "Perhaps I should intervene." Seeing her so violent bothered him.

"Maeve! Maeve! I cannot believe I am running towards a werewolf and a notorious gangster! I think you have handled the situation quite thoroughly!" Bud ran to the opponents.

The ghostly Capone was a blue bloody mess. His face was literally covered with scars. Maeve shoulders and chest raised and lowered quickly. She stepped back from the mess of Al Capone. She looked up at Bud then fell to the ground in a growl.

Bud ran to Maeve, who, in wolf form, was badly injured. The need to repair her to a healthy state was ever more pressing. When the moon went down she would go back to being undead. If she wasn't repaired, this would further damage whatever tissue was worthy of saving.

He held her and watched Capone's form vanish. All that was left were bones. Whatever supernatural menace resurrected the bones of the gangster was still at large.

CHAPTER EIGHT

IVY OUT OF HER LEAGUE

Ivy Zheng walked through the broad, heavy, medieval wooden double doors of the Archaeology Institute at Chicago Metro University. The lobby had a small gift shop to the right of the entrance and an info desk on the far wall that usually had a volunteer monitoring bags that needed checking for those interested in walking the gallery of the Institute. It was after hours so no one was at the desk. Ivy walked to the left away from the gallery and up a broad staircase to the office of Professor Covington. Ivy had scheduled a meeting to meet with her Teacher's Assistant, Tricia. The doors were left open for her.

Ivy was hard on herself to achieve. She had hardly any use for mathematics anymore, and consistently scored high and aced every class. The challenge of antiquity and the constant debate combined with a lack of knowledge of the past fueled her ambitions and drive for perfection these days. She was a perpetual student, who had more than enough credit hours to graduate. She just wanted to stay in class until she figured out exactly what to do with her life. Right now the path was leading her to archaeology.

Ivy walked up one flight then turned and climbed another set of steps to a hallway lined with offices. All were framed by old treated wood. Covington's office lay ahead a few doors on the right. Ivy reached the door when she heard a muffled conversation.

"Don't tell me what I can and can't do! This is my research!" A guttural, gravelly male voice yelled.

"You are making yourself sick. You can't continue like this." Tricia's voice was calmer than the man's, yet trembled.

"I told you! Do not tell me what to do! I will do as I please! You won't stop me! Neither will he!"

"Listen and just look at yourself! You're not yourself!" Tricia's voice shook with fear.

Ivy heard a loud crack, like a big book being pulled by gravity to the old floor. Ivy's heart beat faster. Covington's door was ajar. She pushed her way in. To her left was a series of rooms with open doorways. "Tricia must be in one of these," Ivy thought.

She heard another loud noise. This time it was followed by someone gagging. Ivy froze and peeked out from behind the door. Tricia smashed into the wall closest to the hallway. Someone had thrown her. Tricia lay motionless and her head drooped to her chest. Ivy pulled back and into hallway. She fumbled for the cellphone in her backpack to call the police. She heard footsteps bounding from inside the office toward the door she had just exited. Ivy stopped fumbling for her backpack and ran across the hallway. She prayed someone had left their office unlocked.

The first one she tried opened, and she stepped into a random office. She didn't close the door all the way as to not make any noise. She crouched under a desk. The heavy footfalls resounded in the hallway; they were coming towards the office where Ivy hid.

She heard the door creak open. She figured the person was scanning the room for someone, anyone. The person was in the room with her. He wasn't making a sound, but Ivy could sense a presence. The feeling seemed to last forever. Then she heard the door to her safe haven office shut. Heavy steps headed down the hall way towards the stairs. She peeked over the top of the desk. There was no one in sight.

Terrified, Ivy ran into Covington's office and down the hallway to Tricia. She was immobile and her chin was pinned to her chest. Blood dripped down on the wall behind her. The force of the throw must have cause a severe contusion to the back of her head. Ivy fished her phone from her backpack and called an ambulance.

CHAPTER NINE

COVINGTON CALLING

Bert, Bud, and Maeve returned to Bud's grandfather's home. They had dragged a panting Maeve to the basement. The damage the ghost of Al Capone had doled out was quite severe.

"This is most concerning, Maeve. When you return to your human undead form there will be considerably more damage to your tissue. Since your cells will not technically be in a live state, there will be no way to heal you without trying to keep you in a live state with a beating heart. This would pump the blood with the necessary antibodies to fight off infection." Bud examined her back which had suffered the greatest wounds. Deep gashes from the ramming bar of the squad car marked Maeve's furry back. Bud kept pressure on some of the wounds while Bert stitched her up.

"My medical protocols have come in quite handily, I might add. What form of the supernatural attacked you Maeve?" Bert sewed up the smaller lacerations, best he could. The large gashes would take considerably more work.

Maeve's muffled vocal box eked and growled out the word, "Poltergeist."

Bert processed the information and searched the internet wirelessly via an antenna in his head.

"A ghost with the ability to interact with the physical world and inflict damage upon the living. I would say that this definition is most accurate," Bert said.

Bud chimed in, "The larger wound's blood will coagulate when dawn hits in a few hours. She will need new blood when we get her back to a live state, which reminds me... Bert did the wire transfer from Ms. Covington come through yet?"

Bert looked up from Maeve's back. She growled as the sudden stitching stoppage hurt her.

"I believe so, but the dollar amount didn't reach the amount needed to purchase more of the equipment needed for a successful attempt at Maeve's reanimation."

Bud's phone vibrated from the insular pocket of his black leather jacket. Bud reached into his jacket and brought out his phone. "Speak of the devil."

Bud cleared his throat.

"Greetings, Mrs. Covington. How may I assist you?"

"I need your help again Mr. Hutchins." Mrs. Covington's smoke-affected voice sounded through the phone's receiver.

"It would appear so. I assumed the evidence we submitted to you was sufficient to prove your husband's infidelity." Bud paced the basement floor, stepping on the green tiles only.

"His mistress has just been murdered in his office. One can only assume the police will be coming to interview my husband. As far as I know, you and I are the only people who know of the affair, so they should not suspect me. I need you to help prove my husband's innocence."

"Wait! You didn't kill Ms. Pazinski did you?"

"No, no of course not. I have no idea who did. The sad part is how crushed my husband is. He must have really loved her." Her voice trembled.

"Were you with your husband this evening? The whole of the evening?"

"Yes, yes. We went to our favorite pizza place and I was pretending everything was normal. Have not brought myself to filing for the divorce papers... I just don't want him to go to jail."

"If he was with you the whole of the evening, he should have a legitimate alibi. My service may not be needed." Bud shook his head since he could really use the money.

"There is one more thing..." Mrs. Covington sighed and paused.

"Yes, what is it my dear?" Bud asked. His brow furrowed. He continued to walk-- the green tiles.

"I sent her a series of text messages saying I knew about the affair and that I would ruin her career."

"So this is not about your husband. This is about proving your innocence. The police have her mobile phone and will search through it. Now I may be of assistance. I can do a simultaneous investigation. My assistant, Bert, will be able to procure any documents the CPD acquires. We have access to every major system in the world. In the meantime, procure a lawyer. Your husband will know that you know when the police arrive. Right now you are a suspect. Depending on the conviction requirements set by the City you may be in trouble."

"That is why I am calling my crack private investigator. Shit, the police are here."

"I will commence with my investigation promptly."

"Thank you Bud. I already doubled your last fee and sent it to you. Keep in touch." Mrs. Covington ended the call.

"Well, Bert, it appears we now have the necessary funds to reanimate our dear friend Maeve." Bud walked over to a closet. He reached for a book on the shelf. He pulled it down and blew the dust off the cover. The book was old and leather-bound. The side of the book was titled, "The Diary of Victor von Frankenstein."

CHAPTER TEN

FLOATING INVESTIGATION

Bud Hutchins had left a destination marker near the Museum of Science and Industry for sentimental reasons. It was one of the favorite places he and his Grandfather frequented with much regularity, especially in Bud's formative years. He teleported to the lawn in front of the huge marble staircase near the parking garage entrance. The Archaeology Institute was only a few blocks away. The late winter/early spring air held a chill near Lake Michigan. Bud popped the collar of his leather jacket. He stopped to look at the Museum and smiled. The lights on the green dome provided a great deal of warmth to Bud on a chilly night. His Grandfather had understood him best and much of their relationship was spent walking the halls of the grand old building that was once housed the Fine Arts exhibition for the Chicago World's Fair in 1893.

His phone vibrated in his interior breast pocket.

"Bert. Yes. I only left you a minute ago. What could you possibly be in need of?"

Bert's voice rattled through the receiver. "Bud, I just wanted to let you know I found the phone call that pointed the police to the top floor of the Institute and the scene of Ms Pazinski's grisly murder..."

"Bert, out with it. Why must you overuse the pregnant pause when information is vital?"

"The number is registered to an Ivy Zheng, a student at CMU. She lives on campus in Oxford Hall. Her dormitory is number 344. It is highly likely she will still be with the police."

"Excellent. Inform when you have reviewed the surveillance footage in the Institute."

"Working on that now."

"Good." Bud ended the call.

He walked towards the Archaeology Institute. There was Chicago Met University Hospital in front of him. To the left of the hospital, were the Oxford-inspired buildings aplomb with gothic spires, much like Talbot Castle in Wales where Maeve and Bud visited last Autumn.

Bud could see the Institute ahead. There were still CPD squad cars in front of the large wooden doors. The typical yellow tape across the doorway. Bud had anticipated the busy nature of the crime scene. He pulled from his other jacket pocket, a smaller version of a drone he had used earlier. Under cover of night, he could easily use the drone without having to employ the battery-draining cloak function. Bud held the drone up in his left hand and used his right to trigger its start with his phone. The whisper-quiet propellers rotated and lifted the drone from Bud's hand. He raised it and used the night vision of the camera to see the way. He flew it high above the squad cars. Bud sat on a bench then hunched over to concentrate on flight, maintaining stealth, but also hoped to manage enough visual fidelity to get as much info on the murder as he possibly could. The layout of the building that Bert and he had viewed before he arrived on campus, showed there were a series of windows, albeit small windows, in almost every office.

The drone reached the exterior of the top floor of the three-storied Institute. Bud made it strafe the sides of the building. The drone's cam showed a window. He flew it closer. No light was emitting. He moved it to the next window. Still no light. He moved the drone further down. The night vision cam of the drone now bore bright light. Bud adjusted the settings on his phone from night vision to normal vision mode. The lights were on. He moved the drone closer to the window. About 15 feet away on the opposite wall was a blood streak, above the body of Tricia Pazinski. Bud zoomed in to get as many photos as he could.

Bud kept the drone in a stable hover. From the pictures on the screen of his phone, he surmised that Tricia was beaten to death. There were no visible signs of any stab wounds. The office space between her body and the window was filled with papers, an open file cabinet, and a tray with artifacts that had spilled on the floor. Ms. Pazinski had put up a fight with whomever savagely dispensed with her life.

Bud knew he would have to get in and examine the scene much more thoroughly. He moved the drone back to the stone windowsill of an office with no lights on, spun the drone around 180 degrees and hit an icon within the drone app that said "payload." A destination marker dropped from underbelly of the drone. Bud flew the drone back to where he sat. He stood up and grabbed it. With the drone secured to his jacket pocket, he walked past the squad cars and around to the office windows. He readied his teleportation wristband. A risky but not impossible use of his teleportation tech played out in his mind. A murder investigation meant that time was always the enemy; Bud needed to get into the offices unseen.

CHAPTER ELEVEN

WINDOWING

Bud's phone buzzed. It was Bert. "I see you activated a destination marker on a windowsill. The likelihood of that succeeding is rather, well, unlikely."

"We have no time for debate Bert. The new markers are pinpointed to my feet. I shall succeed in the endeavor by balancing and securing the rest of my person with my hands on the window frame."

"Bud, Maeve thinks this a fool's move as well," Bert said.

"I assume you were able to get her to a stable undead state?" Bud asked.

"The moon is still full and she is in wolf form. She has been stitched and wrapped with great care. I don't want to employ the same medic subroutines on you when you fall from the windowsill, unable to recover successfully from your teleportation."

"Nonsense, it will work." Bud ended the phone call. He stared at the third story of the Institute and found the darkened window where he dropped the marker. Bud flailed his arms to warm up for grabbing the window frame. He had done it several times over. Bud took a deep breath then exhaled and cocked his head, pretending he was a formidable physical presence and not a wiry, lanky young man. With his legs shoulder-length apart, he initiated teleportation on his wristband.

Bud found himself on the windowsill. His feet were partially planted but soon uprooted. He flailed his arms hoping to catch the window frame. Bud's hands scraped the glass window. He wished so desperately that the tips of fingers were like that of an arachnid's and would stick. Instead, they helped propel his backwards fall off the small ledge. The shock of falling overwhelmed Bud and he could not bring himself to teleport his way out of the dire situation. The third story was high enough to do major damage, but also too short a distance to actually react accordingly. Bud opened his eyes wide and hoped his inevitable incapacitation would be short and manageable.

Just as Bud figured his short trip would come to an end, he saw his teleportation wristband light up.

Bud's felt a soft cushion give way to the springs of his twin bed that coiled underneath him. The metal frame of his bed collapsed.

"Holy shit." Bud dropped his fake English accent in times of distress.

He did not move. He looked around at the spare bedroom of his Grandfather's home. The walls were off-white. There were old movie posters decorating the walls, some framed, some tacked on to the wall. Stacks of VHS tapes on a shelf and he could not have felt happier to be home. He lay and stared at the 1980s physical media.

Bert entered the room. "You are welcome Bud."

Bud recovered quickly upon seeing Bert and readied his defense. "It will work. The night blocked my perception of how much room I actually had in the window frame. You will get no thanks from me. I did not ask that you remotely initiate teleportation."

"Even if it was to safety, sir?" Bert asked.

"I still need to investigate the Institute. Again, only call me when you have the surveillance information."

Bud teleported back to the grounds of the Museum of Science and Industry. He did not want to tell Bert, his android assistant, that he had been right. Pride that was grossly impregnable to any criticism made Bud friendless. He only had become acquainted with Maeve when he had investigated her Uncle's death.

He would revise his strategy: visit Oxford Hall and hope that Ivy Zheng was done answering questions and filing reports with the police.

CHAPTER TWELVE

CONCENTRATED EBB AND FLOW

The single light bulb swung back and forth in the small room. The glass beakers had been replaced. A few shards from their predecessors still glistened from the floor in the yellow glow of the bulb.

The huddled man sat on a stool with his head in his hands. That idiot Covington only had a partial understanding of what needed to be done. His emphasis on physical components in a solid state had been his folly. The chemical nature of the research still seemed lost to the tenured Archaeology professor. This frustrated the man more and more with each passing day. The deadline approached and the Board still favored Covington over him. This bias was not official but the egregiously gracious nature of their behavior towards Covington enraged him.

Still he must push on. He'll try the mixture again with this new material. He felt he was close and a calm washed over him when he focused solely on his work. He prepped his lab for another experiment. His work would be considered revolutionary and would change the world. He took solace in the dreams of his victory, no matter the means of his accomplishment. The end-game would bring him glory and frankly, no one would be able to stop him from success once he found the right mixture. A rare smile adorned his face, not borne of happiness, but of visceral dominance. It was a smile that a fierce competitor employs to mock a fallen foe.

CHAPTER THIRTEEN

BUD MEETS IVY

Oxford Hall had a gothic bell tower spire similar to other buildings on campus yet that was the only similarity. It also had a redesigned front adorned with panes of glass and a modern look, similar in nature to Soldier Field in Chicago where architectural contrast is on full display. The stadium that was once purely Greco-Roman now had a modern glass bowl around its interior. It jutted over the stone columns in places as if a spaceship had landed in it but couldn't quite fit. Bud shook his head as he approached the dormitory. He checked his phone and scrolled through the long text message thread from Bert. He had sent him Ivy's information including door codes after he informed Bud of her call to the police.

He entered Oxford Hall. A security guard sat a desk. Bud casually walked past the security guard who was watching a video on his phone.

The upgrade to electronic keypad locks made Bud's life much easier. Bud used a camera filter on his phone to scan the keypad for its model number and the most likely lock combinations. Bud's camera gave him actionable intel, door keypads of this model, usually had a six-digit combo with the first three digits being the same and then varying after that. Through the filter Bud could see glowing fingerprints which were the most concentrated on digits 2, 5, and 7. He entered that combination then remembered Bert told him Ivy's room number 344. It worked. The door lock opened.

"This system is incredibly stupid. Parents of students should be bursting with lividity," Bud thought.

He entered a hall with elevators to the left and a stairwell on the right. He chose to wait for the elevator. A group of students spilled out of the elevator, and Bud quickly covered his nose and mouth with his sleeve. Hypochondria. The students smelled of booze. They each held laptops and components of a computer to assemble it for a night of intense PC gaming. Chicago Met was not your typical party school.

Bud was glad the elevator was empty. He used his sleeve to hit the button for the third floor. The elevator moved swiftly. 344 was to his right. He knocked on the door. A young, thin Chinese woman with black-rimmed glasses opened the door.

"Ivy, I presume." Bud held his P.I. License in the air. The one that Officer Hanks scoffed at the autumn before in Salem.

"Ugh, I just got done talking to the police. I want to be left alone! I just told them I don't want any counsel. I just want to be alone. Leave me alone." She slammed the door in Bud's face.

Bud knocked again and said, "I can help find the killer much faster than the cops can. Alas, we need to converse in order to fulfill my audacious claim."

Ivy opened the door; her logic and curiosity drove her. "Who are you? How did you know to come here?"

"I am Bud Hutchins. I am a private investigator working for Mrs. Covington, the wife of your professor. It was his teacher's assistant, Tricia who was so viciously murdered. In order to clear my client, I need your help."

She examined Bud's license, his weak stature, and eyes. She shut the door in his face again.

Bud shook his head.

She opened the door with her backpack on her shoulder.

"Let's go. Tricia was my friend. I will help in any way I can." She locked her door. Ivy bumped into Bud as she brushed ahead of him back toward the elevator. Bud was actually flustered and somewhat intimidated.

"Can you get us into the Institute past the police tape?" Bud asked.

"I know another way in."

CHAPTER FOURTEEN

NO EXIT

Ivy and Bud headed back to the Institute. Ivy brought Bud around the building to a set of stairs that led underground to the basement of the Institute. The police had not even thought to block this area off with the procedural caution tape. The steps were dirty; the ambient light from the city helped guide Ivy and Bud down to a door.

"I didn't want anyone to know that I know about this door. Technically, no one uses it, but the maintenance team," Ivy said.

"Why the secrecy?" Bud inquired.

"I come down here to study the artifacts stored here. Tricia did not know I would sneak in. Earlier I had an appointment with her and she left the front doors open for me. That is when I saw what happened. It was brutal and loud. We have to find out who did this." Ivy opened the door with a special padlock key.

She moved with a forward momentum so pronounced that even the hyperactive Bud Hutchins was reeling.

"Do you think it wise to move so quickly? The murderer could be sequestered in the basement. Perhaps we should employ a slower gait."

"I did hear heavy footfalls run away and down the stairs to the lobby. I wonder if the cops checked the camera footage yet? I suppose you are right. You said you had resources available to you so why haven't you checked yet?"

Ivy opened the door and stamped her feet. She then flipped a switch which caused a fluorescent wave of lights; some blinked on while others pulsed with power. The basement of the Institute had row upon row of casing and labels, shelves, and trays, all marked with numbers of a Dewey decimal system.

"Well, so much for a stealthy approach." Bud slapped his forehead.

"If the killer is in here, lights help make him or her easier to find," Ivy said.

"Right, right. Let me...let me check with Bert. He was supposed to have been compiling the necessary surveillance footage."

Bert called Bud.

"Speak of the devil. Yes, Bert," Bud said.

The robotic voice burst from the speaker of Bud's phone. Ivy listened intently.

"I have accessed the footage. A hooded figure dressed darkly runs down the stairs to the lobby of the Institute but does not leave out the front door. The figure heads into the gallery of the Institute," Bert said.

"I have been freshly made privy to another door around the back or south end of the building. It is a basement door at the base of a stairwell. The hooded figure may have exited via that door. Any cameras near the south end of the building?"

"Yes, of course, I scanned every camera around the building. The only footage bearing any person that is not Ms. Ivy, was the hooded figure that headed into the gallery."

"Peruse the footage again," Bud said.

"No need to sir. My hard drive is solid state. My memory is locked down. Checking things twice is only derived from the mistakes of humanity. I am no human Bud. You designed me that way."

Bud shook his head. He knew Bert was right. In a way, Bud wanted Bert to be wrong because of the windowsill incident.

"So the killer is still in this building and somehow eluded the police search of the building."

"It appears to be so Bud," Bert said.

Ivy interjected: "Enough talk. Let's find this asshole."

CHAPTER FIFTEEN

ILLUSORY INSTITUTION

Bud followed Ivy into the rows of artifacts.

"I assure you the police would have found the culprit by the present time," Bud said.

"Like they cordoned off the basement door?" Ivy retorted.

"Your point is most astutely taken." Bud watched as she crouched down and looked below some of the long tables. "Bert told us of the hooded figure entering the gallery perhaps we should check there first."

"How do we get up there without being seen? I am sure the cops have the area blocked off by now and the doors locked," Ivy asked.

"You granted us entry to the basement. Now let me work. This means your pace must be more controlled and slowed Ms. Zheng."

"I have been through a lot and I don't need a lecture from a sleazy private investigator." Her face was visibly upset. Her brow wrinkled above her black rim glasses.

"I am not lecturing. It would be better if we worked together instead of exacting futile levels of inertia on each other." Bud missed Maeve, his original female companion in a similar situation. She was more patient with him.

Bud called Bert, "Has the CPD removed the body yet?"

"Yes Bud. They brought her out eight minutes ago. The police are patrolling the area heavily and campus security will be on duty in the Institute the rest of the evening. It would be wise to use a stealthier approach." Bud looked at Ivy and knew she could hear Bert's advice.

She shrugged.

"Thank you, Bert." Bud ended the call and headed towards the stairwell that led to the lobby.

"You can't just walk up the stairs if campus security is on watch," Ivy said.

"I am not walking up the stairs to my capture. I am positioning myself for our entry into the gallery."

Bud stopped at the base of the stairwell. He brought out the mini-drone from his leather jacket pocket and his phone. He initiated the flight control. The drone hovered, whisper-quiet. He initiated the cloak. The battery drained substantially but the drone would not have to fly far. Bud could see the lobby desk through the drone's camera. Two campus security guards in white and blue uniforms sat at the desk, talking. Neither seemed to be doing or attempting to be doing any rounds.

The doors to the gallery were set back to the left of the desk. The gallery's lights were off.

"One would think they would leave the lights on," Bud commented.

"If you said the cops searched everywhere then there is no need to have the lights on. Plus, light damages some of the art pieces in the gallery," Ivy said.

"I am aware of light damage, but this is certainly an exceptional evening."

"What are you planning to do with the drone? It's impressive you made it disappear. I will admit it."

Bud flew the drone up the stairwell leading from the lobby towards the scene of the crime. He turned the camera towards the guards. Their conversation was engaging. Bud then pressed an orange icon on the screen of his phone. The drone began to click.

SNIK! SNIK! SNIK!

The guards looked towards the ascending stairs then at each other.

One yelled, "What the fuck was that?"

"Probably nothing. Don't worry about it."

Bud pressed the orange button over and over again. The drone was farther up the stairs.

SNIK! SNIK! SNIK! SNIK! SNIK!

"Okay we should check it out!"

"This place has to be haunted. What the shit?"

Ivy and Bud heard the rolling wheels of a chair, then two sets of footsteps moving towards the upper stairwell. The long strides of a walk turned to short hops of climbing stairs.

Bud piloted the drone all the way to end of the office hallway and pressed the orange button a few more times. He moved the drone into an office, dropped the mini-drone into a garbage can, and turned off the cloak.

"Now is our time to move."

Bud climbed the stairs. The guards were in pursuit of his phantom drone. The way to the gallery doors was clear.

"What if the gallery doors are locked?" Ivy was right behind Bud.

"That is of no matter. I need you to wear this." Bud brought out a wristband.

Ivy secured the band to her narrow wrist. Bud pulled a marker from his pocket and slid it under the double door.

"I think you will find this ever more impressive than a cloaked drone." Bud smiled.

CHAPTER SIXTEEN

GHOULISH GALLERY

"I shall go into the gallery first then I will activate your wristband."

Bud pulled back his black leather sleeve to reveal a similar band to the one Bud had just given Ivy. He suddenly disappeared. She was listening to the guards clearing the various offices upstairs when she realized that she was no longer in the lobby but in the gallery. She turned around to see the lights of the lobby through the glass double doors of the interior of the Babylonian gallery. Her nerves were rattled. She was shaking from the sudden shift through space she had experienced. Adrenaline pumped through her veins at a quickening pace and her heart pounded.

"You are officially the first student of Chicago Met to have teleported. Certainly, there must be no equal to that distinction in the annals of this great institution. Now gather yourself. We must find Ms. Tricia Pazinski's murderer."

Bud brought up the camera on his phone. He activated the flashlight and a list of different filters for three-dimensional space. A thermal camera, a motion detector, and fingerprint scanner-- the very same tech he used to enter Ivy's dormitory.

"How? Is this possible?" Ivy asked looking towards Bud's face softly illuminated by the phone's flashlight.

"Certainly you can surmise various theories on how I was able to accomplish teleportation but I will spare you the details. We must press our advantage and figure out where this hooded figure is."

"I mean I understand how you are able to break down your molecular mass but how do you transport and rebuild it in a different space? How did you do this?" Ivy's innate curiosity sparked. She became ravenous for answers.

"Ivy, if I tell you then the novelty would wear off. I cannot reveal too much especially to someone of your intellect. It will not be contained, nor would my patent for it be my own. I hope you understand my need for safeguarding my technology. Now we must stick to the sides of the gallery behind the cabinets so as to not arouse the guards' suspicion upon their return to the lobby."

Bud moved off the main walkway and in between two large show cabinets. He scanned the area for the culprit.

Ivy followed Bud shaking her head in disbelief. Respect for Bud began to grow. Perhaps he was not a typical private investigator who chased adulterers and people who stole credit card numbers from gas stations.

"I don't think her murderer would be hiding in this corner of pottery shards and demon figurines," Ivy said.

Bud scanned the glass cabinet. Ivy was not wrong. Shards and small figurines. One figure of which had a human body, a dog's head, and two pairs of large wings.

"Oh, dear, that is Pazuzu. Is it not?" Bud asked.

"Yes. A Babylonian demon associated with rain and drought. Inherently evil but also a champion against other evil spirits and the nemesis of Lamashtu, the demon that attacks pregnant woman," Ivy said.

"Hmm, keeps evil spirits at bay not unlike the Order of St. Michael..." Bud said.

"What's that? Anyway, Pazuzu is associated with horror films and people don't focus on the good efforts of the demon. Pregnant women would keep a figurine of Pazuzu in their home to keep away Lamashtu."

"Sounds perfectly logical..." Bud couldn't believe he had said that. His experiences with Maeve and the Order had been slowly turning him away from always thinking there is a scientific, practical reason for everything.

"...yet ludicrous." Bud finished. He still had a way to go even after all he had gone through. He moved on to the next section of the gallery and perhaps the most impressive.

"We are heading towards the giant Assyrian King Sargon relief. The one thing that might be of note is that the relief is not flush to the wall. There is a backside to it. Be careful. It is a pretty good hiding spot especially given how careless the cops were on their initial search," Ivy said.

Bud shined his cell light on the large stone raised relief section of a palace wall. The relief depicted King Sargon combined with a beast that had five legs and hooves for feet. Bud was impressed with the craftsmanship. He stepped closer to the ancient stone grey wall and slowly moved to the side to light the back of the wall.

Ivy followed Bud. She kept both hands on his back and peeked over his shoulder. Bud lifted his phone to eye level and initiated a thermal scan. The space behind the relief, which was only about a three-feet wide, showed a slight reading.

Bud and Ivy moved closer to the space. He looked at the screen of his phone. Ivy looked at what the phone's flashlight showed.

"There is no one there Bud," Ivy whispered.

Bud looked up from the screen of his thermal imaging app. "It appears to be so, yet someone may have rested here. I am still seeing a slight thermal signature."

POP!

Ivy jumped on Bud's back. He nearly lost his balance. One of the track lights that illuminated the writing above the rear of the relief had broken.

"A faulty light bulb! Even with the lights off, a loose wire can still carry a charge. It could have merely loosened from a poor job at screwing the bulb in. The wiring in this old building must not be to code. Anyway, what does this writing say?" Bud asked.

Ivy slid off Bud's back.

"Sorry about that. It is just the typical boasting of the king's greatness. His biography and achievements are written here but not necessarily for the purpose of being read. Knowing that it has been recorded is what mattered to the Assyrians. They would write on keystones implanted into the ground. It was not important that anyone knew the writing was there," Ivy said.

"How strange the ancient customs were." Bud turned away from the Assyrian gallery and headed to the next section. They had to make a right turn as the layout of the entire gallery was a U shape.

They heard the sound of something heavy, like a large piece of furniture, being dragged on the marble floor. It came from somewhere ahead of Ivy and Bud.

"One can assume the custodial staff does not respond that quickly to broken light vessels. What is the content of the next gallery?"

"The Egyptian mummies," Ivy said.

CHAPTER SEVENTEEN

MUMMIFIED REMAINS

Bud and Ivy pushed farther into the Archaeological Institute's world famous gallery. The sound of rolling wheels ceased. Bud turned his phone's flashlight function off. He brought up the night vision filter.

Ivy knew the gallery backwards and forwards.

"A fourteen-foot statue of King Tut marks the entrance to the Egyptian section," Ivy whispered.

Bud moved the screen of his phone and saw the cobra headdress of King Tutankhamen colored green by the night vision filter. He and Ivy moved around the statue and into the Egyptian section. Bud switched quickly to the motion sensor app. A few feet into the gallery something moved. The reading on his phone marked a slight three out of a possible ten rating. He kept the phone aimed in the exact same spot as the movement. Nothing.

Bud checked the night vision screen and only saw a square box approximately six by six foot in size. Then he quickly switched back to the thermal app. Again nothing. It could have been a rat or some other critter taking refuge underneath the large square display case.

"No one is there. I think it safe to use the flashlight again. Let's examine this box over here." Bud said.

"This is an Old Kingdom burial display. Look at how this person was mummified in the fetal position. Most Egyptians were buried in this way. Only the royals and upper class could afford the ornate and detailed sarcophagus burial," Ivy said.

Bud examined the mummy. It's carbon-colored exterior and brittle bones both fascinated Bud and gave him a slight chill considering the situation he and Ivy were in, searching for a killer among corpses. The small resting place the mummy had was both comforting but also terribly claustrophobic. Around the mummy's body were pottery shards and other things that this fellow needed for his sojourn into the afterlife. Bud's close examination of the body caused the square burial display case to move and reproduce the same grinding sound that had prompted their investigation of the area.

"Bud you moved it!" Ivy said.

"It appears to be so."

Bud dropped to the floor and flashed the light underneath the case. There was a small two-inch separation between the case and the tiles. This case could be moved and swapped out easily. It had wheels underneath it.

"Ivy, we must examine what is under this case. Help me push it."

Bud stood up and Ivy assisted him with moving the case about six feet away from its original spot.

"That was easier than I expected," Ivy said.

"Indeed, I am not known for my physical prowess," Bud added.

"Unequivocally not." Ivy mimicked Bud's fake English accent.

Bud shone the flashlight on the floor. There was a panel with a depressed handle. Bud grabbed it expecting it to lift.

"Oh poppycock. I can't be that weak," Bud said.

"You might actually be that weak," Ivy said.

Bud's grip on the handle started to move the panel. It did not raise, it actually slid over the floor revealing a dark passage.

"Perhaps we have the reason for Trish's murderer's prompt run into the gallery-- an underground passage. I am all too familiar with subterranean environs. I was almost sacrificed to a pagan god in one." Bud ignored Ivy's last jab.

Ivy's intense focus caused her to be apathetic to Bud's past plight. Her friend was murdered. She wanted to find the killer now.

"I really don't need to hear a story right now. It is almost morning. Are we going down or what? We have to make it back up here if the Institute opens or should we just send for the police?" Ivy asked.

"I prefer not having to explain myself to the police. I will most certainly be shackled for my sarcasm and condescending tone."

Bud shined the light down into the passage. There was a small ladder descending to a stone floor. He lowered himself down and Ivy followed.

There was a long corridor in front of them. Gothic light fixtures that looked as if they were converted from gas to electric, provided dim light along the walls. The floor was haphazardly cobbled together with brick and mortar.

Ivy stepped off the ladder to the uneven ground.

"Shall we?" Bud motioned towards the long corridor.

"We shall." Ivy took a deep breath and walked ahead of Bud.

Bud's phone buzzed. Bert said: "Maeve and I have surmised another possible sighting of our poltergeist along Archer Avenue. The police and emergency scanner indicates a few auto crashes throughout the night on a forest preserve road. All reported a female hitchhiker as the cause."

"Clever poltergeist, assuming the forms of Chicago legends Al Capone and now Resurrection Mary. She is rumored to have died in an accident along Archer Avenue in the 1930s. Since then she has haunted drivers using said avenue. I would start your investigation around Resurrection Cemetery near the grave which many ghost hunters claim is the remains of Mary. Then make your way down the road. How is Maeve? Back in undead form?"

"She is no longer the beast and her wounds from the grill of the squad car are stitched and holding. I have since ordered the remaining components for our restorative experiment. They will be delivered shortly. Spared no expense," Bert said.

"Excellent. Ivy and I remain ever vigilant on the hunt for our killer. Keep me apprised of the resurrection of Resurrection Mary." Bud ended the call and followed Ivy down the old, underground tunnel on the path of a cold-blooded killer.

CHAPTER EIGHTEEN

LAB OF RENOWN

The corridor seemed to go on forever with no entrances or exits anywhere. No offshoots, nooks, or crannies surprised them. It was a long march. They were at least a mile from the Institute.

"This is crazy. Is there no end to this!" Ivy exclaimed.

"Perhaps it would be wise to not yell," Bud said.

They kept on down the path. It felt humid in the tunnel. There was a smell that emanated from further down the tunnel. They hadn't smelled anything until this point.

"Smells like a Bunsen burner," Ivy observed.

The end of the line seemed near. The dim lamps that lit the path showed a grey steel door on the right wall of the tunnel, like the kind found in a submarine. A hatch mechanism stood between Ivy and Bud and entry into the only room they had found along the corridor.

The smell of a recently used Bunsen burner grew stronger.

Bud used his phone to examine for fingerprints. There

were many, but all seemed to be concentrated in the same spots on the hatch handles which most likely meant that only one person had used this room in the past few hours.

"The door is too thick and made of steel so my thermal camera won't work. We will just have to open it and see who or what is inside. Be ready. I may have to teleport us out of here should danger strike. Stand to the side."

Bud grasped the hatch handles and pulled clockwise. He grimaced but was able to open the door. Ivy stood ready to pounce on whomever was in the room. They both froze and looked at each other. They could be facing someone willing to beat a woman to death. Ivy and Bud nodded to each other and simultaneously entered the room.

The room was a laboratory. A single lightbulb descending from a wire attached to the ceiling showed a table with the Bunsen burner, beakers, a microscope. The room was much bigger than the light indicated. No signs of life in the room either.

"This couldn't be what I think it is..." Bud said.

"What are you thinking?"

"The labs where Chicago Met helped to develop the atomic bomb."

"You may be right. It's big enough for a team of scientists. This is strange." Ivy examined the table under the lightbulb.

"This whole night has been strange. Thankfully, the sun will be up shortly. What have you got?"

"There are artifacts all over this table. Pottery, figurines, tablets, even some cylinder seals. They've all been shaved or heated. Broken down in some way. Chipped away..." She picked up a bowl that had powder in it that had been ground from various artifacts from the Institute. "Why destroy ancient artifacts from the Institute?"

"Perhaps they have some properties while in another form?" Bud asked.

"Maybe. I should take sample of this. I was a chem major before I turned to Archaeology."

"You don't seem the type to be decisive. A career student I presume." Bud picked up a cylinder seal.

"You really are a jerk aren't you? If we want to do this right, this will take some time. Maybe you should collect some evidence with your phone while I actually try and figure out what the hell is going on," Ivy said.

"Gather what you need. I shall examine the lab further."

Bud picked up a book on the floor next the table of artifacts. It was a history book. It had bookmarks jutting from various sections. He opened to the first one. Inside were notes. One scribble pointing to a spot on the map between the Tigris and Euphrates rivers read, "The origin of the Elixir".

He showed the book to Ivy. "Perhaps these artifacts are needed to make this? An elixir of the ancients as it were?"

CHAPTER NINETEEN

BLOCKADE AND BEEPER

Bert and Maeve finally reached Archer Avenue after making a considerable trek through many traffic lights all the way down 79th street. Traffic was light as the sun was just beginning to peek over the eastern horizon. Maeve stared at the sky. She remembered her early morning hikes with her Uncle through the forests of New England. Those were simpler, happier times.

Her Uncle was a caring yet demanding man. Her long hikes were lessons in discipline and sacrifice for her training in The Order of St. Michael. Maeve did not live the life of a typical American teenager. No smartphone. No game consoles. No frequent shopping jaunts. She lived a life of sworn poverty. The life of a monk.

"It is indeed strange that all these auto accidents occurred in the same evening. Is it not Maeve?" Bert's conversation protocol kicked in every 15 minutes.

"It has to be the poltergeist from Mt. Olivet taking the form of another Chicago legend. The monks of the Order in

Chicago have certainly been sealing their trees every night. This ghost followed us from Llanwelly," Maeve responded with the same voice as Bert.

"Have you any contact with the Chicago members of the Order?" Bert asked while driving the speed limit along the forested roads of Archer Avenue, just outside the city limits.

"When we settled in Bud's house, I alerted them with our secret pager system that I was in Chicago. Other than that, there has been no contact, but that is normal for a hermit Order. If we do hear from them then serious shit is hitting the fan."

"Pager? I am sorry what does shit have to do with it?"

"A pager or beeper from the early 90s. A form of wireless communication...just google it in your head. Bud needs to update your slang database. Up ahead must be an accident site."

Two squad cars' lights spun as a tow truck hauling a wrecked crossover SUV drove towards Bert and Maeve.

"Drive on. Further down the road. Maybe we will see our hitchhiker."

They made it another hundred yards when they noticed the squad cars formed a blockade. They closed Archer. The morning commute would be rough for many workers emerging from sleep.

Bert drove to the blockade when a cop signaled for him to turn around. Bert kept driving forward.

"What seems to be the problem officer?" Bert said as he rolled his window down. An officer walked to the car.

"We have had a rash of accidents. People seriously hurt. We have an inspection team checking the road for potholes and whatnot. Please turn around." The young police officer put his hands on his hips.

"Thank you officer. We shall take another route to our destination." Bert stared at the officer.

"Okay move along now. Let's go." The officer shooed him away.

"Bert!" Maeve urged Bert to turn around and drive.

Bert finally made a move.

"You are so awkward," Maeve said. "We had better find a way onto Archer even if it is on foot. If there really is a road inspection team they are in grave danger."

"I believe there is a short parallel street to Archer that ends in a small residential neighborhood. We can park there then traverse on foot."

Bert turned off Archer and onto La Grange Road south to the next light and the parallel road.

Maeve heard a beeping sound. If she could properly feel anything her heart would have dropped. She grabbed the pager from her hoodie. The Order needed help.

"Shit!" Maeve illuminated the green LED screen of the obsolete device.

"Is this where serious shit hits a fan?" Bert asked as he parked the car in the residential neighborhood.

"Yes Bert. I need you to trace the number now." She held the pager in front of Bert's face.

He scanned the number. "It is from a landline in a St. James of the Sag Church just down Archer Avenue past the blockade."

"Oh no. Let's go Bert! A monk needs our help!"

"Walking will take around 45 minutes."

"I am a zombie! It will take me forever. I can barely walk as it is. We have to break the blockade."

CHAPTER TWENTY

BLOCKADE RUN

"I am afraid that my driving protocols restrict me from putting us in any danger and breaking the blockade of municipal police vehicles is very dangerous." Bert stopped next to a gray ranch house in the neighborhood parallel to Archer Avenue.

"I am driving. Move." Maeve opened the passenger door.

"I don't think this wise." Bert put his hands up.

Maeve walked around the car and pulled the driver door open.

"It does not matter what you think. A monk is in danger down the road and that damn inspection team. Now get out." Maeve's artificial vocal chord eked out monotone commands but their content gave her voice a menacing feel, like an evil A.I. voice in a sci-fi film.

Bert exited the car and hopped in the passenger seat.

Maeve slammed her door, best she could with the use of her stiff undead muscles.

The dawn's light hit the street in front of them. Maeve pushed the pedal to the floor. A man emerged to grab his morning paper and barked at her to slow down. She didn't.

"My map application shows no exit from this neighborhood. There is a slight elevation to consider as we are higher up than Archer Avenue. So we will most likely roll the vehicle if we continue on our current route." If Bert could cover his optics he would.

Maeve drove between two homes without backyard fences.

"Beyond this yard is a considerable drop off. I urge you to not continue----" Bert stopped.

The red beater Grand Am rumbled through the backyard and down the hill. Bert's head hit the window then the interior roof of the car. Maeve gripped the steering wheel. The car rumbled down the hill. The morning dew may have helped quicken their descent. It created a slippery surface for the tires to roll down the grassy, muddy hillside. The yellow dashes on Archer Avenue fast approached. Maeve turned the wheel to the left in anticipation of hitting the pavement. The car hit another big bump and Bert flew out of his seat and again hit his head. Maeve applied the brakes again and skidded sideways onto Archer Avenue.

Maeve pumped the brakes. The car stopped facing the proper direction towards St. James of the Sag, home to monk who reached out for help. She pushed down on the accelerator. Maeve looked in the rearview mirror to see the police blockade grow smaller and smaller.

"We did it Bert!" Her robotic voice adulated.

"We have done nothing but jeopardize the safety of ourselves and others," Bert said.

"How much longer 'til we get to the church?" Maeve asked, ignoring his previous comment.

"At the current rate of speed approximately four minutes. Alas, be on the lookout for the road inspection team."

"You mean them?" Maeve pointed towards a team with reflective vests running towards the car about a hundred yards ahead. Three men waved their hands at Maeve and Bert and kept a steady run.

"Bert, you will have to talk with them. Maeve secured her hood over her head. She did not want to scare the already frightened men with her zombie face. She pulled up to the men and slowed the car to a gentle stop. Bert rolled down his window and popped his head out.

"How may we be of assistance?"

"Let us in! Let us in!" The burly man pulled at the back door handle. The two other men gathered behind him, yelling, "Hurry up! She's right there! Fucking Resurrection Mary!"

Maeve looked ahead and in front of the car was a ghostly woman, with the same blue hue as Capone. She wore a party dress commonly worn in the clubs of the Prohibition era. The dress was short. Her hair cropped, yet her bangs hung low across her face blocking her eyes. She walked towards the car. As she moved closer, she lifted her arm in a hitchhiking pose and beckoned for their car to pick her up.

Maeve unlocked the doors. The men still scrambled with the handle.

Resurrection Mary walked closer to the car only a few feet away.

The first man piled into the backseat.

Mary reached the front bumper.

The second man fell into the car. The third man slipped and fell to his knees failing to reach the backseat.

"Back the car up! Back it up! It's too late for Jerry! Go!" The burly man yelled from the backseat.

Maeve refused to move the car. The third man got up and started running into the forest off the right side of the road.

Resurrection Mary walked over to Bert's front passenger door. Her head began to shake. Her bangs receded. The skin melted off her face. Her mouth opened.

Mary's skull caved in on the right side of her skull. Her ghostly tongue hung out of her mouth in a wrangled, serpentine mess. The gore was too much to bear even for Bert. He shut down his optics.

Maeve hit the accelerator, jolting the car forward.

"What are you doing?! Don't go this way! That's what she wants!" The burly man warned.

Maeve drove. She needed to save the monk of the Order at St. James Church. Suddenly, the trees that lined the sides of Archer Avenue began to crack with a splintering, thundering boom. They swayed violently and began to fall on the road ahead.

CHAPTER TWENTY-ONE

MAEVE AND MARY SITTING IN A TREE...

Maeve drove underneath one of the falling maple trees before it hit the ground, but would not evade the fallen pine that lay in large chunks in front of them. She pushed hard on the brakes. Bert hit his head on the windshield. The two road workers jolted forward and almost landed in Maeve's lap. The car was now essentially trapped between two trees. The pine tree split apart into logs, which then rolled and began to levitate in front of the car. Another tree fell and cracked in front of them. This one did not split into large chunks as the first pine had. Mary did not want Maeve to accelerate. The logs swayed back and forth in the air as if on a pendulum readying to smash through the windshield of Bud's car.

"Everyone get out of the car now!" Maeve urged. Her voice apparatus was strained.

The road workers each jumped through their respective passenger doors and rolled onto the pavement. They ran into the woods away from Resurrection Mary.

Bert exited the vehicle and turned to face Resurrection Mary who was approaching the rear of the vehicle. The remnants of her grotesque ghastly skin hung off her skull and twitched as she moved closer. Bert struggled to look at her.

Maeve stood up out of the car, grasped her crucifix and faced the swaying logs. One of them flew towards Bert, who was still facing Mary. The log smashed into his back and splintered. Bert's metal frame held up, but Maeve's body would not be able to withstand such a blow.

Bert dove headfirst over the hood of the car. Another log swung and spun towards Maeve. He intended on shielding her, but the log burst into flames then shattered just as it was about to crush her head.

"Still got it." Maeve lowered her crucifix. Bert slipped off the hood of the car as he marveled at Maeve's ability to set matter on fire at will. She developed this power in her training with her Uncle to become a monk of the Order of St. Michael.

"Impressive Maeve. Alas, we are not out of the woods yet. Literally."

More trees swayed, creaked, and cracked. Resurrection Mary stood on the street next to passenger side of the car, Maeve and Bert were on the driver side. Mary put her hands on the car and began to push it towards Bert and Maeve. The trees behind them splintered into spears. Trunks jutted from the ground. Pikes, spears, and other impaling shapes formed at their rear and hovered forming a horrendous trap.

"This is most precarious." Bert's head spun around 360 degrees to see the trap.

"Oh dear. Don't ever do that again. In fact, run as fast as

you can to St. James and see what happened to the monk. I will handle this bitch," Maeve said.

Resurrection Mary pushed the car closer to the spears that were hovering at the side of the road.

"I shall be off then. Be safe and try not to sustain any more soft tissue damage. Bud is worried you are beyond repair." Bert slid under a tree spear and ran down Archer Avenue.

A spear flew at Maeve. She ducked. The spear smashed through the driver door window. The space between the car and the jutting wooden death dealers slimmed to at least two feet. Maeve reached into the car and grabbed the spear. She secured it between her legs. She hoped that in her undead state, she could still use the power she had absorbed from the witches of Salem- the power of flight.

CHAPTER TWENTY-TWO

...K-I-L-L-I-N-G

Maeve hopped up and down once. Nothing happened. She grasped the stick and crouched. She prayed. Suddenly, the stick lifted her off the ground. If Maeve could smile, she would have. She quickly flew up and away from the vice-like trap Resurrection Mary had so effortlessly assembled. Maeve ascended to the tops of the trees; Mary looked up and let out a blood-curdling scream. The remaining windows and windshield of Bud' car shattered from the sonic ferocity of a tortured banshee. Mary flipped the car over. This was the same tactic that had caused all of the other accidents throughout the course of the last evening.

Maeve flew over the carnage then readied herself to charge at Mary with the pointed end of the spear turned rocket. Her hands gripped just under the jagged edge.

Resurrection Mary anticipated Maeve's tactical advantage and commanded her broken tree fragments to angle upwards like an anti-air battery from World War 2.

"Not good." Maeve leaned forward and began a fast, but controlled descent towards Resurrection Mary.

The flak in the form of jagged sticks, spears, and blunt wooden objects cut through the chilled morning air and flew towards Maeve. There was no way she would be able to avoid all of it.

A few small jagged sticks peppered Maeve's arms and shoulders. She flew further down and avoided a huge tree trunk that barreled toward her head. She leaned to the left then recovered to center. She maintained a direct path to Mary who was now only a few feet below.

Mary let out another scream. This time her audible angst was cut short as Maeve drove the spear she rode into the belly of the reanimated and corporeal Resurrection Mary. The same general form that the poltergeist assumed after absconding and disturbing the remains of Alphonse Capone.

Maeve lifted Mary off the ground. Mary reeled and gripped the spear in agony. Her disgusting, deathly, decaying face didn't scare Maeve, given her own personal situation at the moment. She flew the impaled Mary towards the trunk of a tree on the other side of the road, and slammed Mary into the pinewood. Maeve flew off the spear and skidded on her stomach into the woods.

Maeve stood up and brushed off. The lack of a functioning nervous system had impaired her pain receptors-- an advantage of being undead.

Maeve walked toward Mary. The ghostly legend was hunched over, immobile. Her torso was pierced all the way through. Maeve was satisfied that she had summarily defeated the poltergeist within the remains of a seemingly innocent woman, named Mary.

Maeve began the slow walk to St. James, but Bud's car

began to spin on its roof. She saw Mary's head was raised from the slumped position. She shook it. The car careened and struck Maeve square in the chest. She lay motionless while Mary's form began to wither into bones and dust. Maeve couldn't move as she watched the poltergeist leave the remains of Mary.

CHAPTER TWENTY-THREE

GHOSTLY GUARDIANS

Bert reached the long gravel driveway that led to St. James Church and the cemetery therein. Nothing appeared to be out of place until he reached the gateway. The gravestones to the left of the church were randomly placed and weathered in disrepair, crooked and cracked. The wrought iron bars of the gate were bent as he approached the limestone-stained exterior of the church building. He entered the Church through the front doors which faced away from Archer Avenue and looked around for a member of the Order of St. Michael.

"Hello? Anyone present?" Bert searched around with his advanced optics for any signs of life. Nothing.

He examined the large wooden cross hanging over the altar and then tried to move closer to examine a golden-trimmed box. Some kind of force prevented him from going further. His optics could not see any physical barrier. Ever stubborn, Bert continued pushing, but this time the force shoved back and almost knocked him off the altar.

"What the hell is limiting my progress?"

As if in reply, a form took shape by the box. It looked like a young, pale man wearing suspenders and holding a pick ax. Next to the ghostly apparition, another taller man with broad shoulders appeared holding a piece of jagged limestone. His face looked older than the first and weathered from hard work. They both floated in front of the golden box behind the altar.

"Oh dear, oh dear." The voice came from behind Bert.

He turned around and saw an older man with a bald head. He wore robes down past his ankles.

"It's okay Flannery boys. I can take it from here. This boy seems harmless," the older man said. The two ghosts disappeared from the altar.

"I presume you are a monk of the Order," Bert said facing the older man.

"Father Martinez, and yes, I am the monk assigned to this parish. One can only assume you are here because of the poltergeist that afflicted and disturbed the remains of Mary Sobieksi. Where is Maeve? I did page her correctly, didn't I?"

"Yes, we received your summons. Maeve is currently battling said poltergeist now further down Archer. Who were those ghosts on the altar?"

"Those were the Flannery boys. Two Irish brothers who died building the I and M canal a long, long, time ago. They are guardian angels. I only call up them in times of great duress, which has been happening more and more frequently, sadly. I have been sealing the tree in the area every night per my duty. Yet, still there is much evil paranormal activity like, for instance, this poltergeist. Are you sure Maeve can handle this poltergeist? I tried sealing it with the power of the sacred tree but it broke away from my power. I was hoping the power of multiple monks would be able to contain it." Father Martinez sat in the pew in front of Bert. His breath was labored.

"Maeve has unique abilities. I am sure she will be up to the battle..." Bert's internal warning system sounded. Maeve triggered the alarm as Bert pinpointed the alarm with his internal GPS. "...I am afraid we must go to the aid of Maeve now!"

"We can take my car," Father Martinez said, standing up from the pew.

"I can get us there faster. Climb on my back." Bert turned around and crouched.

"A piggy-back ride...I am too old for such nonsense."

Bert turned his head. "Trust me. We must hurry."

Father Martinez hopped on and Bert held the monk's legs.

"Tighten your grip. I won't feel it. I am a synthetic android. Be not afraid."

Bert began a brisk walk out of the church with Father Martinez on his back then gradually increased his speed.

"Hold on." Bert moved faster and faster. By the time he hit Archer Avenue, he was moving the speed limit of 45 mph.

"AH! HAHAHAHAHAHA!" The good priest yelled and laughed as Bert took him on a thrill ride. Bert began to slow upon seeing Bud's totaled car and Maeve laying on the side of the road. Father Martinez hopped off his back, collected himself, then ran to Maeve. He knelt down next to her.

"Oh no my dear. En el nombre del Padre, y del Hilo, y del Espirtu Santo..."

Bert scanned Maeve's injuries then called Bud.

"We have an emergency situation. The poltergeist is

still at large and Maeve is badly injured. Severe chest contusions. Head trauma. She still has some fine motor skills as she was able to trigger the silent alarm I connected to her cross. How is the investigation going?"

Bud's voice burst from the receiver. "Bert! The investigation is of no matter. This is not a casual conversation. A friend is in need. Her body can only take so much. She will be beyond repair if we don't restart her heart. Teleport her to the Tower. Then transfer all the equipment. The final pieces were delivered via a rush order to the house this morning. Let's move now. There are storms coming. We are fortunate. Time for the Frankenstein Protocol."

CHAPTER TWENTY-FOUR

SEARS TOWER OF TERROR

"Have you gathered all the samples you need of this so-called elixir?" Bud walked over to Ivy who was putting more shavings into a plastic bag. She was on her fifth bag.

"Almost done. I did tell you it would take some time. Okay, we can go." Ivy sealed the last plastic bag.

"We shall teleport out of here to my original spot on campus near the Museum of Science and Industry. I must make haste." Bud stood next to Ivy, who held all her samples.

"Wait will these be intact with teleportation?" Ivy asked.

"Yes, of course. Don't drop them." Bud readied the app on his phone to trigger teleportation. "Anything else you need?"

Ivy and Bud looked around one more time at the dimly lit, old laboratory where the atomic bomb had been developed.

"Wait." Ivy pulled the string of the singular light bulb hanging from the ceiling.

"Here we go." Bud triggered teleportation.

The early morning light was dim. Storm clouds gathered. Ivy reeled from the experience of suddenly shifting from one spot in three-dimensional space to another. She dropped the bags, knelt down and felt the grass on a field in front of the Museum as a comforting reminder of reality.

"When you have recovered, I would suggest furthering your study of these samples. Also, I would suggest staking out the Institute. It is unclear if the gallery will still be closed today or just the offices upstairs. Needless to say we should watch for any suspicious people entering or exiting the building."

"Bud, I know I have been difficult but I hope your friend is okay. I hope you can help her because I could have helped Trish and I didn't. I was too scared." Ivy looked down. Her bottom lip quivered.

"It is highly likely that you would not be standing here if you entered the fray. You notified the police and that was the right thing to do, Ivy. We will catch her killer. We have solid leads. Tally ho."

Bud found himself reeling from a gust of wind atop the tubular-constructed icon, the Sears Tower, now known as the Willis Tower. Once the world's tallest building, the view from the top was incredible. Bud was not afraid of heights, but one could not help but be intimidated by this extreme. The cars below were ant-like. The massive white antennae next to Bud acted as the ant queen. The Tower commanded Chicago's skyline.

Bert was setting up Maeve's medical bed. The storm clouds rolled in from the west and covered Chicagoland. Around the medical bed were dynamos ready to collect electricity and channel it into Maeve's undead body through a series of ports that were strategically placed near her major arteries and heart. A helmet would be used to stimulate and remind Maeve's brain to signal a heartbeat. Signals from the heart to the brain and from the brain to the heart were needed to stimulate human life.

"The deep brain stimulation electrodes are ready in that helmet Bert?"

"Yes, sir they should implant with no problem as it has already been tested on Parkinson's patients."

"I know they work, Bert. I just wanted to know if they were ready."

"I assembled them myself," Bert answered.

"That is why I asked Bert. You are the one who assembled them."

Bud examined Maeve who lay on the medical bed as Bert bounced around setting everything up. Her skull was exposed and cracked in the back of her head. Her chest was severely bruised when Mary hit her with Bud's car. These new injuries added to her already bruised back from the Capone battle.

Her vocal apparatus still worked, "What are you going to do to me, Bud?"

"We are going to employ the same principles outlined in the Diary of Victor Frankenstein to stimulate your brain and heart."

"You are going to electrocute me?" Maeve said.

"In a way yes. A very controlled amount of electricity will flow through your body. Be not afflicted with anxiety, dear Maeve."

"This isn't the way. What happened to me is of a supernatural origin Bud. Practical medicine won't reverse this."

Maeve struggled to sit up while Bud applied butterfly

stitches to open wounds and wrapped her torso and the back of her head with medical wrappings. She was weak.

"Nonsense Maeve. If I invented a working teleportation system, I most confidently and stridently can reverse undeath."

The first raindrops hit Bud's forehead. The wind kicked up. Clouds shielded their view to the city below.

"Bud, don't do this," Maeve pleaded.

"This will work." Bud lay her down on the medical bed.

Thunder rumbled. The sound traveled from west to east and grew louder and louder.

"Bert, it is time. Plug everything in to that access panel. Get the laptop up and running. I will monitor the current. We will pull from the Tower's internal electric power then generate the rest from the lightning strikes. Once we channel the power from the building into the equipment and then to the antennae, we should attract some lighting strikes."

BOOM! CRACK! A lightning strike sounded from a couple miles away.

The rain pelted Bud and Bert. Bud wiped the rain from his eyebrows. Bert slipped but secured the laptop into a protective shell and handed it to Bud.

Bud sat on the roof. Puddles formed in different spots around him. Bud adjusted the dynamos and made sure Maeve's DBS helmet was secure over her head.

"Step away Bert. In fact, perhaps you should go as you don't want to get struck by lightning."

"It appears I can't teleport out of here, sir, with the storm interference."

"Okay then step away. I am about to boot everything up."

"Bad idea." Maeve said.

BOOM! CRACK! BOOM!

Bud started the laptop and secured the power from the Tower into the dynamos and equipment. He pulled so much power from the Tower it started to vibrate. Bud and Bert slid sideways. The mighty wind was causing the top of the Sears Tower to sway.

"Oh shit!" Bud exclaimed.

They only slid a few feet before sliding back. The rain pelted them.

CRACK!

The lightning bolts increased. One hit one of the large, white antenna, the power traveled down to the dynamos surrounding Maeve. The foot end of the medical bed moved with the sway but it's weight kept her stable.

Bud wiped his brow and checked the levels of the laptop then tried to initiate and control the flow of the electrical current into Maeve. He failed to register a heartbeat.

The sway caused Bud and Bert to slide again. This time a dynamo fell over and rolled away from Maeve's medical bed. It was still connected to power from the Tower. Bud lay in a puddle in front of the rolling dynamo that sparked its way toward him. Bert jumped in front of the dynamo and caught it. The electrical current enveloped and jolted Bert. Bud could smell the synthetic skin melting.

His android assistant had saved him.

CHAPTER TWENTY-FIVE

BEDKNOBS NO BROOMSTICKS

Bert vibrated and flailed. His voice apparatus buzzed loudly. The sound of Bert's suffering sickened Bud. Even though Bert was just a robot. Bud still cared. He did not know how much more Bert could take. The current that was supposed to revive Maeve was now destroying Bert.

Bud pulled his leather jacket over his head and walked, preferring not to run and slip, to the generator. Another lightning strike coursed through the antennae and sparked the dynamos around Maeve. She was still safe as Bud was not able to activate the helmet or the ports connected to her.

The rain dwindled for a moment and Bud was able to unplug the equipment from the electrical generator underneath the antennae. He looked towards Bert who still couldn't pull away from the dynamo. The current from the antenna was too strong. Suddenly, Bert was able to throw the dynamo off of himself but did so with such incredible force that it flew off the side of the building. The bed was attached to the dynamo. Maeve's bed rolled away from the spot in front of the antennae and towards the eastern section of the roof.

"Oh dear!"

Bud ran to grab Maeve. His heart beat rapidly. His disbelief was suspended by imminent doom. The bed rolled closer and closer to the edge of the rooftop. Maeve attempted to scoot off the foot of the bed but was too weak.

"I've got you! I've got you!" Bud jumped towards the bed, reaching for Maeve's foot. The head of bed tipped over the edge. Bud's leap seemed to last forever. His fingertips touched the tip of her shoe, but he ultimately failed and fell on his hands.

The middle of the bed tipped over the edge if it went any further Maeve would have to submit to the power of gravity.

Bud popped back up. He leaned over the edge and secured Maeve's ankle with one hand and pulled back on the bed to hold it in place with the other. Bud's lack of strength was temporarily rendered irrelevant due to the adrenaline pumping through his veins in a stream as mighty as the torrential rain.

"Maeve I am going to need to you to disconnect yourself. The wires in the ports need to be disconnected or you will go down with the ship as it were." Bud's grip was still strong.

Maeve was angled, not quite upside down, but close to it.

She pushed off the helmet.

"Don't drop me, Bud."

Bud could only grimace.

She removed the plugs from her chest, then her arms, but couldn't reach her legs. A sit up from a nearly upside down position would prove difficult, given her weakened state.

Another dynamo connected to the bed blew off the roof which made the weight pulling against Bud greater.

His grip weakened.

Maeve's arms reached for the plugs near her femoral arteries. She leaned up with all her might, but fell back.

"One more... time... you can... can do it, my dear," Bud urged.

BOOM. More thunder rolled.

Maeve reached up and unplugged both of her legs with one fell swoop.

Bud loosed his grip on the bed. The bed and dynamos crashed down the carbon-tinted tubular structure towards the ground. It skated off the sides of the building. Glass shattered and sprayed out into wind.

Bud used both hands to pull Maeve up to the roof. The thunderstorm rolled toward the lake to the east. The rain remained steady. Maeve and Bud laid next to each other exhausted.

"Um, where's Bert? Couldn't he have helped you?" Maeve asked.

"I am afraid he may be incapacitated."

Bert appeared. He is face had been burnt off. The cold metal of his skeletal face remained. His optics were huge and terrifying to look at. He buzzed and sparked.

"Bert...you...still operational?" Bud asked as he sat up.

Bert let out a low, guttural growl then jumped off the top of the Tower.

CHAPTER TWENTY-SIX

SINKHOLES AND SURPRISES

"Bert!" Bud lifted himself off the ground and ran to the edge Bert had jumped off. The clouds still blocked his vision to the ground. He heard Bert hit the ground. The sound was not unlike an artillery cannon. Bud's heart dropped. His grand plan to revive Maeve had failed and led to disastrous consequences.

"Don't you think you ought to get down there." Maeve was still on her back.

She raised herself up on her elbows. "Let's hope he didn't kill anyone."

"It is still a bit early for the heaviest throes of rush hour. I am sure Bert survived the fall. What is most worrisome is why he jumped off one of the tallest buildings in the world? With the storm past our current vector, I should be able to check his programming with the mobile."

Bud reached for his phone and found himself surprised it was still in his jacket pocket. A diagram of Bert's body showed on Bud's screen. Bert's body flashed red. Emergency mode.

"This is most unfortunate. Bert is in an elevated emergency mode which means all his processing resources are being spent on physicality. He is basically as strong as Frankenstein's original monster. With the damage from the storm, who knows what damage he can wreak. He will possibly perceive everything as a threat." Bud grabbed the wet hair on the top of his head.

"Well, can't you just shut him down?" Maeve said.

Bud attempted to hack into Bert with his mobile. Nothing.

"I am afraid the damage from the storm has severed my direct connection with his operating system. I can monitor him but not control him."

"Bud, get down there. Now. Shut him down. Then get up here and help me. I told you your experiment wouldn't work." She laid back down on the rooftop. Her strength was sapped. The rain turned to a drizzle.

"I shall return." Bud teleported to a destination marker he had left near Union Station months ago. The station was only a couple blocks from Willis Tower. The first flood of workers emerged from the station on their daily march to work. Bud joined the crowd but pushed his way through, faster than even the most impatient walkers.

Sirens blared.

"Shit. Shit. Bert, don't let the sound of first responder vehicles lead me to you!"

People largely ignored Bud's outburst.

A block away from the Willis Tower, Bud searched for a sign of Bert. The Fire Department roared to the front of the building. An ambulance and then the CPD, made their way to what Bud surmised was a significant hole in the ground.

Bud ran past the yellow tape to a group of firemen looking into the hole.

"Yeah, gotta be a sinkhole or somethin,'" a fireman said.

"This'll be a nightmare right at frick'n rush hour. And I was almost done with my damn shift," another fireman said.

"Esteemed gentlemen of the Chicago Fire Department, I would suggest you move away from the hole in the ground. I am afraid it is not a natural sinkhole as that would be highly improbable given the nature of this street." Bud stood next to them.

"Who da hell are you?" the fireman next to Bud said.

"It is advisable that we all step away from this fabricated, not-at-all naturally occurring sinkhole," Bud said.

The same low growl Bert let out before jumping, sounded from the hole. It got louder and louder.

Bert flew out of the hole and rose at least twenty feet in the air. Debris from the street sprayed out behind him and pelted Bud and the firemen.

"What da hell is dat?!" a fireman yelled.

"That, my dear civil servant is the cause of the hole in the ground."

Bert landed on the hood of a cop car. The back of the car sprung up as the hood crumpled underneath Bert's weight. The cops inside the vehicle were in shock. Their eyes wide. They froze. A monster had smashed their engine.

Bud Hutchins, the genius-inventor, witnessed his creation nearly kill someone.

Bert stepped off the hood and onto the street. He surveyed his surroundings. Bud could tell the android viewed all the emergency responders as threats.

Another two cops emerged from their squad cars. Their guns were pointed at Bert, "Get down on your knees now."

He turned to the cops, the skin torn from his face, and his optics bulged unnaturally.

Bud had to break one of his rules. He had to lure Bert away from the cops.

He needed a gun.

CHAPTER TWENTY-SEVEN

RAMPAGE

Bud had only a few seconds before Bert would react to the guns the cops wielded and pointed. Bert's emergency code prompted him to respond with extreme prejudice at any gun aimed at him or Bud.

Bud surveilled the situation. Bert's left leg sparked. It must have been damaged in his leap off the Willis Tower, and this would surely slow him. Bud still assessed only risk, but a risk worth taking. Bert acted as the perfect distraction. Bud positioned himself behind one of the police officers and watched as Bert began to limp towards the officers with intent to destroy their weapons.

"You can shackle me later!" Bud tackled one of the officers from behind. The young officer fell to the ground. The grip of his revolver hit the pavement hard and bounced out of his hands. Bert turned away from the cop on the ground. The other police officer shot at Bert, but the bullet bounced off his head, leaving a burn mark on his steel skull.

The cop who had fired his sidearm cowered. Bert overcame the officer. The crunching of the cop's right hand terrified Bud. Bert crushed bones and metal.

Bud grabbed the loose gun from the ground.

"Bert!" Bud pointed the gun.

The dysfunctional android turned to Bud. The cop knelt and screamed from pain as Bert loosed his grip. Bud waved the gun in front of Bert, egging him on. Bud knew Bert's optics tracked the gun.

Bud began to run east on Adams towards Michigan Avenue. He hoped to help Bert jump in the lake away from the city center. Bert limped but limped faster than any human ever could. He was only a couple feet behind Bud's fastest speed.

Bud ran down the middle of Adams, which was a one-way street where traffic moved west. Bert and Bud ran east. Bud kept to middle of the street, hoping that the oncoming traffic would slow his android assistant down as Bert would have to dodge the cars.

Bert didn't dodge. Bert crushed a Mercedes' hood. Then sideswiped a black SUV with his shoulder sending it into a side of a building. The rest of the oncoming traffic braked. A cab rear-ended a small economy car and the frame jolted off the road and hit a hydrant. Water sprayed everywhere.

Bud heard the sounds of twisted, heavy metal and turned around. Still in the center of the street, the cars around Bud had stopped and watched the devastation Bert wrought on rush hour.

"Shit. Shit. Shit. Egregious, excessive mayhem is not in your code Bert!" Bud backtracked toward the dysfunctional droid. Bert's head spun around in circles. He likely was waiting for another car to drive towards him, so he could destroy it.

Bud walked towards Bert. He hoped that perhaps Bert would finally stop his rampage. Maybe the traffic worked in Bud's favor after all.

"Bert, it is I, Bud Hutchins, your creator." The robot's head still spun in circles.

"Bert, if your audio nodules are still operational. I need you to stand down. I am going to lay the firearm down on the ground. There is no need for emergency mode anymore. We are safe." Bud put the revolver on the ground and moved toward Bert, hoping to get close enough to teleport him back home.

Bert's head still rotated like a bad special effect from an iconic 70s horror film.

Bud was two feet away from Bert. A voice from behind yelled, "Freeze!" Another officer pointed a gun at Bud's back. Bert's head stopped rotating. His optics honed in on the officer's gun.

"Put away the gun now, officer. Clearly this is no ordinary perpetrator. As you can see from the devastation around us and the fact that he has no face should indicate the sensitivity of our current quagmire." Bud kept still but his eyes widened.

Bert moved forward and threw Bud onto the sidewalk. Bud landed on his right elbow, but quickly looked towards the street. The police officer was running away with Bert in hot pursuit.

"Good chap." Bud rubbed his elbow then ran back into the street. Bud saw Bert chase the cop toward Michigan Avenue. Bud picked the revolver back up and ran as fast he could while supporting his injured elbow.

The cop and Bert turned left onto Michigan Avenue. Bud had almost reached Michigan when he heard the feint sound of Ravel's "Bolero" coming from Orchestra Hall. The melodious song was rudely interrupted by three loud gunshots.

CHAPTER TWENTY-EIGHT

LION HEAD

Bud turned the corner and onto the ever-busy Michigan Avenue, the world famous street was buzzing as usual with traffic and pedestrians. He noticed Bert rampaging into the lobby of Orchestra Hall, home to the renowned Chicago Symphony Orchestra. Bud rubbed his elbow and sped up to close the gap between him, Bert and the cop, who heeded his advice and ran. Bud didn't think it wise to lead Bert into a rehearsal of the CSO. Alas, here he was.

Bud paused for a moment outside the bronze doors that stood between him and mayhem. He took a breath and barreled into the ticket box office area of Orchestra Hall.

Bert was scanning the room. His artificial skin was now peeling off his neck and his optics looked cold and mechanical. Three bullets had left burn markings on Bert's torso.

The rising, almost deafening, chords of "Bolero" pulsed from the concert hall into the box office. The cop must have jumped through one of the ticket windows. He was hiding behind the counter.

Bud was surprised Bert hadn't picked up on the obvious whereabouts of the officer, but the robot was severely damaged, it is likely that the only scan his optics would pick up would be a gun.

"Bert! You blithering idiot! It is I, Bud Hutchins, your creator. I command you to cease this needless subroutine. There is no emergency. You are the sole cause of current events."

Bert turned his head.

Bud hoped his commands would somehow be obeyed by the destructive android.

They stared each other down. Bud's heart pounded. He hid the revolver behind his back.

Bert took a step.

The music reached its fevered crescendo. The brilliant horn section blasted the rhythmic, repetitive, notes. Bert turned towards the loud music and ran towards the doors of the concert hall.

"Oh no, you bloody don't!" Bud readied the revolver. His reluctance to shoot was vanquished by his monstrous creation's seemingly unending path of devastation.

He pulled the trigger. The bullet bounced off the back of Bert's head. Bert was smashing one of the doors leading into the hall when he felt the ping. He spun towards Bud.

"That's it old chap! Follow me!" Bud ran out of Orchestra Hall and back onto Michigan Avenue.

Bert busted through the bronze doors of Orchestra Hall, leaving them in a contorted mess. Bud weaved across Michigan Avenue between vehicles stopped by the numerous traffic lights that peppered the famous street. He ran towards one of the original buildings of the Columbian Exposition of 1893, the Art Institute. Bud jumped multiple steps of the grand stone staircase at a time. Bert followed.

He'd surprisingly left the cars stopped in traffic alone, but sadly did not spare one of the famous lions that adorned the entrance of the art museum.

Bud thought the Art Institute would be open. He had pulled and pushed the doors. He even had used the butt of the revolver to crack a door. Nothing worked. Defeated, he turned to face his creation. One of the signature Bronze lion's heads roared through the air toward him. Bud dropped to the pavement. The lion's head smashed through the glass doors granting Bud the entry he had desired.

"Most appropriate." Bud gingerly stepped over the proud lion's head and into the foyer.

The alarm blared. A lone security guard rushed to call for help behind the admissions desk.

"Hey! You can't be in here!" The guard yelled.

"Believe me, my presence is not voluntary. Where might I ask is the Medieval Hall of Armor?"

"What the?" He saw the deranged Bert coming up the stairs. "Um, straight ahead and to the right."

"Thank you and you might want to hide behind the admissions counter."

Bert stomped towards Bud.

The guard quickly ducked.

Bert kept on towards Bud.

The white walls of the Institute showcased various galleries of Impressionist and Classical art. Bert left the walls untouched. He had already left his own impression upon the Institute with the lion's head redecoration.

Bud reached the end of the Hall and turned right. Ahead lay the Hall of Armor--the detailed, vast, collection of medieval weaponry and knightly garments. Bullets were not working with Bert but perhaps other weapons would.

Bud recalled the weapon collection in Beauregard and hoped Maeve was okay still on the top of the Willis Tower.

Bullets didn't work on the android, but they did work on glass. Bud shot three through a display case. The mechanized stomping of a severely damaged Bert was getting louder and louder. Bud had little time to prepare.

CHAPTER TWENTY-NINE

MEDIEVAL TIME

Bud's vision was limited yet sufficient. The knight's helmet was heavy. The face guard jutted outwards and he struggled to keep his head from drooping forward. His elbow hurt like hell. He stood to the left of the entrance to Hall of Armor. The metal gauntlets felt tight and very cold. The sword's weight intimidated him, yet he had to find the strength to wield it. He hid behind a full-size knight mannequin. He hoped the pain in his elbow wouldn't weaken his swing or aim too much. He need to strike Bert with a fatal blow.

The wiring in Bert's neck from the main CPU in his head to the power cell in his chest was the android's only structural weakness. Bud gripped the hilt of broadsword as Bert stomped closer and closer to the entrance of the Hall.

The alarm bells rang with a deafening sonic assault and soon more of Chicago's finest would be searching the building. Bert's rampage had to end now.

Bud laid the gun on the ground in front of the display case where he hid. The trap was set.

Bert entered the room.

Bud was just to the right of Bert behind the knight. He saw his creepy optics scan the room.

Bert's head lowered. Bert bent to destroy the gun.

Bud pushed the knight mannequin onto Bert. The clanking of metal on metal pinged louder than the alarms. Bert lay prone under the heavy armor only for a few seconds. He quickly pushed off the armor and struggled to his knees.

Bud raised the broadsword and aimed at Bert's neck. Bud's elbow throbbed as he used all his might to bring the heavy blade down on Bert. The blade stopped abruptly when it sunk into Bert's neck. The robot fell to the ground and spastically shook as he lay prone once again. He attempted to grab the sword. Bud let the hilt go and looked at the medieval weapon embedded in his friend's neck.

Shouts and footfalls down the hall announced the arrival of the cops.

"Sorry to do this Bert!" Bud kicked down on the sword to finish the sever.

Sparks flew. One more kick would do it. SNAP.

"Freeze kid!" Eight police officers reached the Hall of Armor.

Bud picked up Bert's severed head.

"It is not as it seems. Gentlemen, my apologies."

Bud, with Bert's head cradled in his arms, disappeared.

CHAPTER THIRTY

VIOLATED

Someone had been here. They had tried to cover their tracks but had left too much out of place. The microscope had been moved at least two inches. The samples had been tampered with. The book had been picked up and put down in the wrong place.

He couldn't bear to see his research stolen from him, when he was so close. He had to be the first. Lab rats would take too long. No clinical trials.

Now is the time.

The Elixir's missing ingredient had been found.

Who else would be on to him? Who was down here?

Now is the time.

He grabbed a beaker. The proper application of heat should finalize the mix. Then he would consume it and show the world.

The Bunsen burner filled the air with the pungent smell of natural gas. The singular lightbulb swayed from his rapid movements, creating a chaotic atmosphere--one of madness and aggression.

He took shavings from each of the ancient artifacts put them in a mixing bowl. He added water. The brittle shavings dissolved quickly in his mixture. He poured the chunky, thick mix into the beaker that rested on a small dish over the burner. The heat would purify it. His eyes grew wide. A puff of green smoke billowed from the glass beaker.

He could barely contain himself. He lived for the elation of discovery, his mood joyous when fortune smiled upon him, yet dour with misfortune. Dangerously so.

Once the smoke dissipated, he picked up the hot beaker with his bare hands. Never mind the pain. He opened his mouth. His heart pounded with anticipation. He drank.

The burning tore through his esophagus, to the lining of his stomach. His heart rate spiked. He grabbed his chest, certain he would not recover this time. He fell to his knees.

His crouched and smacked the ground with an open palm. He lay on his stomach panting like a rabid dog. Foam bubbled from his mouth.

CHAPTER THIRTY-ONE

HUBRIS

Bud dropped Bert's head on the desk in the computer room. He pulled the knight's helmet off. He quickly attached an intact dangling USB cord hanging from the many wires protruding from Bert's severed neck, and attached it to the desktop computer. It would take quite a while for Bert to recover, should he recover at all. Bud had little time to waste. He had left Maeve on top of one of the world's tallest buildings. He looked on his phone for the marker he used to teleport directly to the Tower. Its beacon did not show on the screen. It must have been damaged in the storm like everything and everyone else.

Bud initiated teleportation back to Union station.

The latter hours of the morning rush filled the station with slackers rushing to work.

His phone buzzed. It was Ivy. "How's your friend, Bud? She okay?"

"I am afraid she is still in a state unsuitable for sustained life. I am on my way back to her now."

"I am so sorry...I see that you had quite the tussle downtown during the middle of rush hour. Way to attract attention to yourself there, Hutchins," Ivy said.

"Oh dear, I was afraid that might happen, considering Chicago is one of the most surveilled cities in America. I've quite the mess to clean up."

"So who was the super-villain you were fighting and being thrown around by?" Ivy asked.

"That is Bert, my robotic companion. He may have suffered some damage to his mainframe..."

"What did you do to him?"

"It would have worked had the weather cooperated," Bud said.

"You can tell me all about it later. The Institute's gallery will be closed but they sent me an email since I am a volunteer, saying the building will be open for staff in the morning. I will begin my stakeout then. The artifacts I found have quite an interesting connection. I will share it with you later." Ivy hung up on him.

Bud hoped the way would be clear now that he was a minor celebrity. The local news stations kept Bert's rampage on a continuous loop. Some of the graphics on the screen said, "Terminator. Real?". They did focus more on Bert than himself which would be to his advantage.

He reached the street and saw police and emergency vehicles were still surrounding the crevice Bert had created with his ill-advised leap.

Bud could easily blend in with the 25,000 people who entered the Willis Tower on a daily basis. He joined the flow of workers filing into the lobby of the tower. He didn't realize he still wore the metal gauntlets from the Art Institute. The metal detectors at the security checkpoint lay ahead. Bud hastily removed the gauntlets from his hand and dropped them on the floor. Two women and one rather large fellow tripped on them.

"Shit! You okay? What the hell are these?" The man yelled.

Bud blended in with the rest of the crowd, creating distance between the medieval mess he made. He kept walking to the checkpoint. He followed a woman wearing a Skydeck badge. The Skydeck is the main tourist attraction of the tower and the elevator to it would bypass the other floors and get him to the 103rd floor the quickest.

Bud cleared the checkpoint, avoided the security desk, and followed the female Skydeck worker. She walked to the express tube elevator and the door opened immediately. Bud hopped in at the last second before the doors closed.

"The Skydeck doesn't open for another half hour, sir. At 9am. You shouldn't be here."

Bud looked like hell. His hair was sweaty and disheveled, sticking out in at least seven places. He held his sore elbow and he was still damp and probably smelled like sweat.

"Oh I understand that. I was called in to repair the antennas."

"You don't have any tools or anything."

"Don't need them." Bud pulled out his cellphone and waved it, "Technology these days. Just have to plug in and make some adjustments. Rough storm this morning."

Bud tried to maintain his American accent but it was so hard for him not to ease into his forced British.

The woman eased up. She had dark circles under her eyes and looked as if she suffered from a lack of sleep. She shook her head and Bud hoped she could sense no danger from him. She was much bigger than he anyway, and could summarily wipe the Skydeck with him.

The 103rd floor was impressive. The view was wonderful and much more peaceful when not having to deal with the prevailing gale-force winds.

Bud located the stairwell to the roof.

"Have a good day."

"You too." The woman was surprisingly pleasant all of a sudden.

Bud ascended the narrow staircase to the roof where Maeve lay. She was in the same exact spot he had left her. Bud wondered if the undead could suffer from paralysis. The notion's absurdity would certainly match the experiences of the day thus far.

"Oh my dear, Maeve. You okay?" Bud shook her shoulder.

"Stop shaking me." Her voice box sounded weak.

"We need to get you back to the house. It will be just a second. We can teleport out of here." Bud grabbed her under the armpits. Maeve was heavy and could barely move or give any assistance. He managed to get his arms around her torso and pushed the button on his teleportation wristband.

They arrived in the living room of his grandfather's home. Maeve became too heavy and Bud dropped her onto the carpet.

Panic built up within Bud. He shook her. She lay unconscious with her eyes wide open. Her state of being undead gave Bud no indication if Maeve, as he knew her, still existed.

"Speak. Speak!" Bud rubbed her cheek. Her big hazel eyes stared at the ceiling.

Bud feared the worst. His insistence on electrocuting her back to live state failed. She had told him it wouldn't work. Perhaps, she had been right.

Bud for the first time in his life, didn't know what to do.

A rapid knock on the front door...

Bud's eyes teared up and a single drop escaped his right eyelid and ran down his cheek. He wiped it.

The knock slowed, but was harder this time.

Bud opened the door to a short man dressed in monk's robes.

"Young man, I am Padre Martinez, a monk of the Order. I must take Maeve with me. She is no longer safe here."

CHAPTER THIRTY-TWO

UNCONVENTIONAL

"Whatever do you mean?" Bud asked, visibly upset.

"I was the monk of the Order who paged for assistance at St. James. The poltergeist is still at large. The violent apparition won't stop until it eliminates those with the power to stop it, the monks of the Order of St. Michael."

"Where are you to take Maeve?"

"A convent near Midway airport, formerly Lourdes High School."

"What is safe about a convent? What will the nuns do? Instill her with a powerful sense of guilt?" Bud was near hysteria.

"No nuns actually physically live there. The convent is largely empty save for a few powerful protectors."

"Do you mean ghost nuns?"

"My boy, do not mock the Lord's servants. Help me get her to the car. The convent is not far."

"How do I know you are not a nefarious foe of the

Order? Show me your scar from the lash of initiation into the Order."

"Hutchins, you have little faith. You will just have to trust our Heavenly Father. Help me my boy." Father Martinez patted Bud's shoulder and looked Bud in the eyes, "She will be safe with me, Bud."

Bud sighed. He looked at Maeve. Another tear dropped down his cheek.

"Given her state, I suppose you arriving here at this time may be considered good fortune," Bud said.

Bud and Father Martinez lifted Maeve. Bud arms wrapped around her torso again and Father Martinez held her legs.

"Is she okay?" Father Martinez said, panting.

"About that I am not certain. This is a rather complex situation. She has been through much turmoil." Bud put her head and shoulders along the backseat of Father Martinez's compact car.

"I will keep her safe my boy. We monks have seen worse." Father pushed her legs into the car. Bud went around the other side of the car and pulled her to a safe position on her back.

Father Martinez drove off with Maeve in the backseat.

Bud hoped the Father could keep her safe--if there was anything left of Maeve to protect. His shoulders slumped from pressure of it all. He needed no nun to spark the guilt. He felt the full measure of his failed experiment as he watched Maeve drive away.

His phone buzzed. Bud took a deep breath. There was still work to do--a murder mystery to solve.

It was Ivy. "Hey Bud, I am on a bench outside of the Institute. I have much to share."

"I shall teleport to you shortly. There is much to..." Bud initiated teleportation.

He arrived again, in front of the Museum of Science and Industry, "...do."

"Did you just teleport while on the phone with me? Amazing," Ivy said.

"I did and it is not that impressive." Bud jogged towards the Institute.

"You are in a mood. Anyway, no suspicious characters have entered the building as of this morning. Just some volunteers and someone to open the door. Also, some of the professors did come to the building early today. They didn't look so good."

"What about the basement entry around back?"

"After you left I set up a camera there. Nothing."

Bud could see Ivy's stark black hair and glasses. She had stacks of books next to her on the bench. He was close. He slowed his jog.

"What is with all the books?" Bud asked.

"The elixir, Bud. I have been dying to tell you!"

Bud was extremely sensitive to the word dying at the moment. He grimaced.

"You really are in a bad mood. Anyway, the books are on neuroscience. It turns out the ancients were on to something. The shavings I got from the ancient artifacts in the lab? They all have one connection: they were believed to hold properties that enhance the mind."

"To what degree of enhancement?" Bud asked.

"Genius level enhancement and not just book smarts either, think charisma, leadership skills, tactical skills, inventiveness...the list goes on and on."

"Oh dear, Ivy. A drink that gives one a high intelligence quotient? What rubbish!"

"We have to get back into Tricia's office. It may very well be all rubbish, but there was a reason all of these items were gathered and connected in that lab. We have to see if there is a tie between what Trish was working on and the elixir."

CHAPTER THIRTY-THREE

THE PROPER APPLICATION

Ivy entered the lobby first. Since she was a regular at the Institute, she likely would not raise alarms. The volunteers were chatting about the previous night's events. They quieted down upon seeing Ivy, knowing she was close with Tricia. The Gallery would be closed today and the offices would close at noon. The staff was allowed to come into recover any work they needed to meet deadlines and class requirements.

Ivy and Bud headed up the stairs together. Bud struggled to keep pace; his exhaustion was great.

"What do you know of Tricia's research?" Bud asked.

"I know that she and Covington were working closely together on something big for the Board of Regents position that Covington wanted. She wanted to keep it under wraps, even from me. Apparently it would have been earth-shattering. That's why I think the elixir may be the key."

Ivy walked down the hall back towards Covington's office, the site where her friend was brutally murdered.

There were two people in other offices working. The police tape was still on Covington's door, but it was open. Bud and Ivy ducked under and into the series of connected offices. Ivy cringed.

"Odd that the door was open. It is technically still a crime scene isn't it?" Bud observed.

"Maybe the cops thought no one would dare enter the area?" Ivy said.

"That is highly unlikely. I think someone has been here. Covington perhaps? Mourning the loss of his mistress? Here to gather his Board of Regents proposal as you said? Did you see him enter the building this morning?"

"No, I didn't see him. I did stop at the library first so he may have gotten here earlier than me. I figured your friend Bert could keep reviewing the video feeds that is until I saw him on the morning news show. Wait. Tricia was Covington's mistress? Did you say that?" Ivy stopped and stared at Bud.

"Yes, I figured she would have told you of her indiscretions. You two were friends."

"No, she didn't tell me. You don't think he killed her do you?"

"According to his wife, he was with her last night at their favorite pizza place. He was devastated upon hearing the news of Tricia's demise," Bud said.

"Did anyone call the pizza place to confirm the Covingtons were there?" Ivy asked.

Bud shook his head, slowly. Another mistake.

"That would be a good idea don't you think, Hutchins?! Mrs. Covington, your client, may be lying to you!" Ivy's face turned red.

"Why would she hire me if she knew her husband did it? Makes not a lick of sense."

"Find out what their favorite pizza place is and call them later when they open. Right now we have to see if we can find any connection to the elixir in here."

Bud scanned the area with his phone the artifacts that had been strewn on the floor were still there.

"Those are more of the same preserved artifacts that we found in the lab," Ivy said.

"What exactly are these?"

"They are dried food containers that must have trace elements of different food that are known to boost brain function: beets, greens, fish, avocado, some carbs, etc. They might not be exactly those foods but foods with similar properties, when mixed and applied properly into liquid form, the elixir is ready to consume."

"What happens if you don't mix and apply properly?"

"Well funny you should mention that because look at this?" Ivy held up a picture of cave paintings that had been circled by Tricia, Ivy noticed her handwriting in an annotation.

"What in the bloody hell does that have to do with anything?"

"You don't know?" Ivy laughed.

"No, I don't bloody know. There, you have me. What is it?"

"Cinnabar, the red paint that contains mercury. Early man used it all the time. Another ingredient is mercury, that if not properly applied could kill you. That is what happens when not properly mixed."

CHAPTER THIRTY-FOUR

HISTORICAL IMPLICATIONS

Ivy and Bud's curious minds were feasting on their newfound revelatory details of Covington's research.

"I do remember from AP World History class, that ShiHuangDi, the emperor of China, drank mercury thinking it would grant him eternal youth." Bud examined the picture.

"Okay, I was a chemistry major before and mercury when introduced to the human brain causes some interesting reactions in neurons. If the other ingredients prepare the brain and energize the amino acids in our neurons then the proper application of mercury could act as binding agent, like a lattice reaching out to other neurons. The lattice would maximize the likelihood of multiple neurotransmitters firing all at once, which many believe is what separates the genius from the moron. Or me from you." Ivy laughed.

"Very amusing. Have you invented teleportation?" Bud scoffed.

"Or it could even mean that the elixir somehow pulls the two hemispheres of the brain closer together? Like in Einstein's brain! The interaction between the two hemispheres is also another reason for explaining genius."

Bud examined more pictures on Tricia's desk including a map of civilizations.

"It is therefore feasible, that Covington thought he could prove man's greatest achievements through the use of the elixir. He has lines crossing the map from Mesopotamia and Africa to China and Japan then to Europe back to the Middle East again to Europe and on to the Americas."

Bud turned the map over. "Look at these names Ivy." Bud showed her.

"Hammurabi, Buddha, Confucius, David, Augustus, Christ, Constantine, Muhammad, Saladin, various popes, Medici, Da Vinci, Louis, Elizabeth...it goes on and on to the Founding Fathers." Ivy grinned.

"It gives whole new meaning to the phrase, 'must be in the water'," Bud said.

"If Covington could prove the elixir is real it would change history. Wars could have been fought not over land and wealth but the elixir itself."

"This is quite intense. Perhaps, Tricia was killed because of this information. Perhaps Covington did want her dead. Wanted all the acclaim for himself? Or someone else in the office wants it and Covington is next on the hit list?"

Bud and Ivy stared at each other in amazement.

"We have to get into the gallery and see if any one comes out of that tunnel. The beaker makes me think that whoever was working down there might actually be consuming it. I did hear Tricia say something like 'you are making yourself sick' right before she was killed. She was talking to a man with a deep voice that I'd never heard before. Lord knows what effect the elixir has on people, if any. It could be dangerous. Safe to say that whoever used that lab is definitely our killer," Ivy said.

CHAPTER THIRTY-FIVE

THE MUMMY

Bud and Ivy teleported back into the Gallery using the same marker they had used the night before. They took up a position behind the Khorsabad relief in the Mesopotamian section to observe the Ancient Egyptian area. They kept particular watch over square mummy case they knew hid a passage to a secret lab underneath Chicago Met University. The lights were off, but there were small windows along the top of the tall ceiling that provided enough light for them to see the mummy case.

Ivy monitored the back door entrance on her phone.

Bud watched the case in short bursts between using his cellphone to search pizza places near the Covington's home in Lakeview. It nagged at him that Ivy had pointed out his trust in Mrs. Covington had blinded him from the details. He also had badly needed the funds for his attempt to revive Maeve. The whole situation made his stomach churn.

"Uh, Bud are you watching the case? What are you doing?" Ivy whispered.

"I can do two things at once," Bud said, scrolling through the pizza place listings.

"Highly unlikely." Ivy stared at her phone as well.

"Just when I commence to find you mildly amusing, you say things of a cutting nature." Bud looked up from his phone. There was movement.

The movement didn't come from the case itself but from the contents within the case. The mummy in the display case unfurled its body. Glass from the case shattered and sprayed all over the floor before Bud's eyes. A blue hue similar to the one surrounding Capone emanated from the dimly lit Egyptian gallery.

"Oh dear, Father Martinez was correct. The poltergeist will stop at nothing to eliminate us." Bud took a step back and knocked into Ivy.

"Who is us? And get off of me?" Ivy pushed him away.

"I failed to mention that I am technically, a monk of the Order of St. Michael, a sect of the Roman Catholic Church tasked with suppressing supernatural beasties like the one coming this way." Bud stayed put. Maybe the poltergeist mummy wouldn't see them.

The reanimated ancient Egyptian hands gripped the side of the display case. Its fingers were thin, brittle, decayed, yet somehow nimble. The mummy pulled itself up out of the case so that the head and torso showed. Its face was an exposed skull with no features but cheekbones framed by gaping holes where its eyes and nose used to be. Wrapping still clung to its head along the sides and top. When it hopped out of the case, Bud could see it looked frail. The power of the poltergeist, however, caused it to move with the fluidity of a professional athlete. It began to run straight towards Bud and Ivy.

Bud turned around and pushed Ivy towards the wall adjacent to the relief and away from the charging mummy. They emerged from behind the relief.

Bud and Ivy expected the mummy to be in hot pursuit as they dashed out in front in front of the Assyrian King's stone memorial.

"Where'd it go?" Ivy asked.

"It seems to have stopped behind the stone relief. Perhaps it dissipated?" Bud took a step forward weighing the decision to check or not.

The top of King Sargon's relief began to move. A rumble vibrated the ground.

"Make way!"

Bud and Ivy ran away from the toppling stone wall that fell towards them. Thousands of years of history wiped away by a bloodthirsty poltergeist. The incredible booming thud rattled and broke some of the glass in the Mesopotamian gallery. Bud and Ivy created enough distance between them and the relief to shield their eyes from all the dust the three-ton wall displaced.

There was a script carved onto the back of the relief. The mummy stood right on top. It raised its arms and the glass display cases around Bud and Ivy lifted off the floor. The mummy moved its arms forward and the cases flew towards the entry doors to the gallery. It was a mangled pile of artifacts, glass, and splintered wood.

Bud quickly searched for available destination markers to teleport to a safe location, but no markers showed. He closed and reopened the app. No markers again. Bud scrambled to check the pockets of his leather jacket, but his pockets were empty.

"Well, that is most unsettling. Someone deactivated all the destination markers. We have been summarily trapped," Bud said.

"No, we haven't! The tunnel Hutchins!" Ivy smacked her forehead.

"How do you suppose we reach said tunnel? There's a monster blocking our path! I was not wrong about our state of entrapment."

"Can't you do some magic or something? You are a monk of the Order, aren't you?"

"I am afraid I am all out of tricks."

The mummy crept towards Ivy and Bud. Its arms outstretched and they rotated clockwise. Bud looked behind him at the blocked over entryway. There was no way through. The shattered glass from the piled display cases spun in the air in a deadly twister that wound its way towards the youthful flesh of Ivy and Bud.

CHAPTER THIRTY-SIX

DEUS EX MARTINEZ

Bud and Ivy ran as fast they could away from the tornado of razors toward the fallen relief and mummy. They had no choice but to run for the tunnel. The mummy kept control of the twister, it preferred to fell Bud and Ivy with glass shards, rather than physically stop them.

The spinning death cloud nipped at the heels of Bud and Ivy as they made the right turn towards the Egyptian gallery. The sound of rushing air and debris fueled their speed. The back of Bud's jacket began to rip into shreds. His eyes widened as he saw the back of Ivy's black hair shoot straight back as if getting sucked into the murderous twister. Ivy slowed down and would soon be overtaken. She fell to the ground

"No!" Bud moved to grab her and drag her to the tunnel entrance.

"Espiritu Santo!"

A great bright light blinded Bud. He felt like he had hit a wall and dropped to his knees. He put his sore elbow in front of his eyes and squinted over and over to see the source of his seeming salvation.

From the center of the light a silhouette formed--a monk of the Order, Father Martinez.

"Grab her my boy! I can hold this poltergeist off for now."

Bud, without hesitation, helped Ivy to her feet. She took her glasses off and rubbed her eyes. "What the hell is happening?"

"Father Martinez has aided us in our endeavors." Bud and Ivy squinted to see the monk, holding his cross high. The light shining from the cross formed a bubble shield around them.

"I can only use my power for defense. We can move together back to the entrance. I created a path through with my light shield," Father Martinez said.

The poltergeist-powered mummy pushed the glass tornado against the light shield with tremendous force. Light vs Dark clashed in an epic struggle, Father Martinez grimaced.

"This poltergeist is too strong. I don't know how much I can hold this shield up."

"You shan't have to for much longer! Behind you is a tunnel entrance. We can escape through there. Just move back a few paces."

The good monk moved the bubble shield in coordination with Ivy and Bud. They pushed the mummy's resting place to the side, revealing the tunnel entrance.

"Okay, Father. We will head down. Can you maintain the shield and descend this ladder simultaneously?"

The light shield flickered as Father Martinez's grip on his cross weakened. The spinning shards of glass pelted the light barrier and disintegrated.

"No I am afraid I cannot but I brought friends with me."

Father Martinez moved towards the tunnel ladder, while Ivy descended into the tunnel. Bud began to follow her but stopped when he saw ghostly blue-collar workers armed with pickaxes and dynamite run towards the mummy.

"AAAAAAH!" The ghostly workers charged the mummy, which dropped its arms. The twister stopped. Father Martinez lowered his cross. The bubble shield dissipated.

"Who are they?" Bud asked.

"They are the brave souls who built the Illinois and Michigan Canal. These immigrants took the toughest and most dangerous jobs and helped build America in order to give a future for their familias, my boy."

A burly ghost threw a rock into the mummy's torso. Another canal worker swung a pick ax that met the bandaged skull. The workers surrounded the mummy.

"Now is our chance to escape down the tunnel. Let's go!" Father Martinez yelled.

CHAPTER THIRTY-SEVEN

ELIXIR OF THE ANCIENTS

Bud, Ivy, and the good Father ran the only direction they could go: down the tunnel towards the lab. Rickety electric lights lit the path.

"We will never defeat that poltergeist. We need Maeve. The ghosts will only be able to fend it off temporarily," Father Martinez, said panting.

"Has she been able to move at all since you took her to the convent?" Bud asked.

"No, it's as if she is paralyzed. She can only move her eyes to indicate she is still with us. I have never seen anything like it. Her heart doesn't beat and she doesn't breathe. Yet, she is still with us."

"How did you know how to find me?" Bud asked.

"I prayed to the Lord. He does listen and answer."

Bud shook his head, keeping two paces ahead of the Father.

"After all this you still struggle to believe Hutchins." Father Martinez stopped to catch his breath.

Ivy was up ahead and reached the lab door.

"Come on Father, we are nearly to our destination."

"Bud, in order for you to truly become a monk of the Order, you must believe." Father Martinez leaned on the tunnel wall.

"We haven't time for a lesson in theological studies Father."

"Bud! Come on! The door is open! I think there may be a way we can save Maeve!" Ivy yelled.

"Father, we must reach Ivy."

Father Martinez stared at Bud.

"My grandfather disappeared. God wouldn't do that. There you have it. Now let us make haste." Bud turned away from the Father and ran to Ivy.

Father Martinez satisfied for the moment, followed with a slow jog.

Ivy entered the lab first. The dangling light bulb buzzed. It flickered.

"Oh hell no," Ivy gasped.

"What is it?" Bud entered the lab.

"Look." Ivy pointed to the floor.

Bud saw Professor Covington face down on the floor with a mess of saliva pooled next to his open mouth.

"Who is this man?" Father Martinez asked.

"This, Father, is Professor Covington, a prime suspect in the murder of a young woman named Tricia Pazinski, who was his teaching assistant." Bud knelt and examined the unconscious faculty member.

"He is out cold." Bud stood back up to see Ivy already fiddling with the artifacts left on the table. She picked up the beaker.

"No, no, no this is all wrong. He used the burner to boil the ingredients of the elixir. That was a mistake, obviously.

Heating it may have caused dangerous chemical reactions due to the mercury in it and poisoned him."

"How can you revive Maeve, Ivy? Certainly not with this elixir? It has knocked the Professor out cold," Bud said.

"I think if I can use the formula he has here I think we should be okay. We just have to let it the formula settle…at a much cooler temperature. Yes, why not. That should work. I mean we can try."

Ivy plopped thin shavings from the ancient artifacts into the beaker. Then she picked up a clear container with a viscous silvery substance in it. Mercury. She dripped a bit into the beaker, then used her thumb to plug the hole and shake it. The contents of the beaker began to bubble.

"Try giving this to Maeve and see what happens." Ivy handed Bud the beaker.

A thundering crash filled the walls of the tunnel.

"We haven't much time. I am afraid there is only so much my ghostly protectors can do away from St James cemetery. Their source of power comes from the Church there and we are too far away for them to maintain their strength for long. The poltergeist will soon be upon us. If that elixir will revive Maeve that will make our odds of defeating our enemy much better," Father Martinez said.

Bud grabbed the elixir from Ivy, "Might as well try it. We all must go."

"No I will stay here and gather all of his research. The poltergeist is after the two of you anyway. Just close the lab door. This material is far too sensitive to just leave here! I will be fine. Just go," Ivy insisted.

"What will you do if Covington comes to?" Bud asked.

Another crash. This time it was closer.

"I will tie him up and when the coast is clear I will call the cops to get him. Now go! Save Maeve!"

"Be safe, Ivy. I don't need another Maeve situation to occur."

"I will be safe. The elixir can possibly save your friend which is more than I could say for Tricia."

Bud nodded at Ivy. He and Father Martinez exited the lab and shut the door behind them. In the direction of the Institute, the tunnel was filled with the ongoing battle between three more canal workers and the mummy. The mummy kicked one through one of the tunnel walls. No damage was left. The worker just disappeared. The last two canal workers lifted their pickaxes and swung wildly. The mummy ducked under their wild swings and punched through both of them. They were gone in a puff of ectoplasm.

Bud and Father Martinez made sure the poltergeist saw them and began to run in the opposite direction.

"Is there a way out, Bud?"

"If the rumors are true there should be an exit that will lead us up to a soccer field on the Midway Plaisance. So yes, in theory, there is a way."

The mummy's athletic prowess was on full display as it ran towards them on its hands and feet. It seemed to double its speed and closed the gap between it and the middle-aged monk and Bud.

CHAPTER THIRTY-EIGHT

MONSTERS OF THE MIDWAY

Somehow adrenaline had kept Bud Hutchins alive and well despite how arduous the last two days have been. He and Father Martinez saw a metal ladder hanging down in the middle of the tunnel.

"That must be the way out!" Bud yelled.

The mummy galloped towards them. They both knew that climbing the ladder would most certainly slow them down enough for the mummy to catch up. They had no choice but to risk it.

"When we get to the ladder, my boy. Let me up first. I will use the power of the Holy Spirit."

Bud reached the ladder first and held the side of it while Father Martinez hurried up the ladder. There was no indication of a hatch or way out.

The mummy bounded towards them. It was only twenty feet away.

The monk stopped his climb and pulled out his wooden cross.

Fifteen feet.

Bud looked up at the Father. Everything seemed to be moving in slow motion.

Ten feet.

"Espiritu Santo!"

The mummy was five feet away.

The light pulsed again from Father Martinez's cross.

The mummy cowered.

"Come up here Hutchins! Find the hatch out of here!" Father Martinez yelled.

Bud ascended the ladder. Father Martinez moved so that one arm and leg were secured to the ladder. Bud pushed the top of the tunnel with his elbow then his head. He held the elixir in his hand. He pushed again, harder this time. Daylight poured into the tunnel.

"Let's go!" Bud climbed through the hole. Father Martinez held his cross and followed suit.

They emerged onto a turf soccer field on the Midway Plaisance, the site of the Chicago World's Fair of 1893.

"I was indeed correct!" Bud said.

"Look out Hutchins!" Father Martinez, yelled as a soccer ball hit Bud in the face.

Bud fell on his ass but managed to not spill the elixir. The women's soccer team ran over, astounded that two men had sprung up in the middle of their practice field.

"Are you okay?" One of the soccer players asked.

Bud's face turned bright red. "Nothing my rather large head can't handle."

"You don't have a big...well, I guess you sorta do." The soccer player laughed.

"Hahahaha, shake it off. There is still a poltergeist on our tail." Father Martinez helped him up.

The mummy hands reached the opening. One of the

soccer players stood shocked as a dead Ancient Egyptian climbed out. Its wrappings and body still intact.

Father Martinez's compact car rumbled onto the field. The soccer team scattered. The car drove through the goal. The net stretched then gave way.

BOOM. CRACK.

The mummy burst into a cloud of dust and frail bones. Father Martinez's car made short work of the poltergeist's frail mummified form.

Bud's jaw dropped. "Who is driving the car?"

The car pulled up to them. Its doors popped open automatically.

"Oh, that would be Andriej. A Polish canal worker."

"He often prefers to stay invisible." Father Martinez entered the car.

"Right." Bud entered the backseat then secured the elixir with both hands.

Ivy gathered all she could of Covington's research. She needed something to carry it. She looked around for a bag like Covington's briefcase. She didn't find a briefcase but she did notice something she would not soon forget. The description of the footage Bud's android friend had relayed to them in the archives. Underneath the lab table was a black hoodie and black jeans. The clothes of the killer! Whatever doubt she had that Covington was responsible for the death of her friend was washed away.

She grabbed the hoodie, opened it up and began piling the books, papers, artifacts into it.

"What are you doing with my things? Give me my hoodie. I can't wear his clothes. I can't stand him. I hate him!"

Covington stood behind Ivy. His hot breath hit the back of her neck. She froze.

"Why must you steal from me like he did?!" He grabbed Ivy's shoulders and spun her around. He towered over her. His face was hairy in places it should not have been. His eyes were bloodshot, his bottom lip was large and drool seeped from it.

"I am not like him. I want to help you."

"Mr. Hyde needs no help from the likes of you."

CHAPTER THIRTY-NINE

HYDE IN HYDE PARK

Ivy tried to maintain her cool and think. Covington's deranged split personality, Hyde, squeezed her arms with an iron grip.

"Let me show you a way to overcome Covington." Ivy took a risk but perhaps this brutish alter-ego would listen to reason no matter how deranged he was.

"I can show you a way to use the elixir to permanently rid yourself of Covington, so that only you will remain and never have to fight him off again."

Hyde's grip loosened.

"How can a girl 'a your small stature and brain possibly hold the knowledge to suppress Covington?" Hyde shook his head, but his eyes were curious and wanted to hear what Ivy had to say.

"You will have to let me work. We have the materials here already. You will have to let me go, so I can show you. Please."

Hyde's grip loosened even more, "Do what ya must.

Know that I will snap that twig of a neck'a yours, should you try anythin' funny lass."

She turned back to the hoodie she had filled with the research materials. Hyde's breath penetrated the hair hanging over the back of her neck. She held the heavy book in her right hand, and she used her left to move the artifacts as if she were looking for something with purpose.

"Stop fuckin' around," Hyde barked.

Ivy had one shot for his testicles. She would have to bend just a little for her elbow to smash his crotch. Her aim had to be true. She let an artifact drop off the table. With the motion to bend down to grab, she twisted and drove her right elbow into the lower regions of Mr. Hyde. He cowered, surprised at the sprite's strength.

"Ah! You bitch!"

"This bitch has two master's degrees you dick!" She held the textbook with both hands. All of her rage from losing her best friend channeled through her swing. The back of the book met Hyde's in violent, jerking, fashion. His head snapped back. Hyde was stunned, but not unconscious.

Ivy dropped the book and ran out of the lab. With her adrenaline pumping, she sprinted back towards the Institute.

Father Martinez drove the car as the invisible Andreij must have returned to his resting place at St. James. Bud was in the backseat and held the elixir safe with both hands.

"How is it that Maeve has suffered so many wounds my boy, especially the nasty one on her neck and back, and now barely lives with no heartbeat?" Father Martinez asked, keeping his eyes to the road.

"Maeve has the ability to set things on fire. She then absorbs the power of any supernatural creature she bests.

We fought off zombies in Louisiana, therefore, she can sustain much damage and was even killed by a werewolf in Wales but lived. Or rather un-lived as it were. She also turns into a werewolf."

"Ah, monks like Maeve are especially rare. Her empathy towards every being causes the absorption. She is a true healer," Father Martinez said.

"Now it is our turn to heal her. Sadly, her human body can only take so much punishment. Upon observation of her undead status over the last few months, I noticed her strength wain. Being a zombie apparently does not give you sustained vitality. Eventually your body weakens. The zombie curse only animates the dead body for so long. So, I have spent the last few months trying to rid her of the curse and restart her heart to hopefully help her regain her live state."

"You will have your chance again soon. We are nearing the convent of Lourdes HS."

Bud looked at the elixir in his hands then out the window to a typical Southside neighborhood. Bungalows and Georgian style houses were all around. The corner of 55th and Pulaski had the typical trappings of this part of town, two gas stations, a donut shop, a bank, currency exchange and many Mexican restaurants. He felt comfort in this neighborhood and hoped Ivy was right, that the elixir would save Maeve.

Ivy reached the ladder. The same type of heavy footfalls that she had heard the night Tricia died echoed down the tunnel. She reached the floor of the dark Archaeological Institute. She pulled herself up next to the disturbed mummy burial. She would have to find a way through the broken display cases that blocked her exit. Ivy ran past the fallen relief and towards the lobby.

"Oh deary! I told ya I'd snap your twig of a' neck! Run all ya want I will catch up!" Hyde roared.

Ivy didn't let him intimidate her or slow her down. Her legs burned. Her heart pumped. Glass from the mummy's tornado crunched under her feet. Light from the lobby was showing through the hole Father Martinez had left earlier in the display case blockade. Ivy could feel her skin crawl as she felt Hyde get closer and closer.

"Love, you can't run or hide from Hyde! Hahaha!" His laugh was throaty, deep, and sinister.

Ivy dove through the path to the entryway and into the Institutes' lobby. Regular voices filled her ears, "Whoa there lady! What the hell is going on?" A security guard helped her up. He was surrounded by two policemen and a cleanup crew of maintenance men.

"Did you cause this mess?" The guard inquired.

Before Ivy could answer, Hyde broke through the display cases. One case almost crushed a janitor, who had opened the doors and had been preparing to clean up the mess.

Hyde emerged from the gallery. He looked bigger to Ivy.

A policeman yelled, "Don't move!" Hyde put his hands up.

"Dr. Covington?" One of the janitor's recognized Covington.

Hyde tore his tweed jacket off then pulled his shirt and tie in one fell swoop. His torso was hairy, muscular, and veiny.

"I said...don't move!" Both cops now had their sidearms drawn.

Hyde jumped at the policemen and tackled them. The guards and cleanup crew ran out of the Institute. Hyde grabbed the policemen's heads and bounced them off the hard floor. Blood pooled around them.

Hyde stood up and wiped the drool off his mouth, "You're next little Ivy."

Ivy ran as fast as she could out of the Institute and into Hyde Park, the neighborhood of Chicago Met University.

CHAPTER FORTY

SAVE MAEVE

The convent was in the west wing of Lourdes High School. It had recently been rented by the Chicago Public Schools, to welcome neighborhood students of the Southside. Nuns no longer lived there and the school used the convent for storage. The yellow brick was typical of Catholic School construction in the early half of the twentieth century. The convent was abandoned until now.

Bud and Father Martinez entered through a back door.

"I couldn't bring her up any more floors. The second floor was the best I could do," Father Martinez said, holding his powerful cross.

"You said she would be safe here. How safe, Padre?" Bud coughed as the dust of the dark, creepy hallway attacked his throat. The hallway was long and there were small dorm rooms that populated each side.

Father Martinez pointed into a room to Bud's left.

"She protected her."

Bud followed the monk and looked into the room to see

a floating nun wearing traditional garb. The habit was a white top surrounded by a black cape that framed her ghostly, old face. She rubbed Maeve's forehead in a comforting, peaceful fashion.

"This school is on all the haunted Chicago websites but she is actually here to protect the children not harm them."

Bud nodded his head. The nun's presence calmed him. He brought the elixir over to Maeve. Her eyes were open and Bud hoped she was glad to see him.

"Sister, could you help me raise her to a sitting position?" The nun smiled then disappeared.

"Sister Marguerite cannot touch the physical world. She was here to keep Maeve's soul with us, Bud."

Bud's eyes teared up. "Well, then thank God for her."

He lifted Maeve's head and torso up.

"Did I just hear you say thank God, Bud?" Father Martinez smiled.

"Not now. Christ! Can't you see we have to get her to ingest the elixir some way? The voice box I implanted should keep the liquid from seeping out of her jugular wound."

Maeve was able to open her mouth and Bud poured the elixir down her throat.

"Gentle my boy," Father Martinez said.

Bud slowed the pour. It took a while but he emptied Ivy's entire concoction into Maeve's stomach.

Bud and Father Martinez held her and stared, hoping something miraculous would happen.

"Perhaps we should lay her back down," Bud said.

Maeve's eyelids grew heavy.

"Maeve, my dear friend, stay with us. Perhaps we should summon Sister Marguerite."

Maeve's eyes closed.

"Father...summon Sister Marguerite!"

"Bud have faith. Give it some time my boy."

Bud was visibly upset. His shoulders raised and lowered quickly as he grabbed Maeve's hand. He cried hard.

"I am so sorry I couldn't help you, Maeve. So sorry!"

Tears rolled down his face in a flood that formed stains on his face.

Bud felt Maeve's hand grip his tightly. His posture straightened. He examined her.

Her color began to return to her face and hand. She pulled herself up to sitting position. The voice box fell out of the wound in her throat. Her vocal chords formed first, then the skin grew and bound her neck to its original pristine state.

She threw her head back as her spine cracked. The damage from her battles with the poltergeist healed.

She grew stronger and stronger before Bud's eyes.

The elixir worked. Ivy saved Maeve.

"Bud, thank you." Maeve's actual voice filled Bud's ears. She no longer sounded like a robot.

Bud tears continued as Maeve embraced and held him tight.

"You really should not thank me. There is someone you have to meet."

Maeve let go of him. Bud pulled out his phone and called Ivy.

She answered immediately, "Bud, did it... work?"

Bud noticed Ivy panting, "Are you running?" Bud asked.

"Yes, from Covington on campus! I am going to the Museum of Science and Industry! Meet me there! He killed Tricia! He is literally Jekyll and Hyde. Not kidding! Call the police!"

"Is that a good idea to lead him into a heavily populated museum?!" Bud asked.

Bud heard nothing. Ivy ended the call.

Bud dialed 9-1-1. "There is a murderer loose on the Chicago Metro campus chasing a petite woman of Chinese descent. You must hurry!"

He pushed the red end call icon.

"Bud, what is wrong with you? Did they even respond to you?" Maeve asked.

"Yes, of course. We must return to campus on the double quick!" Bud said.

Maeve shook her head.

CHAPTER FORTY-ONE

SAVE IVY

"I can drive us back there," Father Martinez said, rushing into the hallway.

"We can get there faster. Bud can't you teleport us there?" Maeve asked.

"For some reason all the markers have been deactivated. I haven't any idea why. Can't we just fly with you?"

Maeve ran into the hallway to find a broom closet.

"Yes!" Maeve grabbed the broom and put it between her legs. Nothing happened. The broom didn't hover.

"Well, I am alive but seemed to have lost all my cool powers." Maeve dropped the broom.

"The car it is!" Bud said, following Father Martinez down the hall.

Ivy climbed the many steps of the green-domed, vast, Greco-Roman influence Museum of Science and Industry. The school groups and main admissions desks were in the basement. She hoped to lead Hyde away from the crowds and school groups clamoring to get in. The Museum had already been open for an hour. Many people were already enjoying the popular exhibits like the human heart, whisper room, the hatchery, a U-boat, etc. She entered the building and pulled the nearest fire alarm.

The noise rattled her ears.

Families enjoying an intricate model train set, looked around to see if the alarm was legitimate. The Museum staff began to usher people to the nearest exits.

Ivy couldn't believe her cardiovascular health was as a good as it was. Sweat beaded on her forehead but she still pushed on. Hyde knocked people out of his way on the steps leading to the entrance. He entered the Museum, the exiting people scattered and screamed when he rushed in.

Ivy stopped to make sure he saw her.

She wanted his focus to still be on her and not the exiting crowds.

"There you are! My little Ivy!"

Ivy was a good hundred yards ahead of him. She ran to the interior of the Museum and took a sharp left and descended the stairs to the main floor to one of her favorite exhibits: the coal mine.

"There is a tree in Jackson Park just behind the Museum. The Order discovered a tree that needed protection there after the serial killer H.H. Holmes used the park to hunt for his victims. We can use it to contain the poltergeist should it attack again. If all of us say the prayer to St. Michael we should be able to defeat it." Father Martinez shared, while speeding eastward on 55th street back to Hyde Park.

"That poltergeist followed us home from Europe, Bud. That period of time we left the tree open for evil to escape, you know, between the werewolf battle and stopping Brother Mike? The poltergeist had to come out of the tree in

Wales. It was haunting us and we didn't even know it until my wolf form could smell the damned thing," Maeve said.

"There was a considerable amount of time that the tree remained unsealed, while we dealt with Brother Mike. It is possible it escaped in that interim," Bud said.

"Why is it targeting us so viciously?" Maeve asked.

"In order for it to subsist in this realm and flourish, it needs to kill and haunt and spread evil. It needs to eliminate those that can stop it. Us." Father Martinez blew a red light, a camera behind the car flashed.

"You just got a ticket, Father."

"Bullshit, I never pay those anyway."

Maeve laughed.

"Could Covington and the poltergeist be connected? The elixir revived Maeve. Is it possible that it showed Covington clues to the elixir's existence to revive it?" Bud asked.

"The nature of poltergeists is to spread evil. Yes, they do form from the death of evil people. It revived evil remains with Capone and Mary but couldn't sustain the connection. The elixir could sustain the connection we can safely say," Maeve added.

"I wonder what evil person this poltergeist originates from?" Bud asked.

"Someone strong. Someone intimidating, who caused much death," Father Martinez added.

CHAPTER FORTY-TWO

CANARY IN A COAL MINE

Ivy lowered herself onto the top of the open shaft elevator that brought guests down to the coal mine exhibit. The elevator was on the lower level which left a space between the top of the elevator and the ceiling of the mine. It was small enough for her to fit through. Ivy laid on her stomach and put her feet through the space first then scooted backwards. She dropped about five feet to the bituminous floor. She ran into the elevator and tried to pull the control panel open to prevent Hyde from using it and ultimately, take refuge in the coal mine.

She felt the elevator bounce.

"Ivy, this foolish game must cease. Are you down there? Did you fit your tiny twig body through this teeny space? Guess I should join you!"

The elevator bounced again. This time weight had been lifted from the top. Hyde was going for the call button.

Ivy pulled with all her might to bend the control panel

to her will. It would not budge. There was no emergency stop in the elevator since it only traveled one floor.

The elevator power pulsed and it began to ascend slowly. Ivy kept pulling at the control panel trying to stop the elevator. She had few seconds to spare before she had to jump off the elevator to avoid Hyde.

"Come on! Come on!" Ivy pulled at the panel one last time. Her efforts proved futile. The elevator reached the main floor. Ivy was too late. Hyde stood over her.

"Hey there." His mouth stretched into a menacing, toothy grin.

The united monks of the Order sped down the Midway of Chicago Met's campus. The Museum of Science and Industry was in sight, as were many first responder vehicles with lights rotating. They were securing the perimeter and helping with the crowds pouring out on to the lawn.

"One can presume my call was effective!" Bud said.

"Not so fast, genius. This looks a fire alarm evacuation. You just called the cops! There are fire engines and trucks everywhere!" Maeve frowned, remembering how frustrating Bud could be.

Father Martinez drove as far as he could before a parked cop car blocked them. He pulled to the side of the road.

The three monks ran out of the car towards the south end of the Museum that borders Jackson Park.

Ivy cowered. Hyde grabbed her by the neck and lifted her up. Ivy clawed at his hands and arms.

"I take will great pleasure in crushin' ya throat little one!"

Suddenly, Hyde's eyes glowed a lightning blue color. He dropped Ivy to the floor. She watched as Hyde shook and the blue glow in his eyes permeated the rest of his body, similar to the reanimated mummy. The poltergeist possessed Hyde.

A group of firemen were clearing the area the coal mine was in.

"Hey big guy, can't you hear the alarm?! Let's go!"

Hyde stopped shaking. The poltergeist had gained full control. Hyde grabbed Ivy and put her over his shoulder.

"According to my master, you are useful to us. Your broken neck will have to wait."

There was a dining area behind the coal mine exhibit and a window that overlooked Jackson Park. Hyde ran and smashed through the window. Ivy screamed. Hyde stomped into a marsh in Jackson Park.

CHAPTER FORTY-THREE

THE ORDER POWER

Bud, Maeve, and Father Martinez heard a scream and saw Hyde, glowing blue bound into Jackson Park's marsh with Ivy on his shoulder. His progress was slow in the muddy water.

"He has Ivy and appears to be enhanced by the poltergeist!" Bud yelled.

"We can kill two birds with one stone! Like I said, there is a tree we can seal the poltergeist in within the Park's grounds!" Father Martinez said.

The three monks of the Order ran to cut off Hyde.

"There it is! By that small bridge where the marsh narrows is the tree we can seal the poltergeist in!" Father Martinez yelled.

"Maeve is it possible for you to still set things ablaze?" Bud ran ahead of his two companions.

"Yes, that I learned from my Uncle with my training. I didn't absorb it from any ghouls," Maeve answered.

"Can you set ablaze the perimeter of the marsh he is in?" Bud asked.

"Yes, I believe I can." Maeve held her cross in stride and said a prayer.

The grass around the marsh burst into flame. Hyde reached the bridge. The fire started to lick at the bridge and Hyde had nowhere to go but forward and towards the tree.

The three monks were now close, just outside the marsh. The flames grew higher. The bridge succumbed to the inferno.

Hyde lifted Ivy over his head with both arms as if to body slam her.

"I will kill her you fools!" Hyde barked.

The haze caused from the flames distorted the scene and Hyde and Ivy appeared to bend.

"Father, is it possible for you to throw a light shield around Ivy as you brilliantly executed earlier?" Bud asked.

Without hesitation, "Espiritu Santo!" A beam of light shot from Father Martinez's cross and showered Ivy in beautiful sparkles.

"Perhaps now would be a good time to pray."

"Has your faith been restored, Bud?" Father Martinez asked.

"I believe so, Father. I believe so." Bud looked at Maeve.

The three monks of the Order recited the prayer:

"St. Michael the Archangel, defend us in battle. Be our defense against the wickedness and snares of the devil. May God rebuke him, we humbly pray, and do thou, O Prince of the heavenly hosts, thrust into hell Satan, and all the evil spirits, who prowl the about the world seeking the ruin of souls. Amen."

Hyde dropped Ivy into the marsh. He keeled over. The poltergeist within him began to separate from his body. The blue ghostly form was being pulled into the tree. It tried to repossess Hyde but failed. The power of three monks of the Order of St. Michael proved too great. The tree behind absorbed the poltergeist, banishing it back into the realm from whence it came.

The flames around the marsh died down. Bud and Maeve jumped in to Ivy's aid. She still glowed from the light shield.

Bud and Maeve helped her out of the muddy water. Hyde had transformed back into Covington. He lay unconscious on his back, slowly sinking in to the marsh. Bud dragged him out.

The threat had been contained. The Order was victorious.

CHAPTER FORTY-FOUR

RESOLUTE AND IRRESOLUTE

"The police have officially arrested your husband for the murder of Tricia Pazinski. One thing I have to ask is what pizza place did you go to the night of her murder and at what time Mrs. Covington?"

Her raspy voice responded through Bud's phone, "We went to D'Ags at about 8:30 after he was done working in his office upstairs. How could it have been him? He was home I swear."

"I am afraid your husband had been experimenting with a poisonous substance that caused dissociative identity disorder. He literally had a split personality. He murdered Tricia then escaped the Institute through a hidden tunnel that exited onto a soccer field on the University's campus. Upon his escape, he must have switched back to his normal self to join you for pizza as if he'd never left."

"But... why would he kill that girl? I thought he loved her?" Mrs. Covington kept her composure, even though that last sentence had to hurt.

"Your husband was drinking a substance that contained mercury. It overstimulated his amygdala, the part of the brain where aggression forms. The chemist on my team believes he killed her while identifying as his more violent dangerous personality. She was helping him with his research. He was trying to get the Board of Regent's position, as I am sure you know. Perhaps stress caused him to turn on her or maybe she was trying to get him to stop experimenting on himself with this phony ancient elixir," Bud explained.

"Well, thank you for your help Hutchins. I truly appreciate it."

"I am sure you will see your husband on television tonight. He caused quite a stir on campus and nearly killed two police officers. Goodbye, ma'am." Bud ended the call.

"That was a bit of a harsh way to end the call Bud!" Maeve said.

"What?" Bud shrugged.

Father Martinez stopped the car in front of Bud's grandfather's home. Maeve, Ivy and Bud exited.

"May God bless and keep you all. I am back to St. James. It was quite an adventure Mr. Hutchins." Father Martinez stuck his head out the car window.

"Indeed it was, Father. Thank you for all your blessed assistance."

Father kissed his cross then drove off.

"Did you ever figure out why your teleport tech failed, Bud?" Ivy asked matching their pace to the front door.

"No, I hope to get Bert back up and running to see what occurred. I have a query for you, Ivy. Why didn't Hyde kill you?"

"I think the poltergeist knew I developed the elixir correctly. Hyde would have killed me but that is when the poltergeist possessed him. He told me I was useful to them." Ivy used air quotes.

"Perhaps." Bud turned the keys in the lock and entered the house. He felt comfort to see his grandparent's home.

"Um, Bud?" Maeve pointed to all the picture frames that were broken and thrown on the floor. Bud's grandfather had been torn from every picture.

Bud picked up the picture of him and his Grandfather downtown at Christmas. His Grandfather's face had been burned from it. Maeve patted his back in comfort.

Bud ran to Bert's computer room. The room had been ransacked and destroyed.

"This is why the teleportation stopped working. They destroyed my computer. That is what maintained the network communication between the band and destination markers." Bud frantically searched his desk. He threw the keyboard. Bert's head was gone.

Underneath the keyboard, burned into the wood was the tree symbol Hanks had showed him a few months ago. It was from the cult that Brother Mike was associated with. This was the cult that had destroyed Bud's home, stole Bert's data, and murdered monks of the Order of St. Michael.

Maeve, Ivy, and Bud Hutchins stared at each other. Their victorious moods had been soured by yet another relentless evil.

END

45

THE FOURTH CHRONICLE...

Time to grab your favorite monster-slaying weapon, raise your torch, and storm the Castle walls.

"THE CASTLE"

AUTHOR'S NOTE ON "THE CASTLE"

Bram Stoker. Bela Lugosi. Dracula. The big bad vampire concept. I wanted to write my own take on the classic vampire tale. "The Castle" not only continues the story but also provides conclusions to many of the series' mysteries and is the most "throw everything and the kitchen sink in" kind of book in the Bud series thus far. Of course, there are more mysteries to solve and adventures to come!

I wanted this book to be epic. I wanted to captivate the reader from start to finish and make the ending so thrilling that you have no choice to but to finish even if it's the damn middle of the night and you need to get up for work the next day.

I actually read Bram Stoker's "Dracula" after I wrote this book. I thoroughly enjoyed the read until the last 100 pages or so. The hunt for Drac just drags on and on for far too long. Van Helsing and the gang's mission to kill Dracula should have been immersive and captivating, instead I was less than thrilled. I did, however, read some academic essays regarding the characterization of Dracula as I really only knew the popular culture tropes and Bela Lugosi's portrayal of the legendary bloodsucker. Some similar characteristics do carry over with the vampire in "The Castle".

Also, there is an even an homage to a Spielberg classic in this book, as well as, the customary Universal Classic Monster nods. "The Castle" deepens the characters, catapults them into uncharted territory, and maintains a steady build to a pulse-pounding finale.

Please enjoy this excerpt from The Castle: A Bud Hutchins Supernatural Thriller #3:

The candlelight flickered. The soft glow accentuated his finely drawn cheekbones and strong jawline. His blue eyes bore a look of joy in the laughter he shared with his female companion. The brunette with the green eyes and ruby-red lipstick closed her eyes and laughed, nearly spilling the wine from her medieval goblet. Before she stopped giggling and her eyes reopened in recovery of her jovial fit, his brow furrowed. His eyes showed his true condition—a menacing yet brief look, one of lust and of hunger in full and equitable measure. The look vanished. His courtly composure retained.

"Oh, my dear Vincentas, who knew you could be so amusing?"

"Shall I take umbrage with your last statement and just kill you right now?" Vincentas grinned.

Another loud burst of laughter.

The Cabernet Sauvignon didn't have a higher level of spirits than any other wine he usually picked from his cellar. Still, Vincentas poured more into her goblet. His attempts at humor could land, but usually with a casual, rather weak effect. She acted as if he'd performed a comedy routine for years and had earned his own television show.

"That is enough wine for me, Vincentas. What are you trying to do me?" She leaned over the small table, giving him full view of her cleavage.

"I do nothing that one does not allow amicably." He smiled, leaned forward, and kissed both of her cheeks then pulled back to survey her reaction.

She stood up from her chair, took another swig from her goblet, walked to his side of the table, and pulled him off his chair. She grasped his shirt collar with both hands and kissed him like a lioness devoured a fresh kill. Her aggression took Vincentas by surprise.

She wasn't the real monster though.

The candlelight moved violently, then the flames extinguished, and darkness overtook the room.

Vincentas didn't need the light. His hands caressed her where they had touched many other women in his long life. He loved discovering the slight variations of the female physique. The curves, the hips, the muscles both hard and soft, the flesh. His particular favorite: the length of the neck.

She moaned.

The sensual and soft sounds of sexual assurance turned to a panicked scream.

A loud crash filled the dark room. In the struggle to free herself, she kicked over the dinner table.

"No! No! Please! Plea—" Her voice gargled with blood.

The wicks of the candles were once again alight with flame.

Vincentas held his prey in both arms and feasted on his favorite body part. Perhaps his enthusiasm got the best of him. He lifted his head from her neck and spit out a piece of her vocal cords, then dropped her on the stone floor.

He sighed, looked up, and shook his head.

"Much needed. Much needed."

A voice from behind him called, "I take it she wasn't suitable."

"Just another eager gold digger, I am afraid. Take this husk away. I need to work on my compositions anyway."

"REVIEWS HELP IMMENSELY!" SO SAYS BERT

If you enjoyed "Bud Hutchins Supernatural Thrillers" please consider leaving a review! Reviews do help immensely! The Order needs you!

Please leave your review at the link below:

PRAISE FOR THE BUD HUTCHINS
SUPERNATURAL THRILLER SERIES

I kept smiling throughout this exciting, original and very entertaining book, which cunningly blends science with the supernatural.
Jack Magnus for Readers' Favorite

J.B. Michaels' novel, *The Elixir*, is a flawless combination of suspense and sci-fi, with a touch of fantasy.

STEPHANIE TILTON FOR WINDY CITY REVIEWS

The intriguing and complex plot is exciting, the gorgeous prose is delightful, and the reader's satisfaction is complete. The Castle is a great literary achievement, original and unpredictable.
Romuald Dzemo for Readers' Favorite

JOIN CAPTAIN BRENDAN AND JANE FAIRY FLYER ON EPIC ADVENTURES THAT WILL CAPTURE YOUR HEART.

Click here for a FREE copy of The Secret Snowball

ALSO BY JB MICHAELS: READERS' FAVORITE GOLD AND BRONZE MEDAL WINNERS. NATIONAL INDIE EXCELLENCE FINALIST. USA TODAY BESTSELLING SERIES.

The Tannenbaum Tailors series- An incredible world in miniature. Mutli-Award-winners. USA Today Bestseller

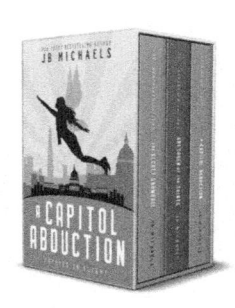

ALSO BY JB MICHAELS

The Viking Throne! Experience the visceral thrills of "Taken" but on the high seas!

Copyright © 2018 by JB Michaels

All rights reserved.

No part of this book may be reproduced in any form or by any electronic or mechanical means, including information storage and retrieval systems, without written permission from the author, except for the use of brief quotations in a book review.

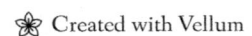

❀ Created with Vellum

Made in the USA
Monee, IL
13 July 2020